**A WASH OF RAINBOW LIGHT,
A DAZZLE OF ULTRAVIOLET ENERGY,
TOLD SPOCK HE HAD FAILED
AGAIN. . . .**

They were fleeing, to some place he would never find, and he could come back again and again and again, earlier and earlier, further fragmenting the very substance of the universe as he attempted futilely to repair the damage being done. But he would *always* fail, he knew it now, something would always happen to cause him to fail. Entropy would always win out.

He cried out in despair.

Fighting the hopelessness that washed over him, somehow he flung himself over onto his chest. Every nerve and muscle in his body shrieked as he reached to drag himself along the floor like the crippled creature he was, like the first primordial amphibian struggling for breath on the shores of a vanishing lake, knowing instinctively in the most primitive interconnections of his brain that he would probably die, if he continued, that he would surely die, if he stayed, that his only chance was to keep going, to try. . . .

Look for other *Star Trek* fiction from Timescape Books

Most Timescape Books are available at special quantity discounts for bulk purchases for sales promotions, premiums or fund raising. Special books or book excerpts can also be created to fit specific needs.

For details write or telephone the office of the Vice President of Special Markets, Pocket Books, 1230 Avenue of the Americas, New York, New York 10020, 212-245-1760.

A STAR TREK® NOVEL

VONDA N. McINTYRE

THE ENTROPY EFFECT

A TIMESCAPE BOOK

PUBLISHED BY POCKET BOOKS NEW YORK

To Gene Roddenberry, for letting me into
his universe for a while,
and
To David Hartwell, a singular friend.

The quotation on page 47 is reprinted from *The Iliad of
Homer,* translated by Richmond Lattimore, by permission
of The University of Chicago Press. Copyright 1951 by the
University of Chicago.

Another *Original* publication of TIMESCAPE BOOKS

A Timescape Book published by
POCKET BOOKS, a Simon & Schuster division of
GULF & WESTERN CORPORATION
1230 Avenue of the Americas, New York, N.Y. 10020

ISBN: 0-671-83692-7

First Timescape Books printing June, 1981

10 9 8 7 6 5 4

Prologue

Captain James T. Kirk sprawled on the couch in the sitting room of his cabin, dozing over a book. The lights flickered and he woke abruptly, startled by the momentary power failure and by the simultaneous lurch in the *Enterprise*'s gravity. The main shields strained to the limits of their strength, drawing all available power in order to protect ship and crew from the almost incalculable radiation of another X-ray storm.

Kirk forced himself to relax, but he still felt uneasy, as if he should be doing something. But there was nothing he *could* do, and he knew it. His ship lay in orbit around a naked singularity, the first and only one ever discovered, and Mr. Spock was observing, measuring, and analyzing it, trying to deduce why it had appeared, suddenly and mysteriously, out of nowhere. The Vulcan science officer had been at his task nearly six weeks now; he was almost finished.

Kirk was not too pleased at having to expose the *Enterprise* to the radiation, the gravity waves, and the twists and turns of space itself. But the work was critical: spreading like a huge carcinoma, the singularity straddled a major warp-space lane. More important, though: if one singularity could appear without warning, so might another. The next one might not simply disarrange interstellar commerce. The next one might writhe into existence near an inhabited planet, and wipe out every living thing on its surface.

Kirk glanced at the screen of his communications terminal, which he had been leaving focussed on the singularity. As the *Enterprise* arced across one of the poles, the energy storm intensified. Dust swirled down toward the puncture in the continuum, disintegrating into energy. The light that he could see, the wavelengths in the visible spectrum, formed only the smallest part of the furious radiation that pounded at his ship.

The forces, shifts, and tidal stresses troubled everyone in the crew; everyone was snappish and bored despite the considerable danger they were in. Nothing would change until Mr. Spock completed his observations.

Spock could have done the work all by himself in a solo ship—if a solo ship were able to withstand the singularity's distortion of space. But it could not, so Spock needed the *Enterprise*. Yet Spock was the only being essential to this mission. That was the worst thing about the entire job: no one was afraid of facing peril, but there was no way to control it or fight it or overcome it. They had nothing to do but wait until it was over.

Kirk thought, with unfocussed gratitude, that at least he could begin to think of the assignment in terms of hours rather than weeks or days. Like the rest of the crew, he would be glad when it was finished.

"Captain Kirk?"

Kirk reached out and opened the channel. The image of the singularity faded out and Lieutenant Uhura appeared on the screen.

"Yes, Lieutenant?—Uhura, what's wrong?"

"We're receiving a subspace transmission, Captain. It's scrambled—"

"Put it through. What's the code?"

"Ultimate, sir."

He sat up abruptly. "Ultimate!"

"Yes, sir, ultimate override, from mining colony Aleph Prime. It came through once, then cut off before it could repeat." She glanced at her instruments and fed the recording to his terminal.

"Thank you, Lieutenant."

The unscrambling key came up out of his memory unbidden. He was prohibited from keeping a written record of it. He was not even allowed to enter it into the ship's computer for automatic decoding. With pencil and paper, he began the laborious job of transforming the jumble of letters and symbols until they sorted themselves out into a coherent message.

Lieutenant Commander Mandala Flynn changed into her judo *gi* and hung her uniform pants and shirt in her locker. For once, her long curly red hair had not begun to stray from its tight knot. She knew she ought to cut it. The border patrol, her last assignment, encouraged a good deal more wildness in appearance, and behavior, than was customary on the *Enterprise:* customary, or, probably, tolerated. She had only been on board two months, and most of her time and attention so far had centered on putting the security team back into some semblance of coherent shape. Consequently, she had not yet felt out the precise informal limitations of life on the *Enterprise.* She did not intend to fit in on the ship, she intended to stand out. But she wanted her visibility to be due to her professionalism and her competence, not to her eccentricities.

She wondered if Mr. Sulu were tired of their half-joking agreement, that she would not cut her waist-length red hair if he would let his hair grow. So far he had kept up his end of the bargain: his hair already touched his shoulders, and he had started a mustache as well. But Flynn did not want him to feel trapped by their deal if he were being harassed or even teased.

She went to the ship's *dojo,* stopping just inside to bow in the traditional way.

On the judo mat, Mr. Sulu completed a sit-up, hands clasped behind his neck, elbows touching knees. But there he stopped, and let his hands fall limply to the floor.

Flynn sat on her heels beside him. "You okay?"

He did not look up. "Ms. Flynn, I'd rather beat off Klingons with a stick than balance a starship around a naked singularity. Not to mention balancing it between Mr. Spock and Mr. Scott."

"It's been entertaining," Flynn said. "Walking innocently along and all of a sudden you're floating through the air."

Mr. Sulu stretched his body and arms forward in a yoga exercise, touching his forehead to his knees.

"Mr. Scott doesn't think the gravity fluctuations, or the power hits, or the rest of the problems are all that funny," he said in a muffled voice. The quilted jacket of his *gi* had hiked up around his ears. He sounded as though he would just as soon stay bundled up as ever come out again. "Mr. Scott's convinced the next time we go through an X-ray storm, the overload on the shields will explode the engines." He grunted in pain and sat up slowly. "All Mr. Spock wants, of course, is a perfectly circular orbit, storms or not."

Flynn nodded in sympathy. It was not as if the danger were something one could stand up to. The responsibility for their course, and therefore for their safety, lay almost entirely on Mr. Sulu's shoulders. He was overworked and overstressed.

"Do you want to skip your lesson?" Flynn asked. "I hate for you to stop when you're doing so well, but it really wouldn't hurt."

"No! I've been looking forward to it all day. Whether it's your fencing lesson or my judo lesson, they're about the only thing that's kept me going the last couple of weeks."

"Okay," she said. Taking his hand, she rose and helped him to his feet. After they had warmed up, Sulu, the student, bowed to Flynn, the instructor. Then they bowed formally to each other, opponent to opponent.

In fencing, Mandala Flynn was just getting the feel of parry six with the foil; Mr. Sulu could get through her guard with ease. In judo, their positions were reversed. Flynn had a fifth-degree black belt in the art, while Mr. Sulu was not too far past the stage of learning how to fall safely.

But today, the first time he came out of a shoulder-throw Flynn felt the position going wrong. She tried to catch him, but she had not expected clumsiness from him. Mr. Sulu hit badly and hard without rolling or slapping at all. Flynn glared down at him, her fists clenched, as he stared blankly up at the ceiling.

"Dammit!" she said. "Have you forgotten everything you've learned in the past two months?" Immediately sorry, she damped her anger. Learning to control her violent temper was one of the reasons she had taken up the discipline of judo. Usually it worked. She knelt beside Mr. Sulu. "Are you all right?"

He pushed himself up, looking embarrassed. "That was dumb."

"I shouldn't have yelled at you," Flynn said, embarrassed herself. "Look, this is no good, you're way too tense, you're going to hurt yourself if we keep it up."

She started to rub his back and shoulders. He made a sound of protest as her thumbs dug into knotted muscles.

"I thought I'd warmed up," he said.

"Warming up wouldn't help." She made him take off his jacket and lie face-down on the mat, then straddled his hips and began to massage his back and neck and shoulders.

At first he flinched every time she kneaded a muscle, but gradually the tightness began to ease and he lay quiet under her hands, his eyes closed. A lock of his glossy black hair fell across his cheek. She would have liked to reach out and brush it back, but instead continued the massage.

When the fierce tautness of his body had relaxed, and her own hands began to cramp, she patted his shoulders gently and sat crosslegged beside him. He did not move.

"Still alive?"

He opened one eye slowly, and smiled. "Just barely."

Flynn laughed. "Come on," she said. "You need a good long soak a whole lot more than you need to be thrown around the gym for an hour."

A few minutes later, they both sank down into the deep hot water of the Japanese-style bath. Flynn untied her hair and let it fall around her shoulders. The water drifted the strands against her back, tickling her; the heat soothed the faint ache where her collarbone had been shattered several years before. Absentmindedly, she rubbed the scar that radiated across her shoulder, silver-white streaks on her light brown skin. The bone had healed adequately, but some day she should go into therapy and get it regrown. Not now, though. She did not have time for that now.

Sulu stretched luxuriously. "You're right," he said. "Just this once, the soak without the workout feels good." He grinned.

She returned the smile.

"Do you realize," Flynn said, "that we've known each

other two months, and we still call each other 'Mr. Sulu' and 'Ms. Flynn'?"

Mr. Sulu hesitated. "I did realize it, yes. I didn't think it was ... proper, for me to initiate any informality."

As commander of security, Flynn was in no analysis of the hierarchy Sulu's immediate superior. If she had been, she would never have permitted herself to find him attractive. But she was used to the traditions of the border patrol, where the established crew decided when to invite new people to use informal names. Rank was not a factor. Here was another case where the *Enterprise* ran along more strictly traditional military lines. Flynn outranked Sulu by a grade.

"I'll start it, then," she said. "My friends call me Mandala. Do you use another name?" She had never heard anyone call him anything but Sulu.

"I don't, usually," he said "But ..."

Mandala waited a few moments. " 'But'?"

He glanced away from her. "When I tell people my first name, if they know Japanese, they laugh."

"And if they don't know Japanese?"

"They ask me what it means, I tell them, and then they laugh."

"I can match anyone in the weird name combination department," Mandala said.

"My given name is Hikaru."

She did not laugh. "That's beautiful. And it fits."

He started to blush. "You know what it means."

"Sure. Hikaru, the shining one. Is it from the novel?"

"Yes," he said, surprised. "You're the only person outside my immediate family I ever met who's even *heard* of the *Tale of Genji*."

She looked at his eyes. He glanced away, glanced back, and then, suddenly, their gazes locked.

"May I call you Hikaru?" Mandala asked, trying to keep her voice steady. He had beautiful, deep, brown eyes that never lost their humor.

"I wish you would," he said softly.

The intercom on the wall whistled, startling them both. "Mr. Sulu to the bridge! On the double!"

Hikaru sank slowly down till he was completely immersed in the hot water. A moment later, he erupted like an outraged dolphin, swung himself out of the tub, and stood dripping on the tile.

"They can find you anywhere!" he shouted, grabbed his towel, and slapped the response button on the intercom panel. "I'm on my way!" He glanced back toward Mandala, who had already got out of the water. "I—"

"Go on," she said. Her adrenaline level shot up; her heart pounded. "We can talk later. Gods only know what's happened."

"Good lord," he said. "You're right." He hurried into the locker room, pulled his pants on fast, and left carrying his boots and shirt. Mandala dressed almost as quickly; she knew security could do very little if the singularity were about to snatch them and gobble them down, but she wanted to be ready for anything.

In the observatory of the *Enterprise,* Mr. Spock stared thoughtfully at his computer's readout. It still did not show anything like what he had expected. He wanted to go through the preliminary analysis again, but it was nearly time to take another instrument reading. He was most anxious to obtain as many extremely accurate observational points as possible.

Since he was to report to Starfleet, and Starfleet was based on Earth, Spock thought about the naked singularity in terms of Earth's scientific traditions. The theories of Tipler and of Penrose were, in fact, the most useful in analyzing the phenomenon. So far, however, Spock had found no explanation for the abrupt appearance of a naked singularity. He expected it to behave in a peculiar fashion, but it was behaving even more peculiarly than theory predicted. The interstellar dust that it was sucking up should cause it to form an event horizon, but it was doing no such thing. If the singularity was growing at all, it was expanding into and through dimensions Spock could not even observe.

But Spock *had* discovered something. The wave functions that described the singularity contained entropic terms such as he had never seen before, terms so unusual they surprised even him.

Many scientific discoveries occur when the observer notices an unexpected, unlikely, even apparently impossible event, and follows it up rather than discarding it as nonsense. Spock was aware of this, never so much as now.

If the first analysis of the data held up in replication, the results would spread shock waves throughout the en-

tire scientific community, and into the public consciousness as well. *If* the first analysis held up: it was possible
that he had made a mistake, or even that the design of
his apparatus was causing unsuspected error.

Spock sat down at his instruments, centered and focussed them, and checked the adjustments.

The *Enterprise* approached a gap in the accretion
sphere around the singularity, a region where the X-ray
storms ebbed abruptly and an observer could stare down
into the eerily featureless mystery that twisted space and
time and reason.

But as Spock's battery of measuring devices scanned
the singularity, the *Enterprise* suddenly and without warning accelerated to full power, ploughed back into the disintegrating matter and energy, burst through to deep
space, and fled toward the stars.

Spock slowly rose to his feet, unable to believe what
had happened. For weeks the *Enterprise* had withstood
the chaotic twists and turns of spatial dimension: now, so
close to the end of his observations, the whole second
series of measurements was destroyed. He needed the
replication, for all alternate possibilities had to be ruled
out. The ramifications of what he had discovered were
tremendous.

If his preliminary conclusions were correct, the expected life of the universe was not thousands of millions
of years.

It was, for all practical purposes, less than a century.

The *Enterprise* sped through interstellar space at a
warp factor that badly strained the already overworked
engines.

At least Mr. Sulu got us out of there with his usual precision, Jim Kirk thought, sitting at his place on the bridge
trying to appear calmer than he felt. He had never responded to an ultimate override before.

The door of the turbo lift slid open, and, for the first
time in weeks, Mr. Spock came onto the bridge. He had
hardly left the observatory since they first reached the
singularity. The Vulcan science officer descended to the
lower level, stopped beside Kirk, and simply gazed at him,
impassively.

"Mr. Spock . . ." Kirk said, "I received an ultimate
override command. I know you haven't finished your

work, but the *Enterprise* had to respond. I have no choice, with an ultimate. I'm very sorry, Mr. Spock."

"An ultimate override command . . ." Spock said. His expression did not change, but Kirk thought he looked rather haggard. All things considered, that was not too surprising.

"Can you salvage anything from your data? Could you reach any conclusion about the singularity at all?"

Spock gazed at the viewscreen. Far ahead, indistinguishable as yet against the brilliant starfield, an ordinary yellow type G star hung waiting for them. Behind them, the singularity lay within its fierce glow.

"The preliminary conclusions were interesting," Spock said. He clasped his hands behind his back. "However, without the completed replication, the data are all essentially worthless."

Kirk muttered a curse, and said again, lamely, "I'm sorry."

"I can see no way in which you are responsible, Captain, nor any logical reason for you to apologize."

Kirk sighed. As always, Spock refused to react to adversity.

It would be a relief if just once he'd put his fist through a bulkhead, Jim Kirk thought. If this doesn't turn out to be extremely serious, I may find something to punch, myself.

"Are you all right, Mr. Spock?" he asked. "You look exhausted."

"I am all right, Captain."

"You could go get some rest—it'll be quite a while before we get close enough to Aleph for me to call general quarters. Why don't you take a nap?"

"Impossible, Captain."

"The bridge really can get along without you for a few more hours."

"I realize that, sir. However, when I began my experiment I psychophysiologically altered my metabolism to permit me to remain alert during the course of my observations. I could return my circadian rhythm to normal now, but it does not seem sensible, to me, to prepare myself for rest when my presence may be required when we reach our destination."

Kirk sorted through the technicalities of his science officer's statement.

"Spock," he said, "you aren't saying you haven't had any sleep in six weeks, are you?"

"No, Captain."

"Good," Kirk said, relieved; and, after a pause, "Then what *are* you saying?"

"It will not be six standard weeks until day after tomorrow."

"Good lord! Didn't you trust anyone else to make the observations?"

"It was not a matter of trust, Captain. The data are sensitive. The difference between two individuals' interpretations of the same datum would cause a break in the observational curve larger than the experimental error."

"You couldn't have run several series and averaged them?"

Spock raised one eyebrow. "No, Captain."

If I didn't know better, Kirk thought, I'd swear he turned a couple of shades paler.

Captain's log, Stardate 5001.1:

We are now a day away from the singularity, but the unease that gripped the *Enterprise* and my crew throughout our mission there has not faded. It has intensified. We have left one mystery behind us, unsolved, in order to confront a second mystery, about which we know even less. The ultimate override emergency command takes precedence over any other order. The *Enterprise* is now under way to the mining colony Aleph Prime, maintaining radio silence as the code requires. I cannot even *ask* why we have been diverted; I can only speculate about the reasons for such urgency, and be sure my crew is prepared to face . . . what?

Chapter 1

Aleph Prime's sun had grown large enough to appear in the viewscreen as a disc rather than a point. The crew stood at general quarters, waiting to face some danger as undefined as the singularity that now lay far behind them. The *Enterprise* approached the mining station with all shields up, phasers at ready, sensors extended to their limits. Kirk still had no more information than the simple implacable command, and he was still restricted by radio silence.

He glanced up at his science officer.

"The star doesn't look like it's in imminent danger of going nova," he said. Incipient nova was one of the very few reasons an ultimate code could be sent out. "That's some comfort."

"Considering its position on the main sequence, Captain, this star is unlikely to go nova now or in the foreseeable future."

"And the other two possibilities are invasion, or critical experimental failure," Kirk said. "Not an inviting choice."

"There is one final category," Spock said.

"Yes," Kirk said thoughtfully. The unclassified reason,

unclassified because unclassifiable: danger never before encountered. "Could be interesting," he said.

"Indeed, Captain."

"Mr. Sulu, what are you getting on the sensors?"

"Nothing unusual, sir. A few ore-carriers in transit between asteroids and Aleph Prime, some sailboats—"

"Sailboats!" People out sailing the solar wind, tacking across magnetic fields, out for a quiet picnic—during such an emergency? Kirk found it hard to believe.

"Yes, sir. It looks like they're having a race. But the course is well out of normal traffic patterns."

"Thank heaven for small favors," Kirk said with considerable sarcasm. Hundreds of years had not changed the tradition that an unpowered sailboat, however small, had right of way over a powered ship, though the pleasure boats drifting across the viewscreen would be like motes of dust compared to the *Enterprise*.

"Captain Kirk," Sulu said, "we're within sensor range of Aleph Prime."

"Thank you, Mr. Sulu. Can we have it on the screen?"

Sulu touched controls and the jewel-like chaos of the station sprang up magnified before them. Its transparent and opaque sections glittered through a rainbow of starlight and refraction. Kirk had never visited Aleph Prime before; he had not expected it to be beautiful. Too many cities were not. But this one was like a congregation of delicate curving glass fibers, and the shells of radiolaria expanded millions of times, and bits of polished semiprecious stones, turquoise and opal, agate and amber.

"Captain, we're receiving a transmission."

"Thank you, Lieutenant Uhura. Let's hear it." Maybe now he would find out why they were needed. If the station had been under attack, it was infiltration rather than invasion, for Kirk could see no structural damage, nor any of the disruption and commotion he would expect after a fight. He did not know whether to be more worried, or less, but his curiosity was certainly piqued.

"It isn't from Aleph Prime, sir," Uhura said. "It's from another starship."

The second ship curved up from beneath the station, and with a sudden shock of perspective Kirk could see, by comparison with the tiny scarlet speck of the other craft, the sheer immense bulk of Aleph Prime. Of course the station was large, it had to be; it held half a million in-

telligent beings, human as well as other life-forms. Sulu
magnified the approaching ship, and Kirk had a brief
glimpse of a tantalizingly familiar shape, painted quite
unmilitarily in the colors of a phoenix eagle, before the
picture dissolved and the video portion of the communication appeared on the screen.

"Hunter!" Kirk said involuntarily.

"Aerfen to *Enterprise,"* said the other starship's captain. "Come in, Jim, is that you?" She paused.

"Captain?" Uhura asked.

"Maintain radio silence, Lieutenant," Kirk said, with
regret. "We'll have to leave greetings for later."

The starship captain paused a moment, gazing out of
the screen. She had changed in the years since Kirk had
seen her last. The lines at the corners of her clear gray
eyes served only to add more character to her face, not to
detract from its elegance. Her black hair was still long,
and the lock that fell down her right cheek to her shoulder she still wore braided and tied with a leather thong
and a scarlet feather. The black now was lightly scattered
with gray, but that merely increased her dignity, her gravity.

Then she grinned, the grin like a child's, and she took
him back years in memory, back to the Academy, back to
the rivalry, friendship, and passion. But he knew her well
enough to detect the trace of reticence in her smile, the
reticence he had caused.

"Aerfen will be at Aleph for a few more days," Hunter
said. "Call me if you've got some time."

The transmission faded. By now Hunter's ship had
swung far enough up the face of Aleph Prime to present its
side to the *Enterprise.* Sulu magnified it again and gazed
at it rapturously.

"Captain Hunter and *Aerfen,"* he said in awe. He
glanced back at Kirk. "You know her, Captain?"

"We . . . went to school together." Kirk had never seen
Sulu in quite such a state of hero-worship; Kirk did not
think Sulu could have been more surprised if D'Artagnan
himself, flexing his épée and twirling the end of his mustache, had appeared and spoken to him.

And far from being amused, Kirk understood completely how Mr. Sulu felt. He felt that way himself, and
with far more reason.

Sulu moved the *Enterprise* expertly into a stable orbit

around Aleph Prime. Relative to the plane of the star system, *Aerfen* circled Aleph in a polar orbit. Instead of choosing a vacant level and inserting the larger ship into equatorial orbit, Sulu used a bit of extra time and a bit of extra fuel to position his ship so that, from the bridge, *Aerfen* would remain in view as long as it kept to its present track. Sulu let its sleek lines fill his gaze. It was much smaller than the *Enterprise,* for it was a fighter. Its design presented the smallest possible cross-section to an enemy in head-on approach, so it appeared to be streamlined. It was painted a fierce scarlet, with points of black and silver. It looked like a swift, powerful avian predator.

As he put the finishing touches on the *Enterprise*'s orbit, the relative orientation of the fighter to the starship changed slightly, and he could see a long bright gash in *Aerfen*'s side, where the paint had been vaporized by an enemy weapon.

"It's seen some action," he said softly. Recently, too, he thought. He knew intuitively that Hunter would not let her ship stay scarred any longer than she absolutely had to.

"Mr. Sulu!"

Sulu started. "Yes, Captain?" He wondered how many times Kirk had spoken to him before gaining his attention —and he wondered if the captain would chide him for the extra use of fuel.

Kirk smiled. "I only wanted to compliment you on the orbit."

Mr. Sulu blushed, but then he realized that the amusement in Kirk's tone was far outweighed by both understanding and approval.

"Thank you, Captain."

Kirk smiled again as Sulu returned his full attention to the fast, powerful little fighter. Sulu was right: *Aerfen* had seen action, and not too long since. Could that be why the *Enterprise* had been brought here so precipitously? An attack on Aleph Prime, and his ship called in as reinforcement? But that made no sense; Hunter had not acted like a commander on alert, and the rest of her squadron was nowhere in range. Besides, the *Enterprise* had already circled the station once and Kirk had still seen no evidence of damage. The sensors revealed no other ships that could conceivably belong to an enemy.

Kirk glanced over at his science officer.

"Have *you* figured out what's going on, Mr. Spock?"

"The evidence is contradictory, but I believe we will not immediately be involved in armed conflict. That is the only justifiable inference I can make with the available information."

"Right," Kirk said.

"Transmission from Aleph Prime, Captain," Uhura said.

Aerfen dissolved from the screen. Sulu sat back, startled by the abrupt change, and his shoulders slumped in disappointment.

A thin young white-haired civilian appeared.

"Captain Kirk!" he said. "I can't tell you how relieved I am that you've come. I'm Ian Braithewaite, Aleph's prosecuting attorney. Can you beam in immediately?" The official spoke with energetic intensity.

"Mr. Braithewaite—" Kirk said.

"The transmitter's still locked down, Captain," Uhura said.

"Open the channel! He asked me a direct question, and I'll be damned if I'll beam anybody into Aleph till I know what's wrong."

"Yes, sir."

"Mr. Braithewaite, can you hear me now?"

"Yes, Captain, of course. Are you having trouble with your transmitter?"

"Trouble with—! You sent us an ultimate override transmission, we've been under radio silence. Technically, I'm violating it right now. What's going on down there?"

"An ultimate?" Braithewaite shook his head in disbelief. "Captain, I'm very sorry, but I just can't discuss this over unsecured channels. Would it be better if I came up there to talk to you?"

Kirk considered the possibility. Whatever was happening down inside Aleph Prime, it was clearly neither a system-wide emergency nor an enemy invasion. Still, he did not want to beam anyone, or anything, into the *Enterprise* till he knew for sure what was going on. He was beginning to believe that what it was was a tremendous mistake. He glanced at Spock, but the Vulcan showed no expression beyond a raised eyebrow. Kirk sighed.

"No, Mr. Braithewaite," he said. "I'll beam down in a few minutes."

"Thank you, Captain," the prosecutor said.

"Kirk out."

The prosecutor's image vanished. Sulu surreptitiously touched a control and the view in front of the *Enterprise*, including *Aerfen*, reappeared.

"Well," Kirk said. "Mysteriouser and mysteriouser." He glanced at Spock, expecting a questioning gaze in response to his poor grammar. Kirk did not feel up to trying to explain Lewis Carroll to a Vulcan, much less Lewis Carroll misquoted.

But then Spock said, straight-faced, "Curious, sir. Most curious, sir."

Kirk laughed, surprise allowing him a sudden release of tension.

"Then shall we go find out what the bloody hell is going on?"

What Jim Kirk actually wanted to do, now that he was out from under the restrictive communications blackout, was call Hunter. But he could not yet justify taking the time. He and Spock beamed down to Ian Braithewaite's office deep inside Aleph Prime.

The tall, slender man bounded forward and shook Kirk's hand energetically. He loomed over the captain; he was half a head taller even than Mr. Spock.

"Captain Kirk, thank you again for coming." He glanced at Spock. "And—we've met, haven't we?"

"I do not believe so," Spock said.

"This is Mr. Spock, my science officer, my second in command."

Braithewaite grabbed Mr. Spock's hand and shook it before Kirk could do anything to stop him. It was the poorest conceivable manners for a stranger to offer to shake hands with a Vulcan.

Spock noticed Kirk's embarrassment, but he knew it would be a serious breach of protocol on his own part not to acknowledge the handshake, if the human were this ignorant. Spock endured the grasp. With a few seconds' warning he could have prepared himself, but there were no extra seconds to be had. Braithewaite's emotions and surface thoughts washed up against Spock in a wave: normal human thoughts, confused and powerful, with an overlay of unexplained grief. Just as preparing for telepathic communication required time and concentration and energy, so did setting one's shields against the echoes of such communication. Spock could not protect himself constantly against every random touch; he had learned to ignore such things, for the most part. But also, for the most part, his shipmates on the *Enterprise* knew better than to touch him.

Trying to return discourtesy with courtesy, Spock did his best not to notice the brief opening into Braithewaite's thoughts, resisting the temptation to intrude directly and discover why the *Enterprise* had been called here. He did not seek out any information, and of the thoughts forced upon him, none was useful.

Spock drew back his hand as he succeeded in sealing his mental shields.

"Please come into the back office," Braithewaite said. "It's a little more secure." He led the way into the next room.

"Sorry, Mr. Spock," Kirk said under his breath. He had seen the muscles harden along Spock's jaw, a faint change anyone who did not know Spock extremely well would be oblivious to.

"I will maintain my shields until we return to the ship, Captain," Spock said tightly.

Braithewaite dragged an extra chair to the inner room so they could all sit down; the cubicle was furnished barely, but crammed with files, data banks, stacks of memory cassettes, transcripts, and the general detritus of an understaffed office. Braithewaite got Kirk a drink in a plastic cup (Spock declined); the prosecutor sat down, then stood up again; his energy-level fairly radiated around him. He paced a few steps one way, a few steps the other. He made Jim Kirk nervous.

"Ordinarily my job is fairly routine," Braithewaite said. "But the last few weeks . . ." He stopped and rubbed his face with both hands. "I'm sorry, gentlemen. A friend of mine died last night and I haven't quite . . ."

Kirk stood up, took Ian by the elbow, led him to the chair, made him sit down, and handed him the plastic cup.

"Have some of that. Relax. Take your time, and tell me what happened."

Braithewaite drew in a long breath and let it out slowly. "I'm sorry," he said. "It hasn't anything to do with why you're here, I just can't keep Lee out of my mind. She didn't seem that sick, but when I stopped by the hospital this morning they said she'd had hypermorphic botulism, and . . ."

"I understand, Mr. Braithewaite," Kirk said. "I see why you're so upset."

"She was Aleph's public defender. Most people expect defense counsel and prosecutor to be enemies, but that's hardly ever true. There's a certain amount of rivalry, but if there's any respect, you can't help but be friends."

Kirk nodded. Spock watched the emotional outburst dispassionately.

"I think I can keep hold of myself now," Braithewaite said. He managed a faint and shaky smile, but it faded immediately. He leaned forward, intense and somber. "You're here to take charge of the case I just finished prosecuting. It's like nothing I've ever faced before. It started out nasty enough—ten people disappeared and it looked like a murderous confidence game. But it was worse than that. It turned out to be unauthorized research on self-aware subjects."

"What kind of research?" Spock asked.

"I'm not allowed to say, beyond proscribed weapons development. It doesn't affect the case, it isn't what the conviction was for. This way it caused less publicity. And publicity would have been awkward. Federation head-quarters has classified everything to do with the case." He smiled wryly. "They're not too pleased that *I* know so much about it. I knew they were concerned, but I didn't expect them to send a ship like the *Enterprise* to take the prisoner to Rehabilitation Colony Seven. It's certainly a secure transport, though."

"Wait a minute," Kirk said. "Wait a minute!" All his sympathy for Ian Braithewaite fled. He was raising his voice but he did not care. "Do you mean to tell me," he shouted, leaping to his feet, "that you diverted the *Enterprise*—you diverted a ship of the line, with a crew of four hundred thirty-five people—to ferry *one* man the width of *one* star system?"

He was leaning over Braithewaite, shouting into his face. He straightened up and stepped back, stopping his outburst but not for an instant regretting it.

The empty plastic cup crumpled loudly in Braithe-waite's clenched fist. "I didn't choose the ship, Captain Kirk," he said. His face had turned nearly as pale as his colorless hair. "Federation HQ said they'd send a ship, and when the *Enterprise* howled in at warp nine I assumed you were it."

"The transmission did not come from Federation Headquarters," Spock said calmly. "Nor from Starfleet Command." He had sat, unperturbed, through Braithewaite's story and Kirk's tantrum. "It did not even come from a Starbase. It came directly from Aleph Prime, with the ultimate override coding that has only been used five times, to my knowledge, in the past standard decade."

"I honestly don't know how that happened, Mr. Spock," Braithewaite said.

"The override is reserved for planetary disasters, unprovoked enemy attack, or unforeseen occurrences in scientific investigation. It is not intended to help deal with petty criminals."

Ian Braithewaite's puppydog intensity vanished in stronger, angry determination. "Petty criminals! Aside from everything else the man's a murderer!"

"I beg your pardon," Spock said, in precisely the same tone he had used before. "Perhaps I misspoke myself."

Braithewaite nodded sharply.

"It is not intended to deal with criminals at all," Spock said. "In fact there are criminal penalties attached to its misuse—as you must know."

Despite himself, Kirk grinned. Spock would deny it, but the science officer was inducing a far more emotional effect with cold facts than Kirk had got by shouting at the top of his lungs. Kirk hoped that somewhere, down in the repressed human half of himself, Spock was enjoying his revenge.

"But *I* didn't use the code," Braithewaite said.

"The communication originated in your office and bore your signature."

"If you've been diverted unnecessarily, I'm very sorry," Braithewaite said with honest sincerity. "I'll try to find out how it happened. Obviously, yes, you should never have been called on the override code."

"Good," Kirk said. "That's that, then. We can be on our way." He stood up.

Braithewaite jumped to his feet and loomed over them. "Captain, you don't understand the problem. We're isolated here, and official ships are few and far between. We simply haven't got the facilities to detain anyone as ruth-

less and charismatic and intelligent as Georges Mordreaux. If he escaped, he could easily drop out of sight,
he could even stow away on a commercial ship and get
completely out of the system. There'd be nothing to stop
his beginning all over again somewhere else. The man's
dangerous: he makes people believe he can fulfill their
dreams! It's essential that he be sent to the rehabilitation
center before he gets a chance to deceive anyone else. If
he gets away—"

"Your neck would be on the line, for one thing," Kirk
said.

Braithewaite slowly flushed. "That goes without saying."

"Captain," Spock said. "I believe we should accede to
Mr. Braithewaite's request."

Astonished, Kirk faced his science officer.

"We should?"

"Yes, Captain. I believe it is vital that we do so."

Kirk flung himself back into his chair.

"What the hell," he said.

Ian Braithewaite wanted to bundle his prisoner off to
the *Enterprise* immediately.

"Sorry, Mr. Braithewaite," Kirk said. "Can't be done.
My ship isn't any more fitted for handling dangerous
criminals than Aleph is. We'll have to make some preparations first."

Kirk and Spock left the prosecutor's officer and headed
toward the central core of the station.

" 'Preparations,' Captain? Security Commander Flynn
is not likely to appreciate the critical implications of that
statement."

"Good Lord, don't tell her I said that. It was just a con-
venient excuse." He realized that he could hardly have
chosen a less tactful excuse: if Flynn heard about it she
would be offended, and justifiably so. Since her arrival,
security had shaped up faster than Kirk would have believed possible. Kirk did not think that his status as
Flynn's commanding officer would protect him from her
fierce loyalty to her people. Or from her brittle temper: it
was so quick to snap that Kirk sometimes wondered if
Flynn really were officer material.

"I have no reason to repeat imprudent remarks to
Commander Flynn," Spock said.

"Good," Kirk said. "Well, I've never been to Aleph

Prime before; I don't see any great harm in staying for a little while, whatever the excuse."

"You will find it most fascinating. There is a small research facility involved in growing bioelectronic crystals, which could revolutionize computer science."

"I'll definitely have to look into that," Kirk said. "Mr. Spock . . ."

"Yes, Captain?"

"Just exactly what's going on? Braithwaite was ready to give up and call for another ship, obviously you realized that. I went along with you, but I'd like to know just what it is I'm going along with."

"Indeed, Captain, I appreciate your trust."

"Well," Kirk said wryly, "what's a captain for?"

"I apologize for my apparent lack of consistency. Until he mentioned the name of the 'vicious criminal,' I had no way of knowing that something far more complex than lawbreaking—however serious—is involved."

Kirk frowned. "I don't remember—Georges Mordreaux? Who is it, Spock? Do you know him?"

"I studied temporal physics under him many years ago. He is a brilliant physicist. In fact, when it became clear that we had not been diverted to deal with any sort of true emergency, the only benefit I could see from our being ordered to Aleph Prime was the possibility of discussing my observations with Dr. Mordreaux before I repeated them."

"This must have been quite a shock to you."

"Jim, the whole matter is absurd!" Spock collected himself instantly and continued, the model of Vulcan calm again. "Dr. Mordreaux is an ethical being. More than that, he is a theoretical scientist, not an experimental one. He was always more likely to work with pencil and paper, even in preference to a computer. Still, supposing he did branch off into experimental work, it is preposterous to think that he would endanger self-aware subjects of any species. I think it unlikely in the extreme that he has metamorphosed into an insane murderer."

"Do you think you can prove him innocent?"

"I would like the chance to discover why he is about to be transported to a rehabilitation center with such dispatch and under such secrecy."

Kirk did not much like the idea of meddling in the business of civilian authorities, but for one thing they had meddled with his ship and for another he was as aware as Spock that if Mordreaux entered a rehabilitation colony he would not emerge improved. He might be happier, he would certainly no longer be troublesome, but he would not be a brilliant physicist anymore, either.

"All right, Spock. There's something weird about this whole business. Maybe your professor *is* being railroaded. At the very least we can nose around."

"Thank you, Captain."

Kirk stopped and pulled out his communicator.

"Kirk to *Enterprise*. Lieutenant Uhura, lift radio silence."

"*Enterprise*, Uhura here. Is everything all right, Captain?"

"I wouldn't go so far as to say that, but there's no emergency. Secure from general quarters. I'll be staying down on Aleph for a while, but you can reach me if you need me."

"Yes, sir."

"Kirk out." He hesitated a moment, then thought better of broadcasting his message to the *Enterprise*'s security commander.

"Mr. Spock, please tell Commander Flynn to back us up if Mr. Braithewaite questions the reasons for our staying here. I think a day is about as long as I can justify, but arrange a rotating skeleton crew so everybody gets some time off. Including you. And particularly Mr. Scott; he's not to spend the layover buried in the engines."

"All right, Captain."

"I assume a day on Aleph and a leisurely trip to Rehab Seven will suit your plans?"

"Admirably, Captain."

The spacious plaza gave the illusion of being under an open sky. In reality it was deep beneath the surface of Aleph Prime. With its mild, random breezes, the scent of flowers in the air, grass a little shaggy, inviting strolls, it was so perfect that Jim Kirk knew he would not be able to tolerate it for long. But until the clichés became obtrusive, he could enjoy it for what it was, the re-creation of a planet's surface by someone who had never walked in the open on a living world. Besides, if he decided he did not like it, he could always go to one of the other parks, one designed for the non-human inhabitants of the station. Jim Kirk glanced around at the nearly empty plaza and wondered if an inhabitant of Gamma Draconis VII would find the nearby tunnel-maze enjoyable for a while, then gradually come to the conclusion that it was just slightly too uniformly-dug, just triflingly too damp, and just faintly, barely perceptibly, too cleverly predictably complex.

Then he saw Hunter, walking out of the shadows of a small grove of trees, and he forgot about tunnel-mazes, about the inhabitants of γ Draconis VII, and even about the balmy, erratic breezes.

Hunter waved, and continued on toward him.

They stopped a few paces apart and looked each other up and down.

Hunter wore black uniform pants and boots that were regulation enough, but she also had on a blue silk shirt and a silver mesh vest, and, of course, the red feather in her hair.

"Still collecting demerits, I see," Jim said.

"And you're still awfully regular navy, you know. Some things never change." She paused. "And I guess I'm glad of it."

They both laughed at the same time, then embraced, hugging for the simple pleasure of seeing each other again. It was not like the old days, and Jim regretted that. He wondered if she did, too. He was afraid to ask, afraid to chance hurting her, or himself, or to put more of the kind of strain on their friendship that had nearly ended it before.

They fell into old patterns with only a little awkwardness, in the way of old friends, with good times and bad times between them, and years to catch up on. They walked together in the park for hours: it came to about an hour per year, by the time they worked their way to the present.

"You didn't get orders to come to Aleph, did you?" Jim asked.

"No. This is the only outpost in my sector that will paint *Aerfen* the way I want it, without throwing stupid regulations at me. And my crew likes it for liberty. Gods know they deserve some right now. How about you?"

"Weirdest thing that ever happened. This fellow, Ian Braithewaite—"

Hunter laughed. "Did he pounce on you, too? He

wanted me to pack up some criminal and take him to Rehab Seven, in *Aerfen!*"

"What did you tell him?" Jim asked, as embarrassment colored his face.

"Where he could put his prisoner, for one thing," Hunter said. "I guess I should have claimed *Aerfen* would practically fall out of orbit without a complete overhaul, but the truth is I was too damned mad to do any tactful dissembling."

"So was I."

"I wondered if he might go after you, too—but, Jim, a ship of the line flying a milk run? Don't keep me in suspense, what did you say to him?"

"I told him I'd take the job."

Hunter started to laugh, then saw that he meant it.

"Okay," she said. "That's got to be a better story than any amount of imaginative profanity. Let's hear it."

Jim told her what had happened, including Spock's analysis. He was glad to have someone more objective to talk to.

"Have you ever heard of Georges Mordreaux?"

"Sure—good gods, you don't mean he's been on Aleph all this time? *He's* the one you're supposed to take off to have his brain drained?"

Jim nodded. "What do you know about him?"

Hunter had always had a serious talent for physics, and had considered specializing in the field. But the academic life was far too quiet for her, and her taste for excitement and adventure won out early on. Still, she kept track of major advances in research in the branches that interested her.

"Well," she said. "There are two schools of thought, and hardly anybody in the middle. The first camp thought he was the finest physicist since Vekesh, if not Einstein. Listen, Jim, do you want to have dinner on *Aerfen,* or shall we find a place around here? I don't know what schedule you're working on, but it's late for me and I'm starved."

"I was hoping you'd come up to the *Enterprise* and let me show you around. What about the other camp?"

She glanced away. "I might have known a diversionary tactic wouldn't work with you." She shrugged. "No offense to your Mr. Spock—but the other camp, which is most people, thought Georges Mordreaux was a loon."

Jim was silent for a moment. "That bad?"

"Afraid so."

"Spock didn't mention it."

"That's fair. I expect he has his own opinion and considers the opposing one scurrilous gossip. Which it surely fell to."

"Why do you keep talking about Mordreaux in the past tense?"

"Oh. I think of him that way. He put out some papers a few years back, and the reaction to them was . . . hm . . . negative, to put it mildly. He still publishes once in a while, but nobody knew where he was. I had no idea he was *here*."

"Do you think it's possible somebody's arranged some kind of vendetta against him?"

"I can't imagine why anybody would, or who would do it. He just isn't a factor in academic circles anymore. Besides, criminal prosecution isn't the way physics professors discredit their rivals, it hasn't got the proper civilized flavor to it."

"What do you think about him?"

"I've never met him; I can't give you a personal opinion."

"What about his work? Do you think he's crazy?"

She toyed with the corner of her vest. "Jim . . . the last time I studied physics formally was fifteen years ago. I still subscribe to a couple of journals, but I keep up a superficial competence at best. I'm far too out of date to even guess at an answer to the question you're asking. The man did good work once, a long time ago. What he's like now—who knows?"

They walked for a while in silence. Hunter shoved her hands in her pockets.

"Sorry I'm not more help. But you can't tell much about anybody's personality from their work, anyway."

"I know. I guess I'm just grabbing at anything to try to figure out why the *Enterprise* got chosen for this duty." He had already told her about Mr. Spock's ruined observations. "Well, Captain, can I offer you a tour of my ship, and some dinner?"

"Well, Captain, that sounds great."

From across the park, Jim heard a faint voice.

"Hey, Jim!"

Leonard McCoy waved happily from the other side of

the park, and, with his companion, came tramping across the grass toward Jim and Hunter.

"Who's that?"

"That's my ship's doctor, Leonard McCoy."

She watched him approach. "He's feeling no pain."

Jim laughed, and he and Hunter walked together through the field to greet McCoy and his friend.

Spock returned to the *Enterprise,* paged Lieutenant Commander Flynn, and started working out a schedule to give the maximum amount of liberty to the maximum number of people, as Captain Kirk had requested. Before he finished, the lift doors slid open and Flynn stepped out onto the bridge.

"Yes, Mr. Spock?"

He turned toward her. "Commander Flynn, our mission here involves your section. Tomorrow morning Dr. Georges Mordreaux will board and we will convey him to Rehabilitation Colony Seven."

She frowned very slightly. Rehab Seven was in this system; it was in opposition to Aleph Prime right now, but still that meant it was only about two astronomical units away: a trivial distance for a starship, almost an insult, and she must realize that.

"If he were a V.I.P. you wouldn't have called me," Flynn said. "I take it that means he'll be in custody."

"That is correct." He knew she was waiting for more information, but he had none to offer. However, Captain Kirk's statement to Ian Braithewaite, that security would have to prepare for Dr. Mordreaux's arrival, suited his plans, and he saw no reason not to make the statement true in retrospect. "We have our orders, Commander Flynn," he said. "Please secure the V.I.P. cabin for Dr. Mordreaux's use."

Spock waited for the stream of questions and objections that would have come from the previous security commander, when he was asked for performance out of the ordinary, but the new commander behaved in quite a different manner.

"All right, Mr. Spock," she said. "What's Dr. Mordreaux been convicted of?"

Spock found it difficult to tell her, because he disbelieved the accusations so strongly. "Unethical research on self-aware subjects," he finally said. "And . . . murder."

"Mr. Spock," Flynn said carefully, in a tone that offered information rather than criticism, "the detention cells are considerably more secure than my people can make a cabin by tomorrow. And the cells aren't dungeons; they're fairly comfortable."

"I am aware of the security problem, Commander Flynn, as is Captain Kirk. I am putting my trust in your abilities. The prisoner will be confined in the V.I.P. cabin."

"Then I will have the cabin secured, Mr. Spock."

"I have posted a liberty schedule for all the crew except your section. I leave that arrangement to your judgment."

She glanced at the terminal, where the screen held the security roster ready for assignment. She picked out several officers with electronics background: four people, as many as could work efficiently on the energy screens.

"Everyone else can go down to Aleph," she said. "Since we aren't responding to a system-wide emergency."

"No, the orders are simply to transport Dr. Mordreaux. Thank you for your cooperation, Commander Flynn. If I can be of any help to you in making the preparations—"

"My people can handle it, Mr. Spock, but thanks."

He nodded, and the security commander left the bridge.

By the time Mandala Flynn got off the turbo lift she could hear the whoops of delight as the liberty schedule went up on all the ship's general communication terminals. She was as glad as the others that a call to a disaster had turned instead into a few hours of freedom. She had to admit, though, that in two months on the *Enterprise* she had sometimes wished for some incident, some conflict, that was real instead of only practice.

You could have stayed in the border patrol, she told herself, flying back and forth and up and down the same limiting plane of space, fighting the occasional skirmish, risking your life and getting shot up, until they retired you to a backwater Starbase somewhere.

Her ambitions aimed higher than that. She was not satisfied with what was known; the unknown fascinated her. That was one reason she had grabbed for the unexpected opportunity to transfer to the *Enterprise:* not for cross-system detours like the current bit of bureaucratic nonsense, but exploration, new worlds, the real thing. Even if once in a while it meant spending six weeks staring down into a naked singularity.

Flynn wanted experience on this ship because, in time, she intended to command it or one like it herself. The limits of Federation worlds were far too narrow for her. She was a child of interstellar space, comfortable with it, attuned to it. She belonged in the vanguard of discovery.

And if you ever find what you're looking for, she thought, if you ever even figure out what it is you're looking for—what will you do then?

She pushed her musings aside as she entered the security duty room, where the four officers she had chosen were already waiting for her.

When Spock was alone, he opened a communications channel to the station and began his real task, that of obtaining as much information about Dr. Mordreaux's recent past as he could find.

First he requested the records on the professor's trial from Aleph Prime's housekeeping computer.

The request bounced back: NO INFORMATION. The tape should be a matter of public record. Spock tried again, appending his security clearance, which should have been sufficient to overcome almost every level of classification. His request was refused.

He tried several other possible repositories of criminal records, and found nothing. The news services carried no notices whatever in their indices of Dr. Mordreaux's arrest, conviction, or sentencing; he held no listing in the station directory. Spock pushed himself away from the information terminal and considered what to do next.

Perhaps the professor had been living under an alias, but that did not explain his disappearance from judicial records, which would have used his real name. Spock considered possibilities, made a decision, and proceeded to deceive the Aleph computers without mercy. Their defenses were adequate for normal purposes—they were not, after all, ordinarily concerned with any particularly sensitive matters—but insubstantial compared to Spock's ability to break them.

And *still* he could find no useful information. The trial tapes simply did not exist, at least in the computer's data banks. Whoever had classified Dr. Mordreaux's case had done an extremely efficient job of it. Either the records had been wiped out—a breach of the constitution of the Federation—or they still existed but no longer interfaced with the information network at all.

Mandala met Hikaru in the gym. He smiled when he saw her, and sealed the collar and shoulder fastenings of his fencing jacket.

"I didn't know if this lesson was still on," she said.

"It'd take a lot more disruption of the schedule for me to cancel it," Hikaru said. "But I didn't know if you'd be able to come."

"I have to check the new shields when they're up," she said, "but till then all I could do would be watch over everybody's shoulders and make them nervous. They'll be finished about the same time you and I are. Then we're all going down to Aleph for some fun. It's on my tab. Want to come?"

"Sure," he said. "Thanks."

Mandala tossed him a book. He caught the small cassette.

"What's this?"

"What do you think of old Earth novels? Pre-space-flight, I mean?"

"I love them," he said. "I think *The Three Musketeers* is my favorite."

"My favorite Dumas is *The Count of Monte Cristo*."

"Have you read *The Virginian?*"

"Sure—it's most fun in Ancient Modern English. How about *The Time Machine?*"

"That's a good one. *Frankenstein?*"

"Sure. *Islandia?*"

"Uh-huh. I read someplace they're finally planning to bring out the unedited facsimile edition."

Mandala laughed. "How long have they been saying that? I wish they would, though."

Hikaru glanced curiously at the cassette she had given him; she gestured toward it with her foil.

"That one's *Babel-17*," she said. "It's just about my favorite. Delany's great."

"I never heard of it. When was it published?"

"Old calendar, nineteen sixty-six."

"That doesn't count as pre-space-flight."

"Sure it does."

"Oh—you must start at the first moon landing. I start from Sputnik I."

"Traditionalist. Hey—that means you haven't read *Sibyl Sue Blue,* either. Are you going to turn down terrific books because we disagree about twelve years?"

"Not a chance," Hikaru said. "Thanks very much."

As they started toward the practice ground, Mandala impulsively put her arm around Hikaru's waist and hugged him.

He did not pull away. Not quite. He was too polite for that. But his whole body stiffened. Surprised, hurt, trying to figure out how and where she had read things wrong, Mandala let him go and strode quickly to her end of the floor.

"Mandala—" He caught up with her; he knew better than to grab her, but he touched her elbow. "I'm sorry," he said. "I . . . are you mad at me?"

"I misunderstood," she said. "Let's not talk about it. I don't want to make a fool of myself twice in one day."

"You haven't," he said softly.

"No?" She faced him. "I thought, yesterday . . ." She shrugged. "I'm usually pretty good at taking hints. I'm sorry I pushed you. I can't claim I didn't mean it but I never meant to pressure you. I'm sorry if I embarrassed you."

"You didn't," he said. "I'm flattered."

"It's okay, never mind. You were a lot more polite about it than I would have been to somebody I wasn't interested in."

"It isn't that I'm not interested."

She could not think of anything to say to that. She had not come out bluntly and told him he was the most attractive man she had ever met, but he had not, after all, been unaware of how she felt. If he found her attractive in turn—and after yesterday she thought he did—then she could not understand his behavior.

"I've been thinking about what happened," he said, his voice strained. "I'm probably leaving. You know I'm thinking about a transfer, we've talked about it. You're the only person I *have* talked about it with!"

"Sure," she said. "So what? None of us really knows what they're going to be doing next week, next month—"

"It wouldn't be fair to you," Hikaru said.

Mandala stared at him; she fought to keep pure astonishment from turning to anger. She flung down her foil. It clattered across the floor. "What the hell do you mean, fair to *me?* Where do you get off, deciding that? You've been honest—what more do you think you could owe me?"

He stood before her, downcast. Mandala wanted to hug him, to take away some of that lost hurt look, but she knew she would not want to stop with a hug. Aside from the absurdity of trying to caress someone while they were both dressed in padded fencing jackets and standing in the middle of a public gym, she did not want to take the chance of embarrassing Hikaru again.

"I just don't think . . ." He paused, and started again. "It seemed so cold, to respond to you when the chances were I'd be taking off almost immediately."

Mandala took his hand, and stroked the hollow of his palm. "It isn't fair to *you,*" she said. "Hikaru, nobody ever makes long-term commitments on the border patrol. It's too chancy, and it's too painful. We used to say to each other: for a little while. I'm not used to anything but that. But you . . . I think you'd rather have something that lasted a long time."

"It *is* better," he said tentatively.

"That's up to you. It's fine. I understand, now. You've been under one hell of a lot of stress these last few weeks, and you're under more because of thinking about transferring off the *Enterprise.* I think you're right not to want to make it any harder on yourself."

"I guess that's part of it."

"Okay."

"Thank you," he said. He hugged her, and she returned the embrace until she was embarrassed herself, by her own response. She drew back, and picked up her foil.

"Come on—I want my lesson."

They saluted each other with the foils. Hikaru put his mask on.

"Hikaru," Mandala said, "if you change your mind, let me know." She pulled her own mask down and slipped into a smooth *en garde* position.

After several hours of fruitless work, Mr. Spock finally broke the communications link to Aleph Prime. He had tried every conceivable route toward the information he wanted, and every conceivable route dead-ended. He could do nothing more on board the *Enterprise*.

Before closing down his terminal he pulled up the duty roster to find someone familiar with the bridge who was still on board. Mr. Sulu's name was first on the list.

Paging the helm officer, Spock reached him in the gymnasium. Sulu appeared on the screen; he pushed his fencing mask to the top of his head. Sweat dripped down his face. Spock ordinarily found Sulu among the easiest of his colleagues to work with. But the other side of the lieutenant's character, the one that emerged when he was in the grip of his very deep streak of romanticism, Spock found virtually incomprehensible.

Mr. Sulu wiped off the sweat, put down his foil, and became once more the epitome of a serious, no-nonsense, one-track-minded Starfleet junior officer.

"Yes, Mr. Spock?"

"Mr. Sulu, can you interrupt what you are doing?"

"I've just finished giving a lesson, sir."

"I must return to Aleph Prime for a short while, and I do not wish to leave the bridge unattended."

"I can be there in ten minutes, Mr. Spock."

"Thank you, Mr. Sulu. Spock out."

But as he reached for the controls he saw Sulu make an involuntary gesture toward him. Spock paused with his hand on the reset button.

"Yes, Mr. Sulu? Is there something else?"

"Mr. Spock—" Sulu hesitated, then spoke all in a rush. "Did the captain say—do you think it's possible—will Captain Hunter come on board?"

Spock gazed impassively at Sulu for several moments. Sulu would, at that juncture, have given almost anything to recall his outburst. Mr. Spock was perhaps the only person on the *Enterprise* who would not, or could not, understand why he had asked the question. As far as Sulu had ever observed, the most effusive reaction Spock ever offered anyone was respect, and that infrequently. He had certainly never shown any signs of hero-worship. Sulu was under no illusions concerning his own feelings about Hunter: they *were* hero-worship, pure, blazing, and undignified. Hunter had been one of Sulu's heroes for half his life. Though he had been born on Earth, his mother was a consulting agronomist and his father was a poet; Hikaru Sulu had spent his childhood and adolescence on the frontier, on a succession of colony planets. His longest stay anywhere was on Ganjitsu, a world far out on the border of a sector that had long been harassed by renegades—the Klingons claimed they were renegades, though of course no one ever believed them—and at the mercy of pirates who were all too human. The Ganjitsu-jin resisted with inadequate means; for a long time they wondered if they had been forgotten, or abandoned. Then Hunter, a very young officer with her first command, swept in like a hunting hawk, beat the pirates back into the hands of the Klingons, and bested the Klingons themselves at their own game.

Sulu had seen things on Ganjitsu that he still had nightmares about, but Hunter had stopped the nightmare-reality. Sulu doubted he could make Mr. Spock understand how he felt about her, even if he had the opportunity to explain. No doubt he had lost the science officer's confidence forever. Sulu wished mightily that he had waited to ask Captain Kirk about Hunter. The captain understood.

However, Spock was not looking at him with disapproval, or even with his eyebrows quizzically raised.

"I have no way of knowing Captain Hunter's plans, Mr. Sulu," he said. "However, the possibility is not beyond the bounds of reason. If she does pay the *Enterprise* the compliment of visiting it, I hope she will receive the reception due an officer with such an exceptional record. Spock out."

Sulu watched the science officer's expressionless, ascetic face fade from the screen. Sulu hoped his own astonishment had not shown too plainly: at least his mouth had not fallen open in surprise.

After all these years I should know better than to make assumptions about Mr. Spock, Sulu thought.

Spock never failed to amaze him—in quite logical and predictable ways, if one happened to look at them from exactly the right perspective—just at the point where Sulu thought he knew most precisely how the Vulcan would behave.

"Hey," Mandala said from behind him, "you better get going, Hikaru—you promised him ten minutes." She pulled off her fencing mask and they formally shook un-gauntleted hands: she was left-handed so her right hand was ungloved.

"Do you think she'll come on board?"

Mandala smiled. "I hope so, it would be great to see her again." She wiped her sweaty face on her sleeve. "You know, if you do transfer, you couldn't do any better than Hunter's squadron." They headed toward the locker room.

"Hunter's squadron!" The possibility of serving with Hunter was so dreamlike that he could not make it sound real. "I wouldn't have a chance!"

Mandala glanced over at him, with an unreadable expression. She quickened her pace and moved ahead of him. Surprised, Hikaru stopped, and, a few steps later, so did Mandala.

She took a deep breath and let it out slowly.

"Where, where in the freezing hell did you pick up such a load of doubt about yourself?"

"If I applied and she turned me down—"

"You have the background," Mandala said. "You have the right specialties. And you have that Academy star."

Hikaru grinned ruefully. "You never saw my grades."

She spun back toward him, a quick fierce fury in her flame-green eyes. "Damn your grades! You got in and you got through, that's all that counts! No low-level knownothing bureaucrat can weed you off a transfer list on the grounds that you couldn't possibly be qualified for anything you really want."

Hikaru knew her well enough by now to hear the pain in her voice, underneath the anger.

"Did that happen to you?" he asked gently. But he already knew it must have; Mandala had never had the chance to attend the Academy. Both literally and figuratively, she had fought her way up from the ranks.

"It's happened . . . several times," she said finally. "And every time it happens, it hurts more. You're the only person I've ever admitted that to. I would not like it said to anyone else."

He shook his head. "It won't be."

"This is the only first-class assignment I've ever had, Hikaru, and I know Kirk didn't ask for me. He demanded the first person available who could replace my predecessor. He would have taken *anybody*." She smiled grimly. "Sometimes I think that's what he thinks he got. I have the job by pure chance. But you can bet I'm not going to waste it. I won't let them stop me, Academy star or not—" She cut off her words, as if she had already revealed far more of herself than she ever meant to. She grasped his shoulders. "Hikaru, let me give you some advice. Nobody will believe in you for you."

But do I dare believe in me enough to try to transfer to Hunter's command? Hikaru wondered. Do I dare take the risk of being turned down?

Mr. Spock beamed back down to Aleph Prime. The city jail was in a short corridor near the government section; it showed evidence of hard use and neglect. The plastic walls were scarred and scratched; in places graffiti cut so deep that the asteroidal stone of the original station showed through from behind. The walls had been refinished again and again, in slightly different colors, leaving intricately layered patterns of chipped and worn and partially replaced surfaces.

A security guard lounged at the front desk. Spock made no comment when she quickly put aside her pocket computer; he had no interest in her activities on duty, whether it was to read some fictional nonsense of the sort humans spent so much time with, or to game with the machine.

"Can I help you?"

"I am Spock, first officer of the U.S.S. *Enterprise*. I have come to interview Dr. Georges Mordreaux before we take him on board."

She frowned. "Mordreaux . . . ? The name sounds familiar but I don't think we've got him here." She glanced at the reception sensor and directed her voice toward it. "Is Georges Mordreaux in detention?"

"No such inmate," the sensor said.

"Sorry," the guard said. "I didn't think we had anybody scheduled to go offstation. Just the usual collection of rowdies. Payday was yesterday."

"Some error has been made," Spock said. "Dr. Mordreaux's trial tapes are not available from public records. Perhaps he is here but the documents have been lost."

"I remember where I heard that name!" she said. "They arrested him for murder. But his lawyer invoked the privacy act so they shut down coverage. She was pleading insanity for him."

"Then he is here."

"No, if that's how he was convicted he wouldn't be here, he'd be at the hospital. But you can look for him if you like." She gestured toward the bank of screens, one per cell, which gave her an overview of the entire jail wing. Spock saw no one who resembled his former teacher, so he took the guard's advice and went looking at the hospital instead.

"Sure, he's here," the duty attendant said in response to Spock's query. "But you'll have a hard time interviewing him."

"What is the difficulty?"

"Severe depression. They've got him on therapy but they haven't got the dosage right yet. He's not very coherent."

"I wish to speak with him," Spock said.

"I guess that's okay. Try not to upset him, though." The attendant verified Spock's identity, then led him down the hall and unlocked the door. "I'll keep an eye on the screen," he said.

"That is unnecessary."

"Maybe, but it's my job." He let Spock go inside.

The hospital cell looked like an inexpensive room at a medium-priced hotel on an out-of-the-way world. It had a bed, armchairs, meals dispenser, even a terminal, though on the latter the control keyboard was limited to the simplest commands for entertainment and information. Mordreaux's jailers were taking no chances that he could work his way into the city's computer programs and use his knowledge to free himself.

The professor lay on the bed, his arms by his sides and his eyes wide open. He was a man of medium height, and he was still spare; he still let his hair grow in a rumpled halo, but it had grayed. His luminous brown eyes no longer glowed with the excitement of discovery; now they revealed distress and despair.

"Dr. Mordreaux?"

The professor did not answer; he did not even blink.

Stress-induced catatonia? Spock wondered. Meditative trance? No, of course it must be the drugs.

Spock had done some of his advanced work in physics at the Makropyrios, one of the finest universities in the Federation. Dr. Mordreaux was a research professor there, but every year he taught a single very small and very concentrated seminar. The year Spock attended, Dr. Mordreaux accepted only fifteen students, and he stretched and challenged them all, even Spock, to their limits.

Dr. Mordreaux had early reached a pinnacle in his career, and what was more remained there; his papers frequently stunned his colleagues, and honors befell him with monotonous regularity.

"Professor Mordreaux, I must speak with you."

For a long time Dr. Mordreaux did not reply, but, finally, he made a harsh, ugly noise that took Spock several seconds to identify as a laugh. He remembered Dr. Mordreaux's laugh, from years ago: it had been full of pleasure and delight; it was almost enough to make a young Vulcan try to understand both humor and joy.

Like so much else, it had changed.

"Why did you come to Aleph Prime, Mr. Spock?"

Dr. Mordreaux pressed his hands flat against the bed and pushed himself to a sitting position.

"I did not think you would remember me, Professor."

"I remember you."

"The ship on which I serve was called to take you on board."

Spock stopped, for large tears began to flow slowly down Dr. Mordreaux's cheeks.

"To take me to prison," he said. "To rehabilitate me."

"What happened, Professor? I find the accusations against you unlikely at best."

Mordreaux lay down on the bed again, curling up in fetal position, crying and laughing the strange harsh laugh, both at the same time.

"Go away," he said. "Go away and leave me alone, I've told you before I only wanted to help people, I only did what they wanted."

"Professor," Spock said, "I have come here to try to help you. Please cooperate with me."

"You want to betray me, like everybody else, you want to betray me, and you want me to betray my friends. I won't, I tell you! Go away!"

The door slid open and the attendant hurried in. "The doctor's on the way," he said. "You'll have to leave. I told you he wouldn't be coherent." He shooed Spock out of the room.

Spock did not protest, for he could do nothing more

here. He left the hospital, carefully considering what the professor had said. It contained little enough information, but what was that about betraying his friends? Could it possibly be true that he had done research on intelligent subjects, and that they had been hurt, or even died? In his madness, could the professor be denying, in his own mind, events that had actually happened? What could he mean, he had only intended to help people?

Spock had no answers. He would have to wait until Dr. Mordreaux came on board the *Enterprise;* he would have to hope the professor became more rational before it was too late.

The science officer drew out his communicator, then changed his mind about returning to the ship immediately. No logical reason demanded that this trip to Aleph Prime be completely wasted. He put his communicator away again and headed toward another part of the station.

As Jim Kirk prepared to call the *Enterprise,* the paging signal went off so unexpectedly that he nearly dropped his communicator.

"Good timing," he said to Hunter with a grin. "And they've let me alone all afternoon, I'll give them that."

Hunter tensed automatically. *Aerfen* did not call her, when she was off the ship, except in a serious emergency: virtually everyone in her crew was capable of taking over when she was not there. She had made sure of that, for *Aerfen*'s assignments left it exposed to the possibility of stunning casualties at any time. Hunter was always, on some level, aware of that fact, and, by extension, of her own mortality. For the good of her ship, she could not afford to be indispensable. She was secure enough in her ability to command to give all her people more responsibility than was strictly essential, or even strictly allowed. The last time Starfleet called her on the carpet, it was for teaching a new ensign, with talent but without the proper formal training credentials, how to pilot *Aerfen* in warp drive.

As a result, Hunter's communicator seldom signalled for her when she was planetside; hearing Jim's go off she unconsciously assumed the call was an emergency. He might need help: her reflexes prepared her for action.

"Kirk here," he said.

Hunter remembered the first time they had met.

He was so spit-and-polish, she thought, and I—I practically still had dust between my toes.

They had regarded each other with equal disdain.

"Captain," said a voice from Jim's communicator, "I have some equipment for the *Enterprise,* but your signature is required before I may beam it on board."

"What kind of equipment, Mr. Spock?"

"Bioelectronic, sir."

"What for?"

"To incorporate into the apparatus for the singularity observations."

"Oh," Kirk said. "All right. Where are you?"

"At the crystal growth station in the zero-g section of Aleph Prime."

"You really need me there right now, Spock?"

"It is quite important, Captain."

Jim glanced at Hunter and grimaced. She shrugged, with understanding, and let herself relax again. No emergency.

"All right, Mr. Spock. I'll meet you there in a few minutes." He closed his communicator. "I'm sorry," he said to Hunter. "Spock worked so hard on those blasted observations, just to have them jerked out from under him. The least I can do is humor him if he wants to put in more equipment."

"I understand," she said. "There's no problem."

"This shouldn't take me too long . . ."

"Jim, it's okay," she said. "I'll go on up to *Aerfen* and take care of a couple of things, then beam directly over to the *Enterprise.*"

"All right," he said. "I'll see you there in a little while."

She gave him directions for getting to where he was going—Aleph's volumetric spherical grid pattern was not nearly as straightforward as it sounded; besides, she knew a good shortcut—and watched him walk away across the field.

Hunter took out her communicator. "Hunter to *Aerfen.* Please beam me up, Ilya."

Waiting for the beam to track her, Hunter thought back over the afternoon. She was glad to see Jim Kirk again, though, as always, a bit surprised that their friendship endured despite their differences, differences that had been obvious from the moment of their acquaintance in the same first-year platoon at the Academy. Jim Kirk was a star student, fitting in with that cosmopolitan home-world flair; Hunter was in trouble even before she arrived, a colonist with proud, prickly, defensive arrogance, who went by a single name and refused to record any other.

Their commander, a senior-class student (whose name mutated instantly from Friendly, which was ridiculous, to Frenzy, which made a certain amount of sense), took exception to her family's tradition of names, and, even more, to the feather Hunter always wore in her hair. By freedom of religion she was entitled to it, but he ordered her to remove it. She refused; he charged her with being out of uniform and with showing contempt for a superior officer.

She had been tempted to plead guilty to the second accusation.

Lawyers were not a custom among Hunter's people, and she did not intend to involve anyone else in her difficulties with the hierarchy. But the court-martial would not convene without a defense counsel. To Hunter's disgust, James T. Kirk volunteered.

Hunter had him firmly typed as the same sort of self-satisfied prig as the platoon commander; he upheld her judgment of him with the first words he spoke.

"I think you're making a big mistake," he said. "I think probably if you apologize to Frenzy he'll cancel the trial."

"Apologize! For what?"

He glanced at her braid of black hair, at the small black-tipped scarlet feather bound to its end. "Look," he said, "if Frenzy adds lying to the charges, you'll be finished."

"Lying!" she shouted. She leapt out of her chair and faced him off across the table, pressing her hands flat on the surface so she would not clench them into fists.

"No one," she said softly, "no one, in the entire world, in my entire life, has ever accused me of lying, and right now I need one good reason, very quick, not to throw you through the wall."

He reached toward the feather. She pulled away, flinging her head back so the braid flipped over her shoulder.

"Don't touch that!"

"I know you don't believe I'm on your side," he said. "But I am. I really am. I did some reading last night and I know what the feather is supposed to mean. It's the last in a long series of tests that only a few people ever complete. I'm not saying you didn't do it—but that feather isn't the real thing. However important it is, it would be better to go without till you can get another real one, because if the board finds out you've made all this fuss over something that has in itself no intrinsic meaning, they'll throw the book at you."

Hunter frowned at him. "Wherever did you get the idea that it isn't real?"

He pulled a text out of his briefcase, slid it into a reader, and keyed up a page. "There," he said, pointing to a picture of a phoenix eagle gliding in the wind, so beautiful Hunter had to fight off a wave of homesickness. Jim Kirk's forefinger touched the white tip of a wing feather. "And there." He keyed up a photo of a young woman. Hunter blinked in surprise. It was her great-aunt, perfectly recognizable. She had been almost as elegant and dignified at that age as she had been well into her eighties, when Hunter first met her. Kirk touched the feather in the photograph: a long one, the span of a hand, with a white tip.

"You see what I mean," he said, nodding toward Hunter's feather, which, though red, was black-tipped, barely the length of her thumb, and far different in shape.

"Either you've got a crappy book, or you missed some spots," she said. "Wearing one of the primaries just means the eagles have accepted you as a reasoning adult being." She stabbed at the reader keyboard, brought back the first picture, and traced her finger along the eagle's crest, which looked darker red through being formed of black-tipped plumage.

"What I wear is a crest feather. It means . . . it's too complicated to explain everything it means. The eagles accept me as a friend."

Kirk looked at her. "One of the eagles gave you the feather?" He sounded rather stunned.

Hunter scowled again. "That's right—good gods, what did you think it was? A trophy?" She was repelled by the idea of injuring one of the magnificent, totally alien, gentle, fierce beings. "They're as intelligent as we are. Maybe more so."

Kirk sat down slowly. "I think I understand now," he said. "I apologize. I jumped to conclusions, and I was wrong. Will you accept my apology?"

Hunter nodded curtly. But her dislike began to ease,

for she too had jumped to conclusions, and she too had been wrong.

The next day, at Hunter's court-martial, the senior platoon commander slowly but surely and irrevocably destroyed his credibility with his superiors. Freedom of religion was a touchy subject with Starfleet. They were committed to it on a theoretical basis, but, practically, it was difficult to administer. Aside from the sheer number of belief systems, the rituals ranged from virtually nonexistent to thoroughly bizarre. So when a stiffnecked undergraduate with his first minor command proved himself guilty of harassing a pantheist whose disruption consisted of wearing a feather in her hair, they showed him very little sympathy at all.

Though she often could have got away with it, Hunter never claimed a religious exemption for her other nonconforming behavior. She succeeded in acting as she thought right, and as she wished, through a combination of fast moves, of giving not a damn about demerits, and of pure, solid, unimpeachable excellence in her performance.

She put aside old memories as she materialized on the transporter platform of her own ship. Her senior weapons officer nodded a greeting to her and tossed his long blond hair back off his forehead.

"Hi, Ilya," Hunter said. "All quiet?"

"I have no complaints," he said, in his clipped, controlled voice. But a moment later, when they passed the aft viewport, he added, "Except one."

"What?"

"Hunter, I would like that damned monster ship off our tail. It makes me very nervous."

Hunter glanced out the port at the *Enterprise,* orbiting behind and above them. She laughed. "Ilya Nikolaievich, they're on *our* side."

Chapter 2

Mr. Sulu was not above imagining himself truly commanding the *Enterprise,* not merely the random high-ranking officer of a crew of all of twenty people. Mandala Flynn had beamed down with the last four security officers, to honor her promise to buy their dinner. Sulu hoped he could join her later.

On the darkened bridge, he slid into the captain's seat and gazed out the viewscreen. The *Enterprise* was oriented so that, with respect to the ship's gravitational field, Aleph Prime loomed overhead, a huge shining Christmas tree ornament set spinning, to Sulu's eyes, by the ship's motion around it; and then, framed by space and multi-colored stars, *Aerfen* hung suspended. Aerfen, Minerva, grey-eyed Athene, defending battle-goddess.

" 'In such likeness Pallas Athene swept flashing earth-ward,' " Sulu said aloud.

"Hunter to *Enterprise,* permission to beam aboard?"

Sulu started, feeling the blood rush to his face, but of course she could not have heard him quoting Homer aloud on the bridge of a starship, no one could have heard him; he was all alone.

"*Enterprise,* Sulu here, permission granted, of course,

Captain." Sulu called for someone to relieve him, on the double, and hurried to the transporter room.

Hunter glittered into reality. Sulu knew instinctively that she would despise effusion. When she stepped down from the platform, he took her outstretched hand and said his name in response to her own introduction. But he bowed to her as well, just slightly, perhaps a breach of Starfleet protocol, but a gesture of respect in his family's traditions. She was not as tall as he expected—he had put her in his mind as some overwhelming demigod or giant, and he was rather relieved that her physical presence was not quite what he had imagined. Her hand was hard and firm, with traces of callus on the palm, and a long angry scar that led up the back of her hand and disappeared beneath her shirt cuff at the wrist. Her silver vest made her shoulders gleam, as if she wore armor.

"Mr. Sulu," she said. "I'm pleased to meet you. Jim spoke of you with a great deal of regard."

Sulu could not think of anything to answer to that; he was too surprised and flattered. "Thank you," he said, finally, lamely. "Captain Kirk hasn't returned from Aleph Prime yet, Captain Hunter. May I show you to the officers' lounge?"

"That would be fine, Mr. Sulu."

They got into the lift, descended, and walked down a long corridor. The *Enterprise* seemed deserted, haunted, surreal, with its crew on liberty and its lights dimmed.

"It isn't shown off at its best right now," Sulu said apologetically.

"Never mind," Hunter said. "A ship like this doesn't need much showing off."

They chatted about *Aerfen* and the *Enterprise* until they reached the lounge. Sulu offered her a drink, or a glass of wine, which she declined; they ended up both with coffee, sitting over a port with a view of deep space, still talking ships.

"That's a nasty gash on *Aerfen*'s side," Sulu said. "I hope there wasn't too much damage."

Hunter looked away. "Not to the ship," she said. "I lost two good people in that fight."

"Captain—I'm sorry, I didn't know . . ."

"How could you? Mr. Sulu, no one volunteers for this particular assignment without knowing the risks."

She appeared, suddenly, very human and very tired,

and Sulu's regard for her increased. To fill the silence, because he did not know what to say, he got up and re- filled their cups.

"Where are you from, Mr. Sulu?" she asked when he returned. Only a hint of tightness in her voice betrayed her. "I feel like I should be able to place your accent, but it's so faint I can't."

"It isn't so much faint as a complete muddle. I lived in a lot of different places when I was a kid, but longest on Shinpai." He used the colloquial name without even thinking.

"Shinpai!" Hunter said. "Ganjitsu? I've been there."

"Yes, ma'am," Sulu said. "I know. I remember. No one there will forget for a long time." It was his turn to look away; he had not meant to tell her anything about him- self or the debt he and a lot of other people owed her, and now he realized why.

I'm afraid she'll say it was nothing, he thought. I'm afraid she'll shrug it all off and laugh at me.

"Thank you, Mr. Sulu."

He looked slowly back at her. Shadows across her face obscured her gray eyes.

"In this career—you must know—you sometimes come to feel like everything you do, the conflict, the friends you lose, it's all for the glory of some faceless, meaningless set of rules and regulations. And that doesn't matter. It doesn't matter a damn. It only matters when you know it makes a difference to a person."

"It made a difference," Sulu said. "Never think it didn't make a difference."

Jim Kirk had to put down the awkward boxes of bio- electronic crystals before he could get out his communi- cator.

"Couldn't you at least have had this stuff delivered, Mr. Spock?" he asked.

"Of course, Captain, but I thought you would not wish to stay at Aleph Prime for several more days."

Kirk grumbled something inarticulate and flipped open his communicator. "Kirk to *Enterprise*."

"*Enterprise*. Sulu here, Captain."

"Mr. Spock and I are ready to beam up, Mr. Sulu."

A few minutes later, Kirk, Spock, and the assorted boxes materialized on the transporter platform. Kirk stepped down to greet Hunter, who had accompanied Sulu to the transporter room.

"You've met Mr. Sulu, I see," Jim said. "This is Mr. Spock, my first officer."

"Mr. Spock," she said, nodding to him. "It's good to meet you after hearing about you for so many years."

"I am honored," Spock said.

Kirk noticed Sulu moving slowly, and, he thought, rather reluctantly, toward the door.

"Mr. Sulu," he said on impulse, "have you had dinner?"

"Dinner?" Sulu asked, surprised by the unusual question. "Captain, I'm afraid my system lost track of time about when we went into the sixth week around the singularity. I wouldn't know what to call the last meal I had."

Kirk chuckled. "I know how you feel. I'm going to show Captain Hunter around the ship, and then she and I and Mr. Spock are going to dine on the observation deck. Hunter, I want you to meet my officers. Mr. Sulu, would you see who else is on board? And would you join us yourself?"

"I'd love to," Sulu said. "Thank you, Captain."

When Kirk and Hunter and Spock had taken the new equipment and left the transporter room, Sulu hurried to the console and opened a channel to Aleph Prime.

"Sulu to Flynn, come in, Commander."

The pause dragged on so long he began to worry; he was about to try calling again when Mandala's voice came through.

"Flynn here."

"Mandala—"

"Hikaru, is anybody else with you?" she said before he could tell her about the invitation.

"No. I'm alone."

"Good. Beam us up, I've got two of my people with me."

He heard the urgency in her voice: he tracked them quickly and energized.

He watched in astonishment as three disheveled figures appeared on the platforms. Mandala was accompanied by two of the more startling members of the *Enterprise*'s security force. Snnanagfashtalli looked rather like a bi-pedal leopard with a pelt of maroon, scarlet, and cream. Everyone called her Snarl, but never to her face. She appeared, crouching down on all fours, her ruby fangs exposed, maroon eyes dilated and reflecting the light like a search beam. Her ears lay flat back against her skull and she had raised her hackles from the back of her neck to the tip of her long spotted tail, now bristling out like a brush. She growled.

"We should go back! I had my eyes on a tender throat!"

Mandala laughed. Her hair had fallen down in a tangled mane. Her red hair, her brilliant green eyes, and her light brown skin made her look as much a lithe, wild, fierce animal as Snarl.

"That tender throat had the bad manners to call for Aleph security, and that's why we got out of there." Mandala looked happier than Hikaru had ever seen her since she had come on board the *Enterprise*.

The third member of the party, Jenniver Aristeides, stood staring down at the floor, her shoulders slumped. She was two hundred fifty centimeters tall, her bones were thick and dense, and she seemed to have more layers of muscle than humans possess. That was quite possible. She *was* human, but she had been genetically engineered to live on a high-gravity planet.

Mandala went to her, and Snarl rubbed against her on the other side.

"Come on, Jenniver," Mandala said gently. She reached up to take the massive woman's hand; she led her from the platform. Jenniver looked up, and against her steel-gray skin her silver eyes glistened with unshed tears.

"I did not want to fight," Jenniver said.

"I know. It wasn't your fault. They'd've deserved it if you'd smashed their heads or if Snnanagfashtalli had ripped away a couple of their faces."

"I have no right to get angry if someone says I am ugly."

"I do," Snarl said.

"But I don't want you to get in trouble."

"I am friendly with trouble." Snarl's voice was a purr.

"She won't, will she? You won't, Commander? Will the captain be mad? It was my fault."

"Jenniver, stop it! It's all right. I was there, I saw what happened. Go get some sleep and don't worry. Particularly don't worry about Kirk."

Snarl took Jenniver's hand. "Come, my friend." They left the transporter room.

Mandala stretched and shook back her hair.

"What happened?" Hikaru asked.

"Some creeps decided it would be a lot of fun to humiliate Jenniver, Snarl took exception to what they said, and about that time I came along," Mandala said. "Thanks for beaming us up."

"You got in a fight."

"Hikaru," Mandala said, laughing, "do I look like I've been out for a quiet stroll?"

"Are you hurt?"

"No, and we didn't damage the other parties too much, either. That takes skill, I want you to know."

He looked after the two security officers. "I wouldn't want to be them when Captain Kirk hears about this, he's going to blow his stack."

Mandala looked at him sharply, narrowing her violent green eyes. "If Kirk has any problems with the way *I* act, he can take that up with me." Fury came so close to the surface in her that Hikaru hardly recognized her. "But if there's any discipline to be handed out in Security, that's my job." Abruptly, her anger vanished and she laughed again. She bunched her loose hair up at the back of her neck, and let it fall again. Hikaru shut his eyes for a moment, at the brink of calling himself a fool for refusing her, however short a time they might have had.

"Oh, gods," Mandala said. "I did need that." She looked after Snarl and Jenniver, with a thoughtful expression. "You know, despite what she looks like Jenniver is very sweet-tempered. I think she's even a little timid. I wonder if she's happy in security?"

"Are you sure you're all right?"

"Yeah. Why did you call me, anyway? Are you finally off duty? Do you want to go back down to Aleph?"

"Have you had dinner?"

"No, I took my people out but I was waiting for you."

"Good," he said. "I have an even better offer."

Jim Kirk would have preferred to welcome Hunter on board the *Enterprise* with a full officers' reception; his own sense of fairness fought with his wish to show his ship and his people off at their best. Fairness finally won; he did not have any of the other *Enterprise* officers called back from Aleph. But when he and Hunter walked into the wide, deserted observation deck, darkened so the brilliant star-field glowed across the entire hundred eighty degrees of the port, he could not maintain his disappointment. He and his old friend stood together looking out into the depths of stars, not talking, not needing to talk; but again, Jim thought of the things he wanted to say to Hunter, all the things he should say. He almost turned to her and spoke her name, her dream-name that only her family and he knew, the name he had not spoken since the last time they made love.

The door opened; Jim drew in a long breath and let it out slowly, feeling mixed regret and relief, as Spock came out onto the observation deck, followed by Mr. Sulu and Lieutenant Commander Flynn. The moment vanished.

"Mandala!" Hunter said. "I didn't know you were on the *Enterprise!*"

"Hi, Hunter. Being here is kind of a surprise to me, too."

"She says she wants my job," Jim said, without thinking.

Color rose in Flynn's face, but Hunter laughed, delighted.

"Then you'll have to recommend her for a better one, if you want to keep this ship yourself."

That was the first time Jim understood what Mandala Flynn had said to him, when he asked her about her career plans at the reception when she first came on board. She really had looked him straight in the eye and said, "I want your job." She had been telling him she expected him to take her very seriously, however doubtful he might be that she had adequate background and education for the job. But he had misunderstood her completely.

Flynn smiled at Hunter.

That's the first time I've seen her smile, Jim thought. A real smile, not an ironic grin. I think I had better re-evaluate this officer.

Hunter and Mandala Flynn embraced with the easy familiarity of the less formal traditions of the border patrols.

"I see I don't have any more introductions to make," Jim said. "When did you serve together?"

Flynn's smile vanished abruptly and her usual air of watchfulness returned. Jim wondered uneasily if his spurof-the-moment excuse to Ian Braithewaite, that it would take security twenty-four hours to prepare for the prisoner, had made its way back to his new security commander. He knew it could not have come from Spock, but it might have reached her more circuitously via Braithewaite himself.

Give me another chance, Ms. Flynn, Kirk thought. I didn't know if you were going to work out. You needed that undercurrent of ferocity to get as far as you have, from where you started, and I didn't know if you could keep it under control. I still don't. But you're an able officer, security is shaping up for the first time in a year, and the last thing in the galaxy I want to do is antagonize you.

"My squadron and the fleet Mandala flew with merged for a while," Hunter said. "Out by the Orion border."

"That got sticky, by all reports," Jim said.

From there, the conversation slipped straight into old times and reminiscences, and even Mr. Spock unbent enough to relate one strange tale from early in his Starfleet career. To Kirk's surprise and relief, Mandala Flynn also began to relax her stiff reserve. Only Mr. Sulu remained on the fringe of the conversation, and he did not seem to feel left out. Rather, he appeared more than content merely to listen. Jim Kirk smiled to himself. He had experienced a few minutes of regret, rather selfish regret, after his impulsive invitation for the others to join him and Hunter, but now he was glad he had done it.

Later that night, Sulu sat in the dark in his small cabin, absently chewing on his thumbnail. He liked the *Enterprise*. His friends were here; his crewmates respected him and his superiors occasionally appreciated him; he admired his captain. And if he decided to stay, he could admit even to himself that he was desperately in love with Mandala Flynn.

Still, he thought, still—what about all those ambitions I used to have? Nothing I've been thinking about for the last six months has changed. My record so far isn't good enough to give me a chance at a real command. I'm going to have to take more risks than I have so far in my life.

What about Mandala?

He knew that if he gave up his ambitions for her she would not understand, and she would begin to despise him. If they were friends, or lovers, it could not be on a basis of guilt or self-denial, not from either side.

If he followed through, he *would* be taking risks. Aside from the sheer physical danger he would be volunteering for, if he applied for a transfer to a fighter squadron—ideally, to *Aerfen*—Captain Kirk would not stand in his way. He was fairly sure of that. But he had no reason to believe Hunter would accept his application. If she did not, and if ultimately no squadron commander accepted him, and he stayed on the *Enterprise*, things would never be quite the same for him here again.

Jim and Hunter walked together to the transporter room.

"I enjoyed today, Jim," she said. "It's been good to see you again."

"I'm sorry we have to leave so soon," he said. "But there's no reason we can't swing past Aleph on the way back."

"I'll be gone by then," she said. "The border's unstable and my squadron is at low strength—I can't afford to keep the flagship off the line any longer than I absolutely have to. As it is I'll probably have to take *Aerfen* out shorthanded." She shook her head, staring down at the floor. "I don't see how I'll replace those two people, Jim," she said.

There was nothing he could say. He knew how it felt to lose crew members, friends, and there was nothing anyone could say.

They reached the transporter room, and Jim fed in the coordinates for Hunter's ship.

"Well."

The only real awkwardness came now, when they did not want to say goodbye. They hugged tightly. Jim had left too long the things he wanted to say. He was afraid it was far too late, not only by today, but by years, to say them. He buried his face against the curve of her neck and shoulder; the scent of her hair brought back memories so strong that he was afraid to look at her again, afraid to try to speak.

"Jim," Hunter said, "don't, please don't." She pulled gently away.

"Hunter—"

"Goodbye, Jim." She stepped up onto the platform.

"Goodbye," he whispered.

She nodded that she was ready. He touched the controls, and she flickered out of existence.

It took Jim Kirk some time to regain his composure. When he succeeded, he headed straight for his cabin, hoping he would not see anyone else. He felt both physically and emotionally drained. For the first time he felt resigned to the *Enterprise*'s carrier mission: nearly grateful for it.

Hunter was right, he thought. This will be a milk run. And maybe that's what we all need right now.

He entered his dark, silent cabin. It was the only place on the ship where he could even begin to relax, and he had not been anywhere near it in over twenty-four hours. Exhaustion began to take him over. He stripped off his shirt and flung it inaccurately at the recycler.

The message light was glowing green on his communications terminal. He cursed softly. A green-coded message was never urgent, but he knew he would not be able to sleep till he had found out what it was. He pushed the accept key.

Mr. Sulu's recorded voice requested a formal meeting.

That was strange. Kirk's last formal meeting with anyone in the crew was so long ago that he could not recall when it had been. He had never had one with Sulu. He prided himself on being so accessible that formal meetings were unnecessary.

Out of curiosity he returned Sulu's call: if the helm officer were sleeping, Kirk would not override a privacy request. But, not entirely to the captain's surprise, Sulu appeared on the screen immediately, wide awake, though looking tired and stressed. Now that Kirk thought of it, Sulu had not had any opportunity to take advantage of liberty on Aleph Prime. Through one circumstance or another he had been more or less on duty ever since they arrived, and he had stood an extra watch to maneuver the *Enterprise* away from the singularity.

I push him too hard, Kirk thought. His competence is so low-key, so overlaid with his sense of humor, that I don't really acknowledge how hard he works or what a good job he does. Oh, lord—I wonder if he had other plans for tonight, but thought my invitation was an order?

"Yes, Mr. Sulu," he said. "I got your message. Is everything all right? I think maybe I owe you an apology."

Sulu's expression turned to blank astonishment. "An apology, Captain? What for?"

"I didn't intend this evening to be compulsory. I have a feeling you had other things to do and I threw a wrench into them."

"No, sir!" Sulu said quickly. "I was afraid we'd all been selfish in accepting, if you and Captain Hunter preferred more privacy—"

"Not at all. Well, I'm glad we got that straightened out. See you in the morning."

"Captain—"

"Yes, Mr. Sulu?"

"That wasn't what I wanted to talk to you about."

Kirk started to ask if whatever it was could wait till they had both had some sleep, but something about Sulu's manner stopped him.

Besides, Kirk thought, isn't this a perfect opportunity to let him know his value to the ship? And to me? That's a good exchange for a little time. And he doesn't look in any state for peaceful sleep; something's really bothering him.

"Why don't you come up to my cabin, Mr. Sulu? We can talk over some brandy."

"Thank you, sir."

This time it was Kirk's turn for blank astonishment. "A transfer?" he asked. "Why? Where? What's happened to make you unhappy on the *Enterprise?*"

"I'm happy here, Captain!" Sulu cupped his hands around the brandy glass. Above all, he wanted Kirk to understand why he had to take this step. The scent of the brandy, almost as intoxicating as the liquor itself, curled up around his face. "Captain, I have an unexceptional record—"

"Your record's exemplary, Mr. Sulu!"

Sulu began again. "Serving on the *Enterprise* is a bright mark on anyone's record. It's the only thing outstanding about mine—and I think I must have got it by sheer luck."

"Oh?" Kirk asked. "Do you think I choose my crew at random?"

Sulu blushed, realizing the tactlessness of his remark.

"No, sir, of course I don't. But I don't know why you did pick me. My marks at the Academy were dead average . . ." He paused, for his own disappointment in himself and his performance at the Starfleet Academy was an ache that had never faded.

"I didn't just look at your cumulative marks," Kirk said. "Moving around the way your family did was bound to leave you less well-prepared than most cadets. So every time you encountered a new subject you started out pretty nearly at the bottom of the class."

Sulu did not look up. He was embarrassed, for that was true.

"And then," Kirk said, "you got better and better, until you mastered the subject completely. That's my idea of a potentially fine officer, Mr. Sulu."

"Thank you, Captain . . ."

"I haven't convinced you, have I?"

"I have to live with my record, sir. Whatever you saw behind it . . ."

"Your next captain might not?"

Sulu nodded.

"I think you're underestimating yourself."

"No, sir! I'm sorry, sir, but maybe for once I'm not. I love this ship, and that's the problem. It would be so easy to stay—but if my name comes up on a couple of promotion lists, I'll be promoted right off it. Eventually I might get a command position. But unless I distinguish myself somehow, unless I get as much experience in as many branches of Starfleet as I can, I'll never be able to hope for more than command of some supply-line barge, or a quiet little outpost somewhere."

Kirk hesitated; Sulu wondered if the captain would try to reassure him, or try to convince him that he did not understand how Starfleet worked and in which direction his career was likely to proceed.

Kirk looked at his drink. "There's no shame in a quiet command."

Sulu took a sip of brandy to give himself some time. "Captain, living my life without shame is important to me. It's necessary—but it isn't sufficient. Watching the diplomacy has been an education in itself, and I wouldn't have missed the exploration for anything. But without something more, my career dead-ends in another two steps."

He watched Kirk's face anxiously, trying to read his expression. Finally Kirk looked up, and his voice carried an edge of coldness.

"I never would have thought Hunter would shanghai my crew—it is *Aerfen* you want to transfer to?"

"Yes, sir—but Captain Hunter said nothing to me of this! I've been thinking about it for a long time. My very first duty preference was for assignment to a fighter squadron, and it was only because the *Enterprise*'s requirements took precedence over everything else that I was assigned here." He was not sure that was the right thing to admit to Captain Kirk, but it was true. "I've discussed the possibility with one friend on board, but otherwise you're the only person I've spoken to." It would have been unethical to apply to Hunter first, and Sulu was rather hurt that Kirk assumed he had done so. "I know she's lost two people in her crew, but I'm not under any illusions: there's got to be a waiting list of volunteers for *Aerfen*. I don't even know what positions need to be filled or whether I'd be suited to fill one. I have no way of knowing how she'll react to my application even if you approve it." He leaned forward earnestly. "Sir, I've never lied to you before, and I'm not about to start now. You can ask Captain Hunter if I've talked to her about this— she doesn't seem to me to be the sort of person who would lie, either."

Sulu could not tell from the far-away, introspective look on Kirk's face how the captain would react now. Perhaps he was only trying to keep anger in check.

"Mr. Sulu," he said, "what happens if she doesn't accept your application, or if Starfleet has already assigned new people?"

"Captain Kirk . . . this is something I've got to try to do, whether it's Captain Hunter's squadron or some other."

For the first time since Sulu had come in, Kirk smiled. Sulu had never been quite so grateful to see that expression on anyone in his life.

"I don't know how Hunter will respond to your application, either, Mr. Sulu," Kirk said. "But if she refuses it she'll be a long time looking for anyone half as good."

The process went faster than Sulu ever imagined possible. He was granted an immediate temporary transfer to *Aerfen*. At first he wondered if perhaps he had been accepted out of desperation, because the fighter was so short-handed. It was possible that Hunter did not really want him on her ship. But Kirk assured him, and Captain Hunter reassured him by her manner, than he was accepted on his merits both past and potential, and that the transfer would be permanent as soon as the red tape threaded its convoluted way through the bureaucratic machinery. So at six hundred hours, barely five hours after he had spoken to Kirk, he stood in the middle of his emptied room, a full duffel bag and a small box of miscellaneous stuff at his feet, and his antique sabre in his hands.

Carrying it, he left his cabin, walked quietly down the corridor, and knocked softly on Mandala's door. The answer was almost instantaneous.

"Come in!"

The lock clicked free; he went into the darkened cabin.

"What's the matter?" Mandala had her uniform shirt half over her head already, assuming an emergency for which she would be needed.

"It's all right," Hikaru said. "It's just me."

She looked out at him from the tangle of her shirt. It covered the lower half of her face like a mask, and pulled loose strands of her hair across her forehead.

"Oh, hi," she said. "You don't look like you've come to get me to help repel an invasion." She pulled her shirt off again, tossed it on a chair with her pants, and waved the light to the next brightest setting. The gold highlights in her red hair gleamed. When she was on duty she never wore her hair down like this, in a mass that curled around her face and shoulders and all the way to the small of her back. In fact Hikaru supposed he was one of the few people on board who had ever seen it down.

Mandala's smile faded. "On the other hand you look like something's wrong. What is it, Hikaru? Sit down."

He sat on the edge of her bunk. She drew up her knees, still under the blanket, and wrapped her arms around them.

"Come on," she said gently. "What's the matter?"

"I did it," he said. "I applied for a transfer to Hunter's squadron."

"She accepted you!" Mandala said with delight.

He nodded.

"You ought to be turning cartwheels," she said. "It's just perfect for you."

"I'm beginning to wonder if I made a mistake. I'm having second thoughts."

"Hikaru, the *Enterprise* is a great assignment, but you haven't been wrong in thinking you need wider experience."

"I wasn't thinking professionally. I was thinking personally."

She glanced away, then back, looked straight into his eyes, and took his hand.

"You see what I meant," she said. "About getting too attached to anybody."

"I'm sorry," he said. "I know how you feel. I didn't even mean to talk about that. I just came to say goodbye, and to give you my sabre. It takes me over the mass allowance."

Mandala accepted the sabre with the dignity due to it: it was an old sword, and a finely-made one.

"Thank you," she said. She bent her head down, resting her face against her knees, and he thought she was crying.

"Mandala, hey, I'm sorry—"

Shaking her head violently without looking up, she grabbed his wrist to stop the apology. When she did raise her head, he saw that she was laughing so hard she was in tears.

"No," she said. *"I'm* sorry. It's beautiful, I'm not laughing at the sabre, only I am, sort of, if I were quick enough on my feet I'd give you—" She glanced around. "Ha, there!" She pulled the heavy ring off the middle finger of her right hand. It was a naturally-formed circle of a stone like ruby, very much the color of her hair, even to the same golden highlights, at the facets. Except when she was practicing judo, she always wore it. She slipped it on his little finger.

In shooting for her promotion to lieutenant commander, one of the subjects Mandala studied was psychology, including its history. Smiling, she told Hikaru about another century's theory of sex and symbols: swords and sheaths, locks and keys. When she was finished, he laughed with her at the quaint ideas of a different age.

They looked at each other soberly.

"Did you mean it, what you said before . . ."

"I very seldom say anything I don't mean," Mandala said. *"Have* you changed your mind?"

"I . . . I don't know."

"It won't make things any easier for you, but I wish you would."

"I've been falling in love with you ever since you came on board," Hikaru said. "But I'm *leaving—*"

She put her hands on his shoulders. "If you do change your mind it won't make things easier for me, either. I love you, too, Hikaru, as much as I've fought it, and I don't know if we're going to be sorrier if we do make love —or if we don't."

Mandala stroked his cheek, the corner of his jaw, the hollow of his throat. He leaned toward her and she responded, kissing him gently, her hands spread against his back.

"You can't imagine how often I've wanted to do that," she whispered. She unfastened his shirt and drew it up over his head, caressing his sides with her fingers. She watched him pull off his boots and his pants; again, she admired his compact athlete's body. She lifted the bedclothes for him to get in beside her, and as he lay down and turned toward her she drew her hand up his thigh, to his hip, to his waist. Her fingers made slow swirling patterns on his skin, and he shivered. Hikaru kissed her face, all over, small warm kisses; he caressed her and stroked her hair and kissed the scar on her shoulder as if he wanted to take away all the pain it represented. Mandala bent over him and let her hair curl down to touch his shoulders. Cautiously at first, then playfully, then joyfully, they loved each other.

Jim Kirk sat in the officers' lounge, his hands wrapped around a mug of hot coffee. He felt depressed.

The door slid open and Dr. McCoy beetled in.

"Mornin', Jim," he said cheerfully, his southern accent strongly in evidence, as it always was when he was under the influence of several drinks, or of a hangover. Kirk could not tell which it was, and he was in no mood to put up with either.

"What a night," McCoy said. He got himself a mug and sat down across from Kirk. "What a night. The same for you, too? You look like I feel."

"Yes," Kirk said, though he was not really listening. "It

was quite a night." He had spent most of it on the sub-space communicator, trying to clear away the red tape for Sulu's transfer, and now he was beginning to think he had made a serious mistake. Perhaps if he had not been so ef-ficient, Mr. Sulu would have changed his mind.

"I thought so," McCoy said. "I sure hope you had as good a time as I did."

"As good a time—?" Kirk went back in his memory over what McCoy had been saying, and realized that since the doctor had only just come back from Aleph, he had no way of knowing about Sulu. In fact, Kirk had seen neither hide nor hair of McCoy since meeting him and his veterinarian friend in the park the day before.

"Bones, *what* are you talking about?"

"Well—I admit I'd had a few when I ran into you yes-terday, but you weren't that subtle."

Kirk just stared at him.

"Jim, boy, you really looked happy. I don't know when I've seen you looking so good. Now, you know I think more constancy in some matters wouldn't hurt you one bit—"

Kirk could not stand it when McCoy got avuncular, es-pecially this early in the morning.

"—so it's a real pleasure to see you with an old friend."

Kirk realized what McCoy had inferred. For some rea-son it irritated him, though, to be fair, McCoy had no particular reason to think anything else. Besides, why should Kirk care what McCoy thought about his and Hunter's friendship? The truth was no one's business but their own.

"You've got the wrong idea, Bones," Kirk said.

McCoy slid into the bantering tone by which, all too of-ten, the two men avoided discussing anythng that was re-ally important.

"What, Don Juan T. Kirk, Casanova of the space-ways—"

"Shut up!"

McCoy looked at him, startled out of joking, realizing that everything he had said so far this morning was as close to perfectly wrong as an imperfect human could de-vise.

"Jim," he said quietly, all traces of the good old boy abandoned, "I'm sorry. I knew you and she used to see a lot of each other, and I just assumed . . . I didn't mean to bring up anything painful."

Kirk shook his head. "It isn't your fault. It isn't even an unfair assumption, given my usual behavior."

"Do you want to talk about it? Or would you rather I slunk away, as best I can with my foot in my mouth?"

"Hunter and I are friends. She's one of the best friends I have. We used to be lovers. We aren't anymore. She's a member of a partnership family—"

"Oh. Well. That explains it."

"No, it doesn't. It doesn't even begin to explain it."

"Jim, now I *am* beginning to get confused."

"Partnerships aren't usually exclusive relationships. Hers certainly isn't. There are nine people in it now, I think—nine adults, I mean. Four or five of them have careers like Hunter's, that keep them away most of the time. But with the larger group, the kids have some stability. I met Hunter's daughter a few years back . . ." At first they had not got along too well; he was not used to being around children. At least he had realized in time that his patronizing manner insulted her, and that she despised him for it. Once he started treating her as a reasoning human being, they began to work out a watchful friendship.

"Her daughter!" McCoy said, surprised. He had not considered Hunter in any but her Starfleet officer incarnation, and he was nearly as startled as he would have been if Jim Kirk himself had started telling stories of his kiddies back home.

"It isn't that often that you meet someone whose father you almost had a chance to be," Kirk said.

McCoy took a long swallow from his coffee mug and rather wished it had something stronger in it.

"I nearly joined Hunter's group, Bones. After I met them the first few times, they invited me—they invited me three different times, over four years. I felt comfortable with them. I liked them all. I think . . . I think I could have loved them all." He stopped and did not continue for several seconds. When he did, his voice grew very quiet. "I thought I wasn't ready for such a big step. I kept turning them down. Maybe I *wasn't* ready. Maybe I wouldn't be ready even now. Maybe I made the right decision. But most of the time I think that saying no was the biggest mistake I ever made in my life."

"It's never too late to correct a mistake."

"I don't think I agree with you about that," Kirk said. "But anyway they never asked me again after I started to wonder if I should have accepted."

"You could ask them."

Kirk shook his head. "It doesn't work that way. It would be such bad manners that they'd almost have to say no."

"But if the partnership isn't exclusive, and you and she are still friends—"

"That's what I thought, for a long while. After the first time they asked me, I thought nothing had changed. Hunter and I were so close for so long . . . But she was growing up and I was still treating everything as nothing more than play. Play is fine up to a point. Play is why the partnership isn't exclusive. But for me and Hunter—especially after the second invitation into the partnership—it was like I was teasing her, all the time, as if I were willing to go just so far but no farther in trusting her, but expected her to trust me completely. She even told me her dream-name. Do you know what that means?"

"No, I guess I don't."

"Either did I, at the time. It's hard to explain, but it's something even deeper than trusting another person with your life."

Kirk paused again, and McCoy waited for him to continue, knowing how hard it was for Jim to speak of such personal matters.

"We had a lot of serious misunderstandings," Jim said. "So much so that when they offered me the invitation for the third time, I was surprised. And when I said no the third time, she was surprised. And hurt. I think she very nearly stopped trusting me at all, then. It's probably a good thing that she got sent one direction and I got sent the other and we didn't see each other again for a couple of years."

McCoy listened to a side of his friend that he seldom saw, realizing that all too often he let the clear and hearty surface obscure the depths. Kirk almost never let anyone detect even a hint of private pain; and he had learned a few things from Spock about concealing it, even as he teased the Vulcan about really being human underneath. Truth to tell, Kirk himself was more deeply human underneath than he cared to admit. McCoy wished he could think of something to say that would help.

Kirk took a deep breath and let it out fast and hard.

"Jim," McCoy said carefully, hoping, as he did so, that he was not pushing even their friendship too far, "couldn't you say to Hunter what you just said to me—about thinking you made a mistake? That wouldn't be the same as asking to join the partnership, would it?"

"I don't know. I've thought about it. But I don't know anymore if she wants to hear that. Why should she? And even if she does, it would put her in an uncomfortable position. What if the rest of the group said no? Bones, what if they said yes and I got cold feet at the last minute? That would be nothing less than a deliberate insult. It's the only strain I don't think our friendship could survive. Not again."

"You don't ordinarily change your mind once you've made it up."

"This is different."

"Why?"

Kirk shrugged. "It just is."

Ten hundred hours. Sulu set his duffel bag and his box of irregularly shaped oddments on one of the transporter platforms, then turned back to all his friends. Word of his transfer had spread almost instantaneously, it appeared, and for once he was glad of the highly efficient ship's grapevine. He would never have had time to find all his friends, much less his acquaintances. But here they were, crowded into the transporter room to wish him well: the members of his beginning fencing class; Pavel Chekov and Janice Rand and Christine Chapel; the elderly yogi of the *Enterprise*, Beatrice Smith; Captain Kirk and Dr. McCoy and Uhura. Even Mr. Spock was there. As Sulu bid them all goodbye, he had a sudden, frightening feeling of apprehension, the conviction that there was something very wrong with what was happening, even though he wanted it, and that the pendulum would swing back very soon, with force and speed enough to crush him. He shrugged off the experience as understandable anxiety; besides, he had never had a prophetic flash before, and his ESP rating was no better than average.

He did not shake hands with Mr. Spock, as he did with Captain Kirk, certainly did not embrace him, as he hugged Uhura, and, then, Dr. McCoy. Instead, Sulu bowed solemnly to the science officer. Spock raised his hand in the Vulcan equivalent.

"Live long and prosper, Mr. Sulu," he said.

"Thank you, Mr. Spock."

Sulu turned. "Mandala . . ."

She put her arms around him. "We were right, Hikaru," she said, too softly for anyone else to hear. "But even that doesn't make it any easier."

"No," he said. His vision blurred; he was embarrassed by the tears.

"Take care of yourself," she said.

"You, too."

He turned abrutly and bounded up onto the transporter platform. He could not stand to remain in Mandala's arms in a place so public. They had said their goodbyes in private.

She raised her hand in a gesture of farewell. Sulu returned it, then glanced at Spock, behind the console, and nodded. The flickering coldness of the beam engulfed him, and he disappeared.

After Sulu had left, the transporter room slowly cleared out. The mood was one of general depression, to which Mandala Flynn was far more than ordinarily susceptible. She gave herself a good mental shake and forcibly turned her attention to her job. In a few minutes their prisoner would arrive. She felt uneasy about the whole assignment, and she knew something unusual was going on. The captain and the science officer knew what it was, but neither had taken her into his confidence.

'Theirs not to make reply,/Theirs not to reason why,/Theirs but to do and die': Flynn thought the line in the same cynical tone in which Tennyson had written it, not with the nonsensical approval or unquestioning attention to obedience that had encrusted it more and more thickly as the centuries passed.

The more she knew about an assignment, the better she could carry it out: she had never encountered an exception to that proposition. But the senior officers of the *Enterprise* did not know her well enough to know how far they could trust her; she wondered if Captain Kirk would ever trust her. He had shown no sign of being willing to do so yet.

Without explanation, he had told her straight out that

he did not expect their carrier's mission to pose much challenge. But he had asked her to arrange an impressive security force. And there was clearly no arguing with Mr. Spock about the use of the guest cabin. So the inexplicable Mister Mordreaux would be hermetically secure from the transporter to his cabin—but after that, Flynn could not be so confident, even putting him under twenty-four-hour guard, even with the new security door on the cabin and the energy-screens around it.

Who, Flynn wondered, is putting on a show for whom? Who is fooling whom? And, more important, why?

Kirk glanced at her.

"We're about ready to receive the prisoner, Commander Flynn."

"Yes, sir. The guard detail is due here at 1015 hours, as you requested." She could hear their footsteps in the corridor.

She could not repress a smile when the team came in. She hoped they did not feel ridiculous, but they knew why they had been chosen: she had thought it best to tell them what little she knew. Each of the five carried a phaser rifle, but the weapons paled before the physical presence of the security officers themselves.

Beranardi al Auriga, her second in command, stood over two meters tall and was as blocky and solid as collapsed matter, black-skinned, fire-eyed, with a bushy red beard and flame-colored hair in all shades of red and orange and blond.

Neon, despite iridescent scales and a long tail spiked like a stegosaurus', most resembled an economy-sized Tyrannosaurus rex. Human beings often thought of her in dinosaur terms: strong and dangerous but slow and stupid. She was quick as electricity and the facets of her I.Q. that Starfleet could measure started at 200 and went up from there.

Snnanagfashtalli and Jenniver Aristeides had been obvious choices for the team. Jenniver towered over even Barry al Auriga. She was like a steel statue. Flynn had, at first, thought Aristeides the most grotesquely ugly human creature she had ever seen, but after a few weeks she began to feel that the quiet woman had a strange, stony, sculptural beauty.

Snnanagfashtalli was the only truly vicious member of the team. After seeing her in action the day before, Flynn had decided to use her only on assignments when she was sure nothing would happen, or when she was certain something would. Snarl did not attack for no reason, and she attacked ferociously when she had cause, but she was not good in the middle ground when restraint and discipline were called for. She possessed neither. Under stress she was more likely to use her ruby fangs than her phaser.

Maximo Alisaunder Arrunja, the last member of the team, had a talent for blending into crowds. He was a craggy-faced, graying, middle-aged man. When he decided not to blend, he emanated the most chillingly dangerous aura of anyone Flynn had ever met. She had seen him break up an incipient fistfight between two irritable crew members: he never had to lay a finger on either of them, he did not even have to threaten them. They surrendered out of pure irrational terror at what he might do.

Flynn glanced at Captain Kirk. "I hope the security force is adequate, sir."

"Yes, Commander Flynn," he said, so poker-faced that she knew her assessment of the situation was not far wrong.

Flynn glanced at al Auriga. "All set, Barry?"

"Yes, ma'am," he said softly.

Then, after half a beat, Jenniver Aristeides said, "If we're waiting for a troop of Klingons."

She just barely smiled. Max laughed, the sound like a growl, Neon made an eerie, tinkling, wind-chime noise, Barry giggled, and Snarl glanced from face to face, rumbling low in her throat, wondering if it were she who was being laughed at. Along with restraint and discipline, Snarl also lacked a sense of humor.

"I appreciate all of you a very great deal," Flynn said. Snarl raised her ears and smoothed her hackles and glided silently to her position by the transporter.

"Captain Kirk," Mr. Spock said, in a tone Flynn would have called very near distress, if anyone had asked her. "Captain Kirk, Dr. Mordreaux is an elderly academic. This . . . this . . . guerrilla strike force is hardly necessary."

"Come now, Mr. Spock—we want Ian Braithewaite to see that we're taking him seriously, don't we?"

Spock's gaze moved from Kirk, to Flynn, and across the security group. He looked at the ceiling for a long moment.

"As you wish, Captain."

The transporter signalled ready, and a moment later the prisoner and Aleph Prime's chief prosecutor materialized. Flynn's quintet put their phaser rifles at ready, and she rested her hand easily on the butt of her holstered phaser pistol.

Why—he's drugged, Flynn thought, as soon as Mordreaux solidified. The blank expression and unfocussed gaze allowed no other interpretation. In addition, the prisoner wore energy-cuffs on his wrists, and a set of inertial-resistance leg restraints that would permit him to walk, but which would snap short and trip him if he overcame the drugs long enough to try to run. It was all as old-fashioned as a set of iron chains, as unnecessary and as humiliating. Mordreaux was in no shape to notice humiliation. Flynn glanced at Spock, but his face remained impassive; he had apparently expended any outburst on the guerrilla strike force.

Braithewaite bounded down from the platform, glanced briefly at the security team, and nodded to Kirk.

"Great," he said. "Where's the detention cell?"

"Mr. Braithewaite," Kirk said, "I'm taking the *Enterprise* out of orbit immediately. There's no time for you to look around, nor any need."

"But Captain—I'm going to Rehab Seven with you."

"That's impossible."

"It's orders, Captain." He handed Kirk a subspace transmission form. Kirk scanned it, frowning.

"You'll be on your own getting back, and as you pointed out yourself there aren't many official ships."

"I know, Captain," Ian Braithewaite said. His expression turned somber and thoughtful. "After what's happened—this trial, and Lee, and . . . well, I need some time by myself. To think some things out. I've arranged for a single-ship; I'm going to sail back." He glanced down at Kirk. "I'll do my best to stay out of your hair till we get to Rehab Seven, and you won't have to worry about me afterward."

He hurried after the security team and his prisoner. Kirk paused a moment, feeling rather nonplussed at being told not to worry about someone who proposed to fly all the way across a star system, all alone, in a tiny, fragile, unpowered sailboat. Shaking his head, he followed the others out of the transporter room.

Jim Kirk returned to his cabin and collapsed in a chair, too tired to move even as far as his bunk. He had had no sleep in thirty-six hours; he had lost the best helm officer the ship ever had; his science officer, trying to salvage some results from his observations of the singularity, some possible explanation for its occurrence, had tied up most of the available computer time working out equations that no one else could even read, let alone understand; and Mr. Scott had just begun irritably demanding engineering's share of the computer time. A brilliant lunatic or a slandered genius—possibly both—was under detention in the V.I.P. cabin, and his unrelentingly energetic watchdog was quartered nearby. The ship flew creaking like a relic, the warp engines needed a complete overhaul, and even the impulse drive was working none too dependably.

One of the reasons Kirk felt so exhausted was that Ian Braithewaite's animation never let up. It would have been far easier to deal with him if he were despicable, but he was only young, inexperienced, likeable . . . and ambitious.

Kirk regretted, now, that he had not explained to Commander Flynn just exactly what was going on—though she obviously knew it was something not quite completely above board. When Kirk pled the press of work and tried to persuade Ian to get settled in, the prosecutor waylaid Flynn for a tour of the security precautions. Kirk hoped she was perceptive enough to continue the show they had set up. He believed she was; now he would find out.

Kirk could not keep his thoughts away from his conversation that morning with Dr. McCoy. Part of him wished it had never happened; he did not often go in for soul-baring, and on the rare occasion that he did, he always felt embarrassed afterward.

Damn, he thought, but that's just what we were talking about. Leonard McCoy and Hunter are the two best friends I've got, and I can't even open up to either of them.

It's absurd. I've been trading my life for a façade of total independence that I know is full of holes even when I'm holding it up in front of me. It isn't worth it anymore —if it ever was.

If Spock succeeds in clearing Mordreaux, we'll have to bring him back to Aleph Prime. Even if he doesn't, the

Enterprise needs a lot of work before we can even think of restarting Spock's observations, and the nearest repair yards are at Aleph. If Hunter has already left, I can hire a racer and fly out to wherever she's got her squadron based. I need to see her again. I need to talk to her— really talk to her this time. Bones was right: even if it doesn't change anything, I've got to tell her I was wrong.

Chapter 3

Chief Engineer Montgomery Scott tramped down the corridor, muttering curses in an obscure Scots dialect. Six weeks' work for nothing, six weeks' work that would have to be done all over again, or more likely abandoned if it were so trivial that it could be interrupted only two days from completion—and for such a foolish reason. Ever since the mysterious emergency message came and they had been diverted, all he had heard was Poor Mr. Spock, poor Mr. Spock, all his work for nothing.

And what, Scott wondered, about poor Mr. Scott? Keeping a starship's engines steady in the proximity of a naked singularity was no picnic, and he had been at it just as long as Spock had been at his task. The engines had been under a terrific strain, and it was Scott's job to be sure they did not fail: if they had given out during a correction of the orbit, the mission would have ended instantly—or it would have lasted a lot longer than six weeks, depending on where one looked at it from. From outside, the *Enterprise* would have fallen toward the deranged metric, growing fainter and fuzzier, till it vanished. From inside the ship, the crew would have seen space itself vanish, then reappear—assuming the ship made the transit whole, rather than in pieces—but it would have been space in some other place, and some other time, and the *Enterprise*'s chances of getting home again would have been so close to zero as to be unmeasurable.

The engines were much of the cause of Scott's foul mood. While everyone on the ship, or so many as made no never-mind, received a day's liberty on Aleph Prime, Scott—rather than relaxing in the best place in this octant to spend liberty—had used every minute hunting up parts and getting them back to the ship. That was only the beginning of the work: he still had to install the new equipment in the disconnected warp engines. He felt far from comfortable, with impulse engines, alone, available to power the *Enterprise*. But they could not dock at Aleph Prime: no, they had to carry out their mission. Mission, hah.

Then there was the matter of Sulu. True, Scott and Sulu were not particularly close, but he had known the helm officer for years and it was downright embarrassing to resurface after six hours fighting energy pods, to find not only that he had left, without so much as a good-to-know-you, but also that virtually everyone except Scott knew he had gone.

He passed the transporter room, then stopped. He thought he saw a flicker of light, as if someone were using the unit. Of course that was impossible: they were too far from anywhere to beam anyone on board. Nevertheless, Scott backtracked.

Mr. Spock stood in the middle of the room, as if he had just materialized on the platform, stepped down, and walked two or three steps before halting: his shoulders were slumped and he looked ready to fall.

"Mr. Spock?"

Spock froze for no more than a second, then straightened up and turned calmly toward the chief engineer.

"Mr. Scott. I should have . . . expected you."

"Did ye page me? Are ye all right? Is something wrong wi' the transporter?" No doubt someone had neglected to ask him to fix it, though that was one of his responsibilities: it seemed as though no one thought Scott worth telling anything to, these days.

"I simply noticed some minor power fluctuations, Mr. Scott," the science officer said. "They could become reason for complaint."

"I can come back and help ye," Scott said, "as soon as I've reported to Captain Kirk about the engines." He frowned. Spock, who never showed any reaction to stress, looked drawn and tired—far more tired even than Scott felt. So everyone—human, superhuman, Vulcan, and even Mr. Spock—had limits after all.

"That is unnecessary," Spock said. "The work is almost complete." He did not move. Scott remained in the doorway a moment longer, then turned on his heel and left Spock alone. After all these years, he should no longer be offended if Spock did not say thank you for an offer of help he had not asked for and did not need. But today Scott was of a mind to be offended by nearly anything.

As the chief engineer approached the turbo lift, a tall thin civilian hurried up: no doubt he was one of the people they had collected on Aleph. When Kirk had not taken Scott into his confidence about the reason for the change in plans, Scott had assumed some essential, vitally secret task had been assigned to them. He had assumed they were working on a strictly need-to-know basis. The assumptions were false, the message was trivial, and Scott had been left in the dark simply because, as usual, no one had troubled to let him know what was going on.

Scott nodded to the civilian as they got into the lift; he wished he were alone because he felt more like being grumpy in private than churlish in public.

"Hold the lift!"

Scott pushed the doors open again and the captain came in. He looked rested; his uniform was fresh: Scott, on the other hand, had spent the six hours since leaving Aleph in the engine room, and he felt grubby.

"Hello, Scotty," Captain Kirk said.

"Captain," Scott replied shortly. It occurred to him suddenly that the civilian must be nearly the last one to have used the transporter, the person Spock implied had complained.

"Sir," Scott said abruptly, "could ye describe to me how ye felt, when ye arrived on the transporter? It would help track down the difficulty."

The civilian looked startled.

"Sorry, sir," Scott said. "I'm the chief engineer, my name is Scott."

"Good lord, Scotty," Kirk said, "is the transporter on the blink too?"

"Your transporter worked fine as far as I could tell," the civilian said. He grinned. "I thought it was supposed to shake you up a little."

The doors opened and they all stepped out onto the bridge.

"I don't know what's wrong wi' it, Captain," Scott said. "Mr. Spock just this moment told me—"

Scott stopped short, and his voice failed him as he stared in astonishment at the science officer's station. There, in his usual place, Spock bent over his computer terminal.

Captain Kirk and the civilian went down to the lower level of the bridge, where Commander Flynn leaned against the railing waiting for them. Scott followed, but he could not drag his gaze away from Spock, and he stumbled on the stairs. Flynn grabbed his arm to steady him.

"You okay?"

"Aye," he said, irked; he pulled away from her.

Kirk took his seat and turned back toward Scott.

"What's the bad news on the engines, Scotty?"

"The engines are no' in very good shape, Captain. I got most of the parts we needed on Aleph, and I can keep things together to do what's needed as long as the warp drive isna pushed, once i' is on line again. 'Twould be better to stay at sublight, till we've had a thorough overhaul . . ."

His voice trailed off as Spock came down to listen.

"What's wrong, Scotty?" Kirk asked.

"Well, nae a thing, really, Captain—but, Mr. Spock, how did ye beat me to the bridge? I came here direct from the transporter room."

Spock cocked one eyebrow. "The transporter room, Mr. Scott? I have been on the bridge since Mr. Sulu left; I have not been near the transporter room for several hours."

"But you said there was something wrong wi' it."

"I am unaware of any malfunction."

"Ye said it had power fluctuations, Mr. Spock, and that i' was nearly fixed. But what I dinna understand is how you got up here before I did." Among the junior officers were one or two inveterate practical jokers, but Spock would never engage in such frivolity, nor cooperate with it. Scott shook his head, as if that would disperse the fog of exhaustion and confusion that surrounded him. Everything would be so much clearer if only he did not feel so tired.

"Mr. Scott, I have been here on the bridge for some time."

"But I just saw ye—I just spoke wi' ye!"

Spock said nothing, but he raised his eyebrow again.

"I *did* see ye!"

"Scotty," Kirk said, "how late did you stay out last night?"

Scott turned toward his captain. "Captain, that isna fair! I took no liberty—I did naught but work on the engines!"

"You were *supposed* to take liberty," Kirk said, in a much more placating tone. "Scotty, we're all tired, we've all been under a lot of stress for a long time. I'm sure there's a reasonable explanation for what you saw——"

"You're saying I'm hallucinating, Captain! I dinna hallucinate Mr. Spock in the transporter room any more than I'm hallucinating him now!"

"I'm saying no such thing. I'm saying I want you to get some rest. We'll talk about this later, if we need to."

Kirk's expression forbade more comment. Scott hesitated, but clearly he was to be excluded from any further conversation. Spock regarded him quizzically, but failed to offer any explanation for his peculiar behavior.

Well, then, Scott thought, with the irritation of generations of lower officers kept in the dark by red tape, high brass, and their own immediate superiors: Well then, so there *is* something unusual going on, after all; this isna a foul-up; this isna a mere courier run. Doubtless I'll find out all abou' it eventually. And perhaps I'll even learn the truth for mysel' wi'out waiting for anyone to deign to say what it may be.

He left the bridge, knowing that the science officer was following him with his gaze, assuming Kirk was even now saying privately to Spock, with admiration and respect, "Well, we can't keep anything from Scotty very long, can we?" and Spock replying, "No, Captain; he has deductive faculties of a power unusual in human beings." Scott entered the lift to return to his quarters, looking forward to a shower—a water shower, hot water, too—and to the quick drink he had denied himself earlier. Then he intended to take a long nap.

He still could not figure out how Spock had got past him

from the transporter room to the bridge. For that was what he had done, whether he was admitting it or not.

Back on the bridge, Kirk would have liked to ask Spock what that scene with Scotty had been all about, but he had to turn his attention immediately to Ian Braithewaite.

"Captain Kirk—*are* we travelling at sublight speed?"

Kirk sighed. "Mr. Braithewaite, Rehab Seven is so close to Aleph Prime—relatively speaking—that if we tried to reach it at warp speed, we'd overshoot. We'd strain the engines far past the danger point with such rapid acceleration and deceleration."

"Wait, Captain, I wasn't objecting—I've never been on a starship before, I'm glad to have the chance to look around. I kind of hoped I'd experience warp speed once in my life, though," he said wistfully.

Kirk began to find it extremely difficult to maintain his irritation at Ian Braithewaite.

"Well, you never know what opportunities will come up," he said. "But you asked to discuss security. I thought Commander Flynn should be here, too."

Flynn had kept her silence; now she stepped forward to join them.

Ian pulled a folded slip of paper from his pocket. "This came while you were asleep, Captain." He handed it over.

Kirk read it: another Aleph citizen had come down with hypermorphic botulism.

"Do you think Aleph will need my ship's medical facilities as backup? Are you worried about an epidemic?"

"I almost wish I were," Ian said. "But since my friend Lee was Dr. Mordreaux's defense counsel, and Judge Desmoulins heard the case, I have to think it could be deliberate."

"Someone *poisoned* them?"

"I have no proof. But I think it's at least possible."

"Why?"

"At this point I could only speculate. But the coincidence makes me very uncomfortable. And scared. The possibility that troubles me most is that someone might be trying to free Dr. Mordreaux. I think we should intensify security."

"Ian," Kirk said tolerantly, "I can certainly understand why you're upset. But you're perfectly safe on the *Enter-*

prise, and Commander Flynn has Dr. Mordreaux's security well in hand." He glanced at Flynn for confirmation, but she avoided his eyes. "Commander Flynn?"

She looked at him straight on, with her crystalline green gaze. "I'd prefer to discuss security less publicly, Captain."

"Oh," said Kirk, and he understood that she expected him to take a hint—that she was not happy with the security arrangements—just as he had counted on her to take hints since this assignment started. "Well. All right. But after all Dr. Mordreaux is an elderly man——"

"Commander Flynn," Braithewaite said, "Dr. Mordreaux is my responsibility as much as yours, and I don't think it's fair to exclude me from discussions about him. Captain Kirk——"

"Kirk!"

Braithewaite spoke at the same moment as the shriek: for an instant Flynn thought it was he who had screamed Kirk's name.

"You destroyed me, Kirk! You deserve to die!"

In shock, everyone turned.

Dr. Mordreaux, wild-eyed, stood at the entrance to the bridge. He thrust out an ugly, heavy pistol, and gestured to Flynn and Braithewaite with its muzzle. "You two, out of the way."

"Dr. Mordreaux," Braithewaite said, "don't make things worse for yourself——"

In the hypersensitivity of a rush of adrenaline, Flynn saw the pistol steady as Braithewaite started toward Mordreaux. She thought, Wrong, wrong, that is *just* the wrong thing to do, brave but stupid, damn all amateurs; as the hammer cocked she had already flung herself forward. Her momentum rammed Braithewaite out of the line of fire and carried her to the upper level of the bridge. One more second's hesitation in Mordreaux and her hand would clamp around his wrist, one more second—Damn Kirk for not telling her what was going on, damn him for making this sound trivial, if he had not she would have kept her phaser on and to hell with general regulations. Another instant—

The gun went off.

The explosion of sound surprised her more than the crushing jolt that hurled her to the deck.

Jim Kirk leaped to his feet. The gun went off a second

time, the sound cutting through the cacophonous disorder on the bridge. The bullet smashed into him, engulfing him in a nova-bright haze of pain.

Mordreaux stepped backwards into the lift and the doors closed, a moment before Spock reached them. The science officer did not waste time trying to force them open. He leaped back down the stairs, past Commander Flynn struggling to her feet, and slapped the paging switch.

"Dr. McCoy to the bridge immediately! Trauma team, emergency nine!"

Spock knelt beside Jim Kirk.

"Jim . . ."

The bridge was in chaos around them. Blood spattered deck and bulkheads and glistened on the illuminated data screens. The security commander, her hand clamped over the wound in her shoulder, gave orders crisply over the intercom, deploying her forces to apprehend Mordreaux. Blood dripped between her fingers and sprinkled the floor beside Spock, like rain.

The second bullet had taken Kirk full in the chest. His blood gushed fresh with each beat of his heart. That meant at least that his heart *was* still beating.

"Spock . . ." Jim fought his way up through massive scarlet light, until he forced enough of it away to see beyond it.

"Lie still, Jim. Dr. McCoy is on his way."

Spock tried to stop the bleeding. Jim cried out and fumbled for Spock's wrist. "Don't," he said. "Please . . ." He felt the blood bubbling up in his lungs.

The wound was too deep, too bad, to quell by direct pressure. Spock ceased the futile effort that only caused pain. Jim felt himself gently lifted, gently supported, and the sensation of drowning eased just perceptibly.

"Is anyone else hurt? Mandala . . . ?"

"I'm all right, Captain." She started up the stairs again.

"Commander Flynn!" Spock said without glancing back.

"What?"

"Do not summon the lift—Dr. McCoy must not be delayed."

She needed to get below to help her people: she *needed* to, it was like an instinct. But Spock was right. She waited, swaying unsteadily.

"Mandala, let me help you." Uhura's gentle hands guided her around and a few steps forward before she balked.

"No, I can't."

"Mandala—"

"Uhura," she whispered, "Uhura, if I sit down I don't know if I'll be able to get back up."

"Lieutenant Uhura," Spock snapped, "page Dr. McCoy again."

Spock did not want to move Jim without a stretcher, but if it and Dr. McCoy did not arrive in another thirty seconds he was going to carry Jim Kirk to sick bay himself.

"What happened, Spock?" Jim whispered. "This was supposed to be . . . a milk run." A light pink froth formed on his lips. The bullet had punctured his lungs. His breathing was irregular, and when he tried to draw breath, pain racked him.

"I don't know, Jim. Please be quiet."

Jim was slipping down into shock, and there was no more time to lose.

The doors opened and McCoy rushed onto the bridge.

"What happened? Oh, my god—" He saw Flynn first and started toward her.

"Not me," she said. "It's the captain."

He hesitated only a moment, but saw that the blood covering her uniform shirt and spattering her face and hands and hair concealed a high and non-critical shoulder wound; he hurried to Kirk's side.

Flynn walked into the lift and the doors closed behind her.

McCoy knelt beside Jim.

"Take it easy, Jim, boy," he said. "We'll have you in sick bay so fast—"

Kirk had never been so aware of his own pulse, throbbing like a thunderstorm through his body. "Bones . . . I . . ."

"Quiet!"

"You were right. What we talked about . . . I was going to tell Hunter . . ."

"You'll still be able to. Shut up, what kind of talk is this?" McCoy waved the tricorder across Kirk's body. Jim's heart was undamaged, but the artery was half severed. The sensor showed a pierced lung, but that was obvious without any mechanical information. The essential thing was to get him on oxygen as fast as possible, then hook him up to a fluid replacer, a heme carrier: he was bleeding so badly that oxygen starvation was the biggest danger.

"Where is the trauma unit?" Spock said, his voice tight.

"On its way," McCoy said, defending his people though he was angry himself that they were not yet here. But he knew he could save Jim Kirk.

"You'll be okay, Jim," he said, and this time he meant it.

But there was something else, a danger signal from the tricorder. McCoy thought immediately of poison, but the readings were in the wrong range. He had never seen anything like this signal before. "What the devil . . ."

Jim thought he had blood in his eyes. A shimmering cloud passed across his vision.

"I can't see," he said. He reached blindly out.

Spock grasped his hand, holding him strongly, deliberately leaving open all the mental and emotional shields he had built during his long association with human beings.

"You will be all right, Jim," Spock said. He put his right hand to Jim's temple, completing the telepathic, mystical circuit linking him with his friend. Pain, fear, and regret welled out into him. He accepted it willingly, and felt it ease in Jim. "My strength to yours," he whispered, too softly for anyone to hear, the words a hypnotic reminder of the techniques he was using. "My strength to yours, my will to yours."

McCoy saw Spock's eyelids lower and his eyes roll back till only a crescent of the whites still showed. But he could not pay any attention to what the Vulcan was doing. The lift doors opened and the trauma team rushed in with the support equipment.

"Get down here!" McCoy shouted. They hurried to obey.

They hooked up the trauma unit and oxygen flooded Jim's body. His starving nerves spread new agony through him. He gasped, and blood choked him. Spock's long fingers clasped his hand. The pain eased infinitesimally, but Jim's sight faded almost to pure darkness.

"Spock?"

"I am here, Jim."

His friend's hand pressed gently against his temple and

the side of his face. Jim felt the closeness, the strength
that was keeping him alive. He could no longer see, even
in his mind, but in some other, unnamed way he sensed
the precision of Spock's thoughts, their order twisted by
Jim's own pain and fear.

Jim Kirk knew that he was going to die, and that Spock
would follow him down the accelerating spiral until he had
fallen too deep to return. He would willingly choose death
to try to save Kirk's life.

James Kirk, too, had one choice left.

"Spock . . ." he whispered, "take good care . . . of my
ship."

He feared he had waited too long, but that terror gave
him the strength he needed. He wrenched away from
Spock, breaking their contact, forsaking Spock's strength
and will, and giving himself up alone to agony, despair,
and death.

The physical resonance of emotional force flung Spock
backward. His body thudded against the railing, and he
slumped to the floor. He lay still, gathering his strength.
The deck felt cool against the side of his face and his
outflung hands. The echoes of Jim Kirk's wounds slowly
ebbed. Spock opened his eyes to a gray haze. He blinked,
and blinked again: the nictitating membrane swept across
the irises, and finally he could see. Spock pushed himself
to his feet, fighting to hide his reactions.

Jim's body now lay on the stretcher of the trauma unit,
hooked up to fluid and respirator, breathing but otherwise
motionless. His eyes—his eyes, wide open, had clouded
over with silver-gray.

"Dr. McCoy—"

"Not now, Spock."

Spock felt himself trembling. He clenched his fists.

McCoy and part of his medical team floated the trauma
unit into the lift, while two of the paramedics stayed behind to take Braithewaite, knocked unconscious in his
fall, down to sick bay.

The captain's body was alive; it could be kept alive in-
definitely now.

But Spock had felt Jim Kirk die.

Mandala Flynn leaned against the back bulkhead of
the turbo lift, closing her eyes and seeking out the damage to her body in her mind. The bullet tracked diago-

nally from her collarbone in front on the left, across her back and down, and lodged against her lower ribs like a molten bit of lead. As far as she could tell, it had cut through without doing critical damage. But her collarbone was shattered, again: she knew what that felt like.

She cursed. The bullet had entered almost exactly where the shrapnel had got her two years before. Now she would have to waste a month in therapy; the jigsaw-puzzle of bone would never return to its original strength.

Her blood pressure was way down: she had to will herself not to go into shock. The biofeedback techniques were working. So far she had even succeeded in holding the pain, most of it, back one level short of consciousness.

She was well aware that she could not stay on her feet much longer. She had lost too much blood, and even with biocontrol, the human body has limits which she had nearly reached.

The lift doors slid open onto an empty corridor.

There should be guards at every level! Fury rose in her, fury and shame, because however badly or insignificantly Captain Kirk was hurt, the responsibility was hers alone. Even if no one at all had been hurt, the prisoner had escaped. There was no excuse for that: she had thought her command of the security force was competent, even out-standing. She had watched morale rise from nothing, but here she was, revealed as a sham.

Face it, Flynn, she told herself savagely, they could have replaced your predecessor with a rock, and morale would have gone up. That doesn't make you adequate to lead. They ought to bust you back to ensign, that's where you belong. They were right all the time.

A lunatic wth a pistol was running around loose in the ship, and not so much as a single guard stood at the bloody-bedamned lift doors.

She stepped out into the hallway. Her feet were numb, as if they had fallen asleep, and her knees felt wobbly and funny.

Is this shock? she wondered. This isn't a symptom of shock. What's going on?

She took a few steps forward. Mordreaux's cabin was right around the corner. Clichés about locking barns after horses got loose crept through her mind along with her usual uncertainty about what a horse actually looked like . . . or a barn . . . she forcibly pulled her attention back.

If her people were not at the lift, Mordreaux's cabin was as good a place as any to begin looking for them. And him.

Could this be a planned assault? she wondered. Was Braithewaite right? All the security people taken on and eliminated, silently, one by one, in an attempt to free Mordreaux? In logistical terms it made no sense to assault a starship instead of the negligible security of Aleph Prime. Here, an attack force would have to get undetected through the ship's sensors; the force would have to board the *Enterprise* through warning systems that included several layers of redundancy, and it would have had to do its work too swiftly, too perfectly, for anyone to be left to set off an alarm.

Mandala stumbled and fell to her knees, but felt nothing. Her legs were numb almost all the way to the hips. She looked stupidly down. That was no help. Somehow she managed to get back to her feet.

An assault made no sense in human terms; in human terms, it was impossible. But she had learned—one of the first lessons she had learned in her life—that the human consciousness was in the minority, and that limiting oneself to thinking in human terms was the quickest way to prove oneself a fool.

Still she had seen no one. She could call them on her communicator, but she was too angry to speak to any of her people any way but face to face. And, truth to tell, she did not think she could lift her left hand. All the strength and feeling had vanished from that arm.

She turned the corner.

There, in front of Mordreaux's cabin, several security people gathered, milling in confusion.

"What the hell is going on?" she said, just loud enough for them to hear. "Mordreaux is loose and you're all standing around like—like—"

Beranardi al Auriga, stooping to peer through the observation port of the V.I.P. cabin's new security door, straightened up. He was head and shoulders taller than his superior. He saw the blood spreading between her fingers and down her arm and side.

"Mandala—Commander, what—? Let me help you—"

"Answer my question!" Flynn could just barely feel the heat of her own blood. The pain had gone.

"Mordreaux is right here, Commander," al Auriga said.

He unlocked the cabin so she could see. She looked inside.

Lying on his bunk, braced on his elbow as if he had just been awakened, Mordreaux gazed blearily out at them.

"What's wrong?" he asked. "What's all the commotion?"

"Neon," Mandala said, "lift, portal, guards?"

"Commander," Neon said in her silvery voice, "prisoner, cell, Neon, intersection; alarm."

"What . . . ?" Flynn's confusion was not because she did not understand Neon's unusual English. Neon had said not only that Mordreaux was in his cell, but that Neon had been guarding him when the alarm sounded.

"Prisoner, bridge, separation," Neon said.

Flynn shook her head, trying to clear her mind of an encroaching grogginess. Any number of possibilities spun through her consciousness. An android duplicate. Clones. Clones, hell, maybe he had a twin brother.

"Barry, get everybody—*everybody*, roust the night watch out of bed—and search this ship. Double the guard here, and put a watch on the shuttlecraft and the airlocks and dammit even the transporter." She gasped: she felt short of breath and dizzy. "Mordreaux just shot Captain Kirk on the bridge—or if it wasn't Mordreaux it was somebody doing a damned good impression. Be sure to warn them that he's armed."

"Aye, Commander."

"Where's Jenniver?" Flynn said. That should have been her first question: she *must* be going into shock. Her vision blurred for a moment. She closed her eyes and held them shut. "Jenniver's supposed to be on duty this watch, where is she?" She opened her eyes again, but her vision had not cleared.

"Sickbay," Neon said.

"I'm all right," Flynn snapped, knowing that was not true.

"Jenniver, sickbay, illness, intersection," Neon said patiently. "Mandala, sickbay, intersection; instant."

Flynn nodded. Neon spoke precisely, even though the only part of speech that matched between her language and English was the noun. If Jenniver had been hurt in an escape attempt that is what Neon would have said. But Jenniver had taken ill, and was in sick bay. Neon thought Flynn should be there, too, quickly. She was right.

"Jiffy," Neon said.

Flynn closed her eyes again. She felt herself losing her balance and tried to catch herself. She flung out her left arm but it moved only weakly; her hand would not work at all. Pain shot across her shoulders and back and vanished into the numbness in her chest and belly; she staggered against the wall with another jolt, and began to slide toward the ground.

Need both hands, she thought dully. That's it.

Her right hand would not move.

Startled, she opened her eyes and looked down, blinking to try to see clearly.

She moaned.

Delicate silver fibrils, glittering through the gray fog, entwined her fingers like silk, binding them to her shoulder. In a panic she ripped her hand away. The fibrils stretched and popped and twanged, like the strings of a musical instrument. The broken ends writhed across her shirt, and the free strands tightened around her hand.

Neon came toward her, making a high, questioning noise.

"Stay back!" Flynn could feel the tendrils growing and twisting inside her, spinning themselves like webs around her spinal cord. Neon and Barry came toward her, trying to help her. "Neon, Mandala, separation, separation! Barry, don't let anybody touch me without a quarantine unit!" Her jaw and tongue began to grow numb, as the threads crept up into her brain. She struggled to get a few words out. Her knees collapsed and she fell forward and sideways, hardly aware of the impact. A film of fast-growing tendrils blinded her.

Now she knew what kind of gun Mordreaux had used.

"Hurry," she whispered. "Barry . . . tell McCoy . . . spiderweb . . . Captain Kirk . . ."

The tendrils reached Mandala Flynn's consciousness and crushed it out.

Spock forced himself not to submit to his body's reactions to what had just happened. Though he understood the human concept of soul, and spirit, his perception of what made a living creature intelligent and self-aware was wholly Vulcan, too subtle and complex to explain in human terms or any human language. But he had contacted that concept, more deeply and intimately than he had ever probed a mind before, and he had watched, no, *felt* all but the last glimmer of it die. If Jim had not broken the hypnotic connection, giving Spock back his will and all the strength he had tried to channel into his friend, Spock too would now be comatose and brain-damaged under the tender, brutal ministrations of Dr. McCoy's life-saving machines.

"Mr. Spock, what happened? Please let me help you." Uhura came toward him, not reaching out to him, but offering her hand half-raised. Spock knew she would not touch him without his permission.

Pavel Chekov leaned over his console, crying uncontrollably with shock and relief, for like the other humans on the bridge he too thought Captain Kirk was going to live.

The emotions raging around Spock were so strong that he could sense them without the aid of touch, and in his weakened state he needed to get away from them. He could not think logically under these conditions and it was essential that someone do so now. A great deal needed to be done.

Though tears flowed slowly and regularly down Uhura's face, she seemed unaware of their presence; outwardly she looked calmer than Spock himself felt.

"Lieutenant—" He stopped. His voice was as hoarse as if he had been screaming. He began again. "I do need your help. Page Commander Flynn and order her to sick bay immediately on my authority. There is reason to think she has been wounded far more seriously than she believes. She must not delay."

"Aye, sir," she said. As the channels signalled ready, she glanced at Spock again. "But you, Mr. Spock?"

"I am not physically damaged." Spock said. It took every bit of strength he had left to walk steadily up the stairs. Behind him he heard Uhura page Mandala Flynn.

"Lieutenant, she's down here." Beranardi al Auriga's voice crept close to the edge of hysteria. "At Mordreaux's cell. She collapsed, but she ordered us not to touch her. She's been shot with a web-slug, dammit, Uhura, she thinks Captain Kirk was, too!"

Spock slammed his hand against the turbo lift controls. As the doors slid closed, every crew member on the bridge looked up at him in shock and horror and terror-stricken surprise.

The lift fell, shutting them away. Spock sagged against the wall, fighting for control of his shaking body. A spider-web: he should have realized it from the first, but it was so peculiarly human in its brutality that he could never have conceived of anyone's using it.

Away from the other members of the crew, he succeeded finally in calming himself. When the doors of the lift opened again, he walked out as steadily as if he had not been an instant from oblivion.

As Spock turned the corner and approached Dr. Mordreaux's cabin, Beranardi al Auriga punched the controls of an intercom.

"Where the hell's the med tech!"

By now the medical section must know about the spiderweb, Spock thought. Sick bay would be in chaos.

Light shimmering on her scales, Neon crouched over Mandala Flynn as if she could protect her with ferocity. Spock knelt beside the security commander's crumpled body. Alive, she had given the impression of complete physical competence and power. It was an accurate impression, but it was the result of her skill and self-confidence, not her size. She was a small and slender woman; life had seeped out of her, revealing the delicacy of her bones and the translucence of her light brown skin. She looked very frail.

"Don't—" al Auriga said as Spock reached toward her. "She said not to touch her."

"I am not under Commander Flynn's authority," Spock said. He reached toward her, but hesitated. His hands were covered with Jim Kirk's blood. Spock brushed his fingertips across Flynn's temple. The wound in her shoulder still bled slowly; the individual cells of her body still maintained a semblance of life. But she had no pulse, and he sensed not the faintest response from her brain.

Her eyes, which had been an unusually intense shade of green, had turned silky gray. Spock had seen the same film begin to thicken over Jim Kirk's eyes as they carried him off the bridge.

"The danger is past," Spock said. He looked up, and met the gaze of each security officer. "The web has ceased to grow. Commander Flynn is dead."

al Auriga turned away; Neon snarled low in her throat. Spock wondered if he would have to defend Mordreaux.

Neon settled back on her haunches. "Revenge," she

whispered wistfully, then, in a stronger voice, "duty. Faithfulness, oath, duty."

Spock stood up. "Where did you capture Dr. Mordreaux?" he asked Flynn's second in command.

"We didn't," al Auriga said dully. Slowly, reluctantly, he faced Mr. Spock again. "He was here. He was locked in. Mandala—Commander Flynn ordered me to have the ship searched. For a double."

Spock raised one eyebrow. "A double." Before he considered that unlikely possibility he had to explore the probability that security had slipped up. "Who was on guard?"

"Neon. It was Jenniver Aristeides' watch, but she's in sick bay—Mr. Spock, I'm sorry, I don't really know what happened yet. I just found out she was ill and I thought it more important to start the search."

"Indeed. What other orders have you given?"

al Auriga took a deep breath. "The guard's to be doubled. What I want is what Commander Flynn wanted all along—to move the prisoner to a security cell. Do the orders to keep him here still stand? Is the captain capable of giving orders?"

"No, Lieutenant, he is not. But those are my orders, and they still stand."

"After what's happened—" The resentment burst out in al Auriga's voice.

"The captain understood my reasoning," Spock said, all too aware that somehow his reasoning had proved faulty.

"This is crazy, Mr. Spock. He got out before. Even with a doubled guard, maybe he could do it again. He could retrieve his gun from wherever he hid it. The description we got was a twelve-shot semi-automatic, so he's got ten more of those damned slugs . . . somewhere."

"The orders stand, Mr. al Auriga."

He heard footsteps and glanced over his shoulder before the sound came within the range of human hearing. A medical technician came pounding around the corner. He looked harried and stunned. Blood smeared his tunic.

He fumbled his medical kit open even before he slid to a stop beside Mandala Flynn's body. Kneeling, he felt for a pulse and looked up in shock.

"For gods' sakes, don't just stand there!" He jerked a heart stimulant out of his bag, to begin resuscitation.

Spock drew him gently but insistently away from Flynn. "There is no need," he said. "There is no reason. She is dead."

"Mr. Spock—!"

"Look at her eyes," Spock said.

The tech glanced down. It was al Auriga who gasped. "That's the way . . ." The technician met Spock's gaze. "That's the way the captain's eyes look. Dr. McCoy is operating on him now."

Spock deliberately turned his back on the technician. He would not think of Jim Kirk's being mutilated further in a useless attempt to save his life.

A thumping noise startled them all.

"Let me out, do you hear?" Dr. Mordreaux shouted, banging on the door again. "I didn't do anything! What am I being accused of this time? I tell you I've been right here since you brought me onto this damned ship!"

al Auriga turned slowly toward the closed door, his body tense with anger. Spock waited to see what the security officer would do; he waited to see if the scarlet-eyed man could control himself sufficiently to take Mandala Flynn's place. al Auriga suddenly shuddered, his hands clenching into fists, and then gradually he relaxed. He turned to the med tech, who was still standing helplessly beside Flynn's body.

"Do you have a sedative you can give him?"

"No!" Spock said sharply.

The two other men stared at him. Neon, ignoring them all, slid the stretcher from its compartment in the abandoned medical kit and began to unfold it.

"Mr. Spock," al Auriga said, "I can't question him when he's hysterical."

"Dr. Mordreaux has been under the influence of far too many drugs administered for far too little reason since before this trip began," Spock said. "Unless he is permitted to recover from their actions we will never hear a coherent story from him. Commander Flynn ordered a search of the ship, did she not?"

"Yes," al Auriga said.

"In that case perhaps you should proceed."

"It's begun," the security officer said. Then he cursed very softly. "And we've got to find that damned gun."

"You have, of course, searched Dr. Mordreaux?"

al Auriga froze. "Oh, my gods," he said. "I don't think anybody has. Neon——?"

"Prisoner, securities, separation," Neon said. She smoothed the rippling stretcher into a flat silver sheet and pushed it down till it nearly touched the deck. "Corridor, cabin, separation."

"None of us has been near him. Commander Flynn was going to search him. I think, but . . ."

"We had better do so now," Spock said. "Unlock the door, and stand away from it."

As al Auriga unlocked the door, Neon lifted Mandala Flynn onto the stretcher, then floated it, and its burden, to waist height. She moved it nearer the med tech, who took hold of the guiding end of the stretcher and stood looking blankly down at it.

"Take her to stasis until after the viewing of her will," Spock said. "Neon: Neon, doorway, offset."

The med tech got out of the way; Neon inclined her head in acquiescence and moved to one side of the door, ready to spring in and help if necessary.

"Dr. Mordreaux," Spock said, loudly enough for the professor to hear, "please calm yourself. I am coming in to speak to you."

The pounding subsided. "Mr. Spock? Is that you, Mr. Spock? Thank gods, a rational person instead of these military-bureaucratic idiots!"

Spock pushed the door open. He was prepared to move with every fiber of strength and speed he possessed to prevent another spiderweb bullet's being fired. But Dr. Mordreaux stood stock-still in the center of his cabin, his arms spread stiffly. When he saw Spock his eyes widened, but he did not move. "Mr. Spock, what happened?"

Spock glanced down at his blood-stained shirt and hands, but did not answer. "I must search you, Dr. Mordreaux."

"Go ahead," Mordreaux said with resignation, and some appreciation of irony. "I'm getting quite good at following the protocol."

Spock searched him swiftly. "He is unarmed."

al Auriga scanned the cabin with his tricorder.

"Mr. Spock, what is it I'm supposed to have done?"

"Captain Kirk has just been shot, Dr. Mordreaux."

"What? And you suspect me?"

"There were several witnesses."

"They're lying. They're lying just like everyone else has lied about me. I haven't hurt anyone, I haven't done anything. All I ever did was help my friends fulfill their dreams."

However damning the truth might be, if Spock withheld it now, the professor would never have reason to trust him again.

"Sir . . . I am one of the witnesses to the assault." He held out his bloody hands.

Mordreaux stared at him, stunned. "You—! Mr. Spock, how can you believe this of me?"

"There's no gun in here," al Auriga said, shutting off his tricorder. "He must have ditched it. I've got to help search, Mr. Spock. I think you'd better come out of here till I can spare another guard."

"You need not be concerned about my safety."

"Mr. Spock—"

"If necessary I will make that an order, Mr. al Auriga." The security officer glared at him a moment, then, abruptly, shrugged. "Whatever you say." He left Spock alone with Dr. Mordreaux.

"I do find it difficult to believe you murdered my captain," Spock said. "However, I have the evidence of my own eyes."

"It wasn't me," Dr. Mordreaux said. "It must have been—an impostor. Someone trying to frame me."

"Dr. Mordreaux, what point would there be to anyone's trying to contrive evidence against you? You are already sentenced to a rehabilitation colony. There is no more severe penalty."

"Only death," Mordreaux said, and began to giggle. "There's nothing left but death, and that's what they have planned for me." From hysterical laughter he dissolved into tears, and collapsed crying on his bunk.

"Dr. Mordreaux!" Spock said. He grabbed Mordreaux's shirt front and dragged him to his feet. Spock's other hand clenched into a fist.

Mordreaux sobbed into his hands. "I can't help it, I'm sorry, I can't help it."

Spock unclenched his fingers, shocked by his own actions. He had come within a nerve-impulse of striking the professor.

"Dr. Mordreaux, I cannot stay here any longer right now. Please try to calm yourself."

"It isn't me," Mordreaux said. through tears. "It isn't me, it's the drugs, please don't drug me anymore."

"No," Spock said. "No more drugs." He gazed down at the man he had respected for so long, now shuddering and sobbing and out of control. "I will come back when I can."

He left Mordreaux behind in his cabin and relocked the door securely behind him. Neon reactivated the power shields.

Chapter 4

Leonard McCoy, M.D.

The name plate on his desk had been knocked half around; Leonard McCoy stared at it as blindly as it stared back at him, mocking him with the very letters of his degree. The brass and plastic were worth as much as his competence. He poured whiskey into his emptied glass: good straight Kentucky bourbon, none of this bizarre alien stuff everyone else on the ship found god knows where and drank and compared hangover stories about. Amazing how many different supposedly intelligent species chose a downright poison, ethanol, as their recreational drug of choice; amazing how many different sorts of biological systems reacted in similar ways to it. He had even seen Spock drunk once, though the Vulcan refused to discuss the occasion. Never mind. Spock was no more fun drunk than sober.

His glass was empty again. He thought he had just filled it. No matter. He filled it again. The things people would drink, even that weird brandy that was Jim's favorite—

He made a small sound of pain and grief deep in his throat. The bourbon was supposed to make him forget, not force him to remember. But now he did remember what had happened, what he had seen and heard and felt, the memory of the silky gray sheen over Jim Kirk's open eyes . . .

He could hear the faint tones and harmonies of the life-support system in the intensive care quarantine unit outside his office. Unwillingly, he got unsteadily to his feet and went to look at the life-systems displays.

The growth of the mechanical web had arrested itself; the molecular fibrils no longer writhed farther and farther into Jim's brain. McCoy had repaired the severed artery and the punctured lung; he had even induced regeneration in the surgical wound so it would heal without a scar.

Yet the scanners gave an utterly misleading pattern. They showed strong breathing, but it was the respirator that forced the movement of air through Jim's lungs; his body made no motion of its own accord. Jim's heartbeat remained regular, but the absence of any signal in the parallel screen showed that the heart contracted because of the nature of the muscle itself, not in response to any nerve impulse. The nerves were destroyed. Even the sinoatrial node and the atrio-ventricular node had been infiltrated and crushed.

Blood chemistry appeared normal: it was an induced normalcy, readings completely level, never changing. pH and electrolytes, blood sugar and heme-carrier were all being stabilized by an extraordinarily sensitive piece of equipment. In a normal, healthy, living human being, the readings would be all over the scale, reacting to everything from breathing patterns and hunger to mood, observation, and fantasy.

McCoy tried to keep his gaze averted from the EEG. As long as he did not look at it he could continue to fool himself. His glass was still in his hand, half-full. He drained it and felt the flow of hope, the sudden certainty that if he looked this time, he would find some proof that Jim's brain had survived and that he would live and recover.

He turned toward the last and most important screen.

All the brain-wave lines were flat, dead flat they had said in medical school, with the self-protective cynicism of young people not yet accustomed to death. Alpha, beta, delta, theta, and all the minor waves through to omega: every pattern that might indicate life showed that Jim Kirk was dead.

The web had completed itself and stopped forming of its own accord. Nothing McCoy or anyone else could do would have stopped it. That was how it was designed. Spiderweb was prohibited on every world in the Federation. No government, however belligerent, manufactured it. Aside from the disgust with which even allies would regard an entity that used it, the weapon could be as dangerous to those who carried it as to its intended victims.

Yet any half-educated moron could construct the stuff in a basement lab. It appeared during the rare outbreaks of terrorism that flared even in the Federation. Spiderweb was nothing *but* a terrorist weapon: it killed surely and certainly, and it caused a slow and ugly death.

Is any death prettier? McCoy wondered. Is death by phaser any less certain? It's death all the same, whether you flash out of existence or slowly dissolve into the universal entropy despite all the resources of modern medicine.

The threads branched out exponentially along axons and dendrites, climbing up the spinal cord and into the brain. The neurophilic metallo-organic molecules concentrated in the cerebrum, and had such a particular affinity for the optic nerve that as they invaded and destroyed the retina they continued growing all around the eye, over the white and the iris, locking the eyelids open.

Jim Kirk stared upward, his dead eyes silk-gray.

McCoy went into his office and poured another drink. Tears running hot down his face, he slumped into his chair, and sat clutching his glass as if the coolness could give him some comfort over blind, screaming grief.

"Dr. McCoy—"

McCoy jerked himself upright, startled by Spock's silent appearance in the doorway of his office. Bourbon sloshed out of his glass and onto his hand, chilling his skin as the alcohol evaporated. Defiantly, he tossed back the last finger of liquor and set the glass down hard.

"What d'you want, Spock?"

Spock looked at him impassively. "I believe you must realize why I have come."

"No, I don't. You'll have to tell me."

Spock left the office and stood, arms folded, before the

quarantine unit. After a moment the doctor rose unwillingly and followed him.

"Dr. McCoy, the captain is dead."

"That's not what my machines say," McCoy said sarcastically, and had a sudden flash of memory, of Jim Kirk laughing, asking, Bones, since when did you put any trust in machines?

"That is precisely what your machines say."

McCoy's shoulders slumped. "Spock, life is more than electrical signals. Maybe, somehow—"

"His brain is dead, Dr. McCoy."

McCoy stiffened, unwilling to agree with what Spock was saying, however true he knew it to be. Somehow his alcohol-fogged consciousness insisted that as long as he believed Jim might recover, the possibility was as good as real.

"I was in his mind until the moment before his death," Spock said. "Doctor, I felt him dying. Do you know how the web functions? Its tendrils coil along nerve fibers. When they tighten they sever the connections between brain cells. They cut the cells themselves."

"I've studied military medicine, Spock. More than you. Even more than you."

"The captain's cerebrum has been crushed. There is no hope of recovery."

"Spock—"

"The body that remains is a shell. It is no more alive than any anencephalic clone, waiting for its owner to butcher it for parts."

McCoy flung himself around, swinging his first in a clumsy roundhouse punch.

"Damn you, Spock! Damn you, damn you—"

Spock grabbed his hand easily. McCoy kept on trying to hit him, flailing ineffectually against the science officer's restraining strength.

"Dr. McCoy, you know that I am right."

McCoy slumped, defeated.

"You cannot hold him any longer. You did your best to save him, but from the moment he was wounded he could not be saved. This failure holds no shame for you, unless you prolong a travesty of life. Let him go, doctor, I beg you. Let him go."

The Vulcan spoke with penetrating intensity. McCoy looked up at him, and Spock pulled away, struggling to hide the powerful feelings of grief and despair that had come perilously close to overwhelming him.

"Yes, Mr. Spock," McCoy said, "you *are* right."

He opened the door of the quarantine chamber. Air sighed past him into the negative-pressure room, and he went inside. Spock followed. McCoy examined the EEG one last time, but he knew better than to hope for any change. The signal remained flat and colorless; all the tracings sounded the same dull tone.

McCoy brushed a lock of hair from Jim's forehead. He could hardly bear to look at his friend's face anymore, because of the eyes.

Precisely, deliberately, he went to work. Once he had made up his mind, his hands moved surely, unaffected by the liquor he had drunk. He withdrew the needles from Jim's arm. The chemistry signals started changing their harmonies immediately. The oxygen tones fell, carbon dioxide rose; nothing filtered out the products of metabolic activity. The signal deteriorated from perfect harmony to minor chords, then to complete discord. McCoy removed the connections that would have restarted Jim's heart when inevitably it failed. Finally, his teeth clenched hard, McCoy disconnected the respirator.

Jim Kirk's heart kept on beating, because the heart will keep on beating even if it is cut out of the chest; the muscle will contract rhythmically till the individual cells fall out of sync, the heart slips into fibrillation, and the cells die one by one.

But the breathing reflex requires a nerve impulse. When McCoy turned off the respirator, Jim's body never even tried to draw another breath. After the final, involuntary exhalation there was no struggle at all, and that, far more than the evidence of the machines, the persuasion of Spock, or his own intellectual certainty, finally convinced McCoy that every spark or whisper of his friend was dead.

All the life-signs stabilized at zero, and the tones faded to silence.

The doctor pulled a sheet over Jim's face, over the dead gray eyes.

McCoy broke down. Sobs racked him and he staggered, suddenly aware of just how much he had drunk. He nearly fell, but Spock caught him, and supported him in the nearest thing to an embrace that the Vulcan could endure.

"Oh, god, Spock, how could this happen?"

McCoy sank gratefully into darkness.

Spock caught McCoy as he fell, and lifted him easily. Loss and regret pulled at Spock so strongly that he could not deny their existence; all he could do was keep them from showing outwardly. That did not lessen his private shame. His face set, he carried McCoy to one of the cubicles and eased him onto a bunk. He removed McCoy's boots and loosened the fastenings of his sweat-stained uniform shirt, covered him with a blanket, and lowered the lights. Then, recalling the single, humiliating, inadvertent time he himself had become inebriated, Spock decided to stay until he was certain the doctor had not ingested enough ethanol to endanger his life. Spock sat in a chair near McCoy's bed and rested his forehead against his hand.

Spock was as oblivious as McCoy to the fact that they had been watched. Across from the quarantine unit, in a half-curtained cubicle, Ian Braithewaite observed everything that happened. He was heavily sedated; he had a hairline fracture of the skull and a severe concussion, from the fall he had taken on the bridge; his head ached fiercely and his vision doubled and redoubled.

At first he did not realize what was happening, and then he thought it must be hallucination or dream. When he realized, with disbelief, that he was observing reality, he tried to struggle up, but the sensors fed more sedative into his system. As the life support displays over Captain Kirk's body went out, one by one, Ian felt himself losing consciousness. He tried to cry out, he tried to make Spock and McCoy stop, but he could not move. He could only watch helplessly, as Mr. Spock and Dr. McCoy argued and then waited for Jim Kirk to die.

Ian fell back into oblivion, believing he would never awaken, but knowing what he had seen.

Spock roused himself abruptly. He had nearly fallen asleep. If he slept now he would be difficult to awaken for several days at least. How long he could hold off the increasing need he was uncertain, but he had no choice. Too many duties lay before him to permit him to rest.

But why *had* he been kept from dozing? He glanced at McCoy, but the doctor slept soundly, in no distress.

In the dimmed space of the main sick bay, the light from the quarantine unit was partially blocked; it was this shadow falling across him that had aroused Spock's attention.

Jenniver Aristeides, the security officer who had been taken ill at Dr. Mordreaux's cabin, gazed through the glass, at the quiet machines, the silent sensors, and the captain's covered body. Her reflection glimmered as two tears fell from her silver eyes down her steel-gray cheeks, and her fingers clenched on the window-ledge.

Christine Chapel hurried across the room.

"Ensign Aristeides, you shouldn't be up."

"The captain is dead," Aristeides said softly.

Chapel hesitated. "I know," she said. "I know. Please go back to bed, you've been extremely ill."

"I cannot stay. I am needed."

Chapel moved in front of Aristeides, blocking her way to the corridor. Aristeides waited patiently, her immense hands hanging loose at her sides, no aggression in her anywhere. The contrast between the two women was so marked that an observer unfamiliar with their backgrounds would have difficulty believing they belonged to the same species. Nurse Chapel was a tall, strong, elegant woman, but next to Aristeides' granite solidity she seemed as delicate as the translucent wind-riders that lived above Vulcan's high deserts, too frail ever to touch the ground.

Spock rose and approached Aristeides quietly. She was the only human being on board the *Enterprise* who was a match for Spock in terms of strength. She was more than a match. He and Chapel together would not be able to stop the security officer if she chose to pass them.

"Ensign," he said, "when you are here you must obey the orders of the medical personnel."

"I am recovered," she said. "I have duties."

"Dr. McCoy took you off duty for at least a week," Chapel said. She glanced beyond Aristeides, to Spock, with relief, and gratitude for at least the moral support: she must be as aware as he that Aristeides could do as she chose. Spock wondered if he could use the nerve-pinch on her, if his hand could span her massive trapezius muscle, if the nerve itself were close enough to the surface to be accessible.

"I should have said honor," Aristeides said. "I have *some* honor left."

"There is no question of your honor," Spock said.

Aristeides did not answer.

"What made her ill?" Spock asked Chapel. "Is she in danger of a relapse?"

Chapel blinked, and passed her hand across her eyes, seeking back in her memory over hours that seemed like days.

"Hypermorphic botulism," she said.

"Most unusual." Spock, like Kirk, had assumed Ian Braithewaite's two colleagues had been felled by infection from a common source on Aleph Prime, but how could Aristeides contract it as well? Neither Aleph Prime nor the *Enterprise* had had a general outbreak of food poisoning. On the contrary, the only point of similarity between the victims was their connection with Dr. Mordreaux.

"I am recovered," Aristeides said. "I cannot stay here. At least let me go to my quarters."

Spock raised a questioning eyebrow at Chapel. "Is there a medical objection to that?"

"It isn't a good idea."

"Please," Aristeides whispered. "I beg of you."

A look of pity softened Chapel's expression. She reached out to touch the metal and plastic band on Jenniver's left wrist, but the security officer flinched back as if—as if Chapel might strike her? That made no sense. Perhaps she simply did not like to be touched.

"Jenniver," Chapel said, "will you promise not to take off your sensor? That way if you're in any distress we'll know to come help you."

"If I require help, the sensor will signal."

That was not a question, Spock thought. She made a statement: she has implied no promise.

"Yes, it will. I suppose it would be all right to stay in your own room," Chapel said. "You need rest more than anything else right now."

Jenniver Aristeides inclined her head in gratitude, and Christine Chapel stood aside so she could leave. The security officer trudged away down the corridor and around a corner, out of sight.

Chapel watched her go, then came a few steps back

into sick bay and stopped. "I hope that was the right thing
to do."

Spock wanted to check on Dr. McCoy again, but as he
turned, Chapel reached out and brushed his sleeve with
her fingertips. Spock faced her again, expecting an outburst of some emotional type, which he would refuse to
understand.

"Mr. Spock," she said, with quiet composure, "someone
must tell the crew what has happened. It isn't fair to
make them find out through rumor, or the way Jenniver
did. The way I did. You're in command now. If you can't
—if you prefer not to do it you must ask someone else
to."

Spock hesitated a moment, then nodded. "You are
right," he said. It was difficult for him to admit he had
bungled, or at the very least neglected, his first duty to
ship and crew; he would be well within his authority to
reprimand Chapel for speaking out of place. But she *was*
right. "Yes, you are right. I will not delay any longer."

She nodded quickly, with no satisfaction, and left him
alone, vanishing into the shadowy depths of rooms of machines and medicines and knowledge that were, right now,
of very little use.

Behind Spock, McCoy moaned. Spock returned to the
cubicle, for if the ethanol had made the doctor ill he
would need help. Spock waved the light to a slightly
higher level.

McCoy flung his arm across his eyes. "Turn it down,"
he muttered, his words so slurred Spock could barely comprehend them.

The light level made no difference to Spock; he could
see in illumination that looked like total darkness to a human being. He complied with McCoy's request.

"Doctor, can you hear me?"

McCoy's answer was totally incomprehensible.

"Dr. McCoy, I must return to my duties."

"I had a dream," McCoy said, each word utterly clear.

Spock straightened. The doctor could be left alone.

McCoy pushed himself abruptly up in the dimness.

"Spock—I dreamed about time."

"Go back to sleep, Doctor. You will be all right in the
morning."

McCoy chuckled cynically. "You think so, do you?"
He rubbed his face with both hands. The lines had deep-

ened since the day before, and his eyes were red and puffy. He peered up at Spock as if the Vulcan were standing in full illumination.

"I know what we have to do," he said.

"Yes," Spock said. "I must tell the rest of the crew of the *Enterprise* what has occurred."

"No!"

"It must be done, Doctor."

"Time, Spock, time. We've done it before—we can do it again."

Spock did not reply. He knew what McCoy was about to say. He had thought of the possibility himself and rejected it out of hand. It was unethical and amoral; and, if certain hypotheses were correct, it was, ultimately, so destructive as to be impossible.

"We've got to rig up the engines to whiplash us back in time. We *can* go back. We can go back and save Jim's life!"

"No, Dr. McCoy. We cannot."

"For god's sake, Spock! You know it's possible!"

Spock wondered what logic would penetrate McCoy's highly emotional state. Perhaps none, but he would have to try to make him understand.

"Yes. It would be possible to go back in time. It might even be possible to prevent what happened. But the stress of our actions would distort space-time itself."

McCoy shook his head, as if flinging away Spock's words without even trying to understand them.

"We'd save Jim's life."

"We would do more damage than we would repair."

"We've done it before! We did it to help other people—why can't we do it to help a friend?"

"Dr. McCoy . . . the other times we were forced to interfere with the flow of events—and we did not always *help* other people—we did it to return the continuum to its line of maximum probability. Not to divert it."

"So what?"

"We did it to prevent the future's being changed. This time, if we change the past, we change the future as well."

"But that was the future that had already occurred. We were living in it. For us now the future hasn't happened yet."

"That is what the people whose lives we affected in the past would have said to us."

"You're saying that the future is irrevocably set—that nothing we do makes any difference because it *can't* make a difference."

"I am saying no such thing. I am saying there are tracks of maximum probability that cannot be stopped and restarted again at will. To do so would cause a discontinuity—a kind of singularity, if you like, no different in effect and in destructive potential from the singularity we orbited only a few days ago. It could drag us to our destruction. Is that what you wish for the future?"

"Right now I don't care about the future! We're living in the present. What difference does it make if something we do now changes it, or something we do a few hours ago?" McCoy frowned, trying, failing, to sort out his verb tenses.

"It makes a difference. That is implicit in every theory put forth about the workings of time, from the Vulcan extrapolations of a millennium ago to the extensions of general relativity in Earth's twenty-first century all the way through even to Dr. Mordreaux's last published work."

McCoy stared at him. "Mordreaux! You're citing his work to prove we can't undo the crime he committed!"

"In effect, that is true."

McCoy lurched to his feet. "To hell with you. You're not the only one on this ship who knows about the whiplash effect. I'm going to find Scotty and—"

Spock halted him with one hand on his shoulder, and McCoy felt a chill down his spine as Spock pressed gently on the nerve at the junction of his neck and shoulder.

"I do not wish to incapacitate you, Dr. McCoy. In your condition it would endanger you. But I will if I am forced to."

"You can't keep me unconscious or locked up forever—"

"No. I cannot."

"So how do you think you're going to stop me?"

"I will confine you to quarters tonight if necessary. I cannot overemphasize the danger of what you are contemplating."

"And after tonight?"

"I hope that in the morning you will be more receptive to reasoning."

"Don't count on it."

"Dr. McCoy, I forbid you to pursue this course of action."

McCoy spun around and turned on Spock in a fury.

"And you think you can command me, now, do you? Because you're the captain? You'll never be the captain of this ship!" His voice was a whiskey-hoarse shout, and only anger kept him from collapse.

Spock took a step backward, then recovered his poise.

"Dr. McCoy, I ask you to give me your word as a Starfleet officer that tonight you will not carry out the action you have threatened." Spock left his own threat unspoken.

McCoy glared at him, then relaxed suddenly and shrugged. "Sure. I won't do anything tonight. I give you my word. What do I care?" He laughed, a sound like tortured steel. "I have all the time in the world!" He turned around and wandered out into sick bay. "What happened to my bottle?"

Lieutenant Uhura sat at her station on the bridge, ready to scream.

Lieutenant Uhura, she told herself. Remember that. *Keep* remembering that.

She knew perfectly well that she would neither scream nor find something to throw at Pavel Chekov, though she wished she could do both. As the strain of the last few hours increased, the excitable Russian distracted himself by alternating incomprehensible mutters in his native language with whistles so tuneless that he must not even be aware of what he was doing. Uhura had perfect pitch; Chekov whistled flat. To Uhura the sound was like the constant scratching of fingernails down blackboards.

Uhura knew, too, that her irritation over Chekov's nervous habits was her own attempt to stop worrying about the captain. Dr. McCoy had issued no bulletin on his condition since immediately after surgery, and that was hours ago. She did not know whether to treat the silence as a hopeful sign, or a sinister one.

It was not so much that Chekov whistled half a phrase of a tune over and over again, or even that he whistled it in the wrong key for the mood of the piece, but that the longer he continued, the flatter his notes became.

Spock had not returned, and Uhura had heard nothing of him over the ship's communicator circuits since he left the bridge. Nor had she heard anything of Mandala Flynn. She must be in sick bay, for Beranardi al Auriga was coordinating the search for an accomplice of the attacker.

Uhura shivered. Spiderweb was little more than a rumor to her; she was from Earth, where there had been no terrorism in decades. She knew what spiderweb was supposed to do; still, she assumed the reports were exaggerated. Captain Kirk and Mandala Flynn were both down in sick bay, perhaps seriously hurt, but they would recover. Uhura was certain of it. After all, Mandala had walked out of here under her own power, so she could hardly be critically wounded.

Pavel hit a particularly off-key note and Uhura glared down at him in annoyance.

The turbo lift doors opened. Pavel stopped whistling.

Mr. Spock walked onto the bridge, and Uhura knew immediately, with an overwhelming wave of despair, that everything had gone terribly wrong.

Without a word, Spock stepped down to the lower level of the bridge. He stopped for a moment, and then he sat in the captain's seat.

Uhura clenched her long fingers. She had an irrational urge to leap up and run from her post, to a place where she would not have to hear what Mr. Spock was about to say.

But Spock had opened the emergency paging circuits: when he spoke, everyone on the *Enterprise* would hear him. There was nowhere to run. Pavel had turned around: he too sensed disaster and his face had paled to a sickly shade.

The silence and the tension increased.

Spock closed his hooded eyes, opened them again, and gazed straight ahead.

"This is Commander Spock."

He hardly ever refers to himself by his rank, Uhura thought, only by his position, science officer, first officer—

"It is my duty to tell you that a few minutes ago, James T. Kirk, captain of the U.S.S. *Enterprise,* died. He was injured beyond hope. He did not regain consciousness after he was taken from the bridge. He experienced no further pain."

Uhura withdrew as far as she could into her own mind, letting the words slide over her consciousness and skid across the slick shiny surface she put up to protect her from the hurt. The realization would have to sink in slowly; for now, she could not accept it.

"In attempting to defend the captain, Commander of Security Mandala Flynn was mortally wounded. She died in the performance of her duty.

"The suspect in the murders is in custody. No concrete evidence of an accomplice has been discovered."

Spock paused, as if searching for some unfamiliar word of comfort to offer to the crew. He failed to find any. He shut off the circuits; the switch made a decisive snap.

"The captain—is dead?" Pavel Chekov spoke in a low and unbelieving tone.

"Yes, Mr. Chekov."

"But—what will we do?"

"We will proceed with our mission," Spock said. "Lieutenant Uhura—"

She looked at him blankly, and replied, finally, as if she had to travel a very long distance just to hear him. "Yes, Mr. Spock?"

"Notify Starfleet of what has happened . . . and the civilian authorities. Mr. al Auriga will undoubtedly wish to take all our statements within the next few hours. We must all do our best to report accurately what occurred."

"Yes, sir," Uhura said dully.

Sulu crept quietly into the minuscule cabin he shared with the senior weapons officer, Ilya Nikolaievich. The cabin was half the size of his private quarters in the *Enterprise*. Perhaps eventually he would find sharing a room unpleasant, but right now his excitement at being on *Aerfen* was impenetrable. Besides, during normal times, when they were on patrol, he and Ilya Nikolaievich would be on watch at different hours and each would have the room to himself for at least a while each day.

Sulu had not felt so good, nor so tired, in years. He had worked for eighteen hours with hardly a break, re-familiarizing himself with the weaponry carried by *Aerfen* and its sibling ships, weapons that depended on precision and finesse rather than brute force, as did those of the *En-*

terprise. He was pleased with his first set of practice scores, but nowhere near satisfied, and he would not be happy till he met or exceeded the scores of the ship's two other weapons officers. The rivalry was a friendly one, but it was rivalry nonetheless.

Ilya slept as peacefully as a child. When he was awake his square-jawed sculptured face held hints of suspicion, watchfulness, and even cruelty. He demonstrated procedures to Sulu efficiently, straightforwardly, and neutrally, showing neither resentment of his new colleague nor enthusiasm for him. Other members of the crew called him Ilyushka, but as he did not invite Sulu to use the diminutive of his name, Sulu stayed carefully with the formal first name and patronymic. Sulu knew he would have to prove himself to everyone: to Hunter, of course, and maybe particularly to Ilya Nikolaievich.

Ilya was shorter than Sulu, but similar in build: compact and well-proportioned, slender but muscular. His heavy straight blond hair fell across his forehead, nearly to his eyebrows, and below his collar in back. He reminded Sulu of Spock, he held himself in such tight control. He was no less somber now, asleep, then he had been earlier, but the tension had gone from his face. He was a human being: the only Vulcan in him, he had put deliberately into his character.

Sulu took off his shirt, then sat down to pull off his boots. They were rather tight and as the left one slid off, his hand slipped. The boot spiralled out of his grasp. He lunged forward to catch it knowing he could not, and winced as the clatter broke the silence of the ship.

Ilya leaped from his bunk, crouching, a knife glinting in his hand. Sulu froze, leaning down with one hand still stretched out toward his boot.

"Sorry," he said, embarrassed, feeling the blood rise to his cheeks.

Ilya straightened up, scowling, and lowered the knife.

"Never mind," he said. "I should have warned you. I spent two years behind the lines during the Orion border skirmish." He slipped his knife back under his pillow. "But please do not touch me when I am asleep, or come up behind me without warning. Do you understand? I react by reflex and I might hurt you."

"I'll remember," Sulu said.

Ilya nodded. The high-collared thigh-length Russian

tunic he wore gaped open above its loose sash, revealing a livid scar that ran down his chest and across his abdomen. Sulu could not help staring, and Ilya noticed his gaze. He shrugged.

"A souvenir," he said, got back into bed, and fell asleep without another word.

Sulu finished undressing and climbed into his own cramped bunk as quietly as he could. He stretched, and rubbed the back of his neck, and closed his eyes for a few moments. But he did not want to go to sleep yet. He pulled the reader away from the wall so it hung suspended over his lap. He had not even had time to program it to his voice, and besides it was bad manners to talk to a computer when someone else was trying to sleep in the same room. He used the keyboard to pull up the schematics for *Aerfen*. He studied for several hours, memorizing the plans and making note of the differences between this ship and the others in the squadron.

While he read, he pushed Mandala's ruby ring around and around on his finger, around and around. He missed her. He did not miss the *Enterprise* yet, and that astonished him. But, oh, he did miss Mandala Flynn. Things kept happening that he wanted to tell her about, he kept thinking, At her fencing lesson, or At my judo lesson, or When I see her later . . . and then remembering that at least for now those times, their times together, were over.

Finally, nearly twenty-four hours after he had come on board Captain Hunter's ship, he fell deeply asleep, with the pale light of the reading screen shining in his face.

Commander Spock walked down the wide corridor of the ship that was, now, his. He was not an unambitious being, but his ambitions lay in other directions than commanding a ship crewed primarily by often incomprehensible human beings. McCoy was right: he was, in fact if not in name, the captain of the *Enterprise*. He would do the job as best he could for as long as he was forced to; he would transfer, as science officer, to another ship as soon as possible. It never entered his mind that he could stay on the *Enterprise;* it did not even occur to him that staying on the *Enterprise* under another captain would be the most logical course of action. With the death of Jim Kirk, this part of Spock's life as well had come to an end, and he saw no point in struggling to prolong it.

He tried to make out what had happened, and how, but failed completely. Every reasonable train of thought ended in paradox or impossibility. No evidence whatever of an accomplice had been found, nor did it appear possible that one could have gained access to the ship and subsequently escaped. In contradiction to this, Mordreaux could not have escaped from his cabin unassisted, yet apparently he had done so. The medical records on Jenniver Aristeides were peculiar. She had been so seriously ill that Spock rejected the possibility that she had freed Mordreaux, then taken poison to cover her guilt. But she could have been a conspirator who was betrayed. It seemed within the limits of possibility, if not probability.

The gun had not been found. Nor had it been disposed of: no anomalous amounts of any unusual element had been found in analyses of the recycling systems.

Had the mysterious accomplice, or even Dr. Mordreaux, somehow managed to get to an airlock before all exits from the ship were put under guard? The gun could then have been sucked away into space, and lost. Or perhaps it had been beamed off the *Enterprise* to no destination, so its subatomic particles were now spread irretrievably over a huge volume of space. That was beginning to look like the only possible conclusion. Yet Mordreaux himself had had no time to perform such a task: Spock could not even work out time enough for him to have done what he was seen to have done.

Spock was slowly coming to the reluctant conclusion that a crew member had arranged and perhaps even performed the so far motiveless crime.

But could he trust his conclusions? He had the evidence of his own observations to prove Mordreaux committed the murder; but he had the evidence of his own observations and what should have been reasonable conclusions to make him believe Mordreaux was not a violent man: and that conclusion, too, appeared false.

Spock hoped Mordreaux had by now recovered. He needed to talk to the professor; he needed to know his perception of the events. Spock strode toward the V.I.P. stateroom.

What had happened on the *Enterprise* bore certain discomforting similarities to what Spock had discovered to be implicit in his observations of the naked singularity. The analysis had seemed to indicate that entropy was increasing far faster than it should; that, in fact, the very rate of increase was growing. Spock found the results extremely difficult to believe, so much so that if he had ever permitted himself to feel either relief or anger he would have been more relieved than enraged when the new orders halted his mission. He needed time to go over his observational apparatus again, to determine if the results were merely an artifact.

The events on the *Enterprise* had that same disquieting aura of wrongness, of occurrences that should not, indeed could not, happen the way they appeared to.

Just as he could make no final determination on the entropy results without more data, he could not understand the events of the past hours without more information. Spock would observe, question, and investigate before he tried to draw more conclusions. Any other plan would be futile.

He would know what happened, and why; he would understand the cause.

The Vulcan language contained no word that corresponded to "coincidence."

"Mr. Spock!"

Spock faced the cry. Snnanagfashtalli bounded down the corridor toward him, on all fours. Furred crew members were not expected to wear uniforms standard-issue for humanoids; Snarl wore a soft leather harness that carried *Enterprise* insignia, communicator, phaser attachment. She came to a silent, smooth halt, muscles rippling beneath maroon and scarlet spots. Her long thin fingers knuckled up in running form, and when she flexed her hands the claws extended.

"Please follow. There is great cause for apprehension."

Spock raised one eyebrow. Snarl spoke in fluent Vulcan, with barely a trace of accent, and none of the lisp that flawed her standard English. Vulcan sibilants were pronounced much differently.

"What is the matter?" He, too, spoke in Vulcan.

"Friend Jenniver. The illness has . . . unsettled her mind. Disarray is in her, and around her, and she sees only one path to her honor."

Spock saw no reason at all to believe Snarl did not understand exactly what that phrase meant.

Snarl switched to English. "She is in despair, Mr.

Spock." That could not be expressed in Vulcan, except by recourse to archaic words. "She wishes only to die."

"Take me to her," Spock said. "Quickly."

Jenniver Aristeides gazed at a painting of her home. It hung on the wall, as if it were a window. She had done it herself, at a time when she felt miserably homesick and lonely, weak and incompetent. Painting was an accomplishment not much admired on her home world, and at times she felt contemptuous of herself for indulging in it. But the scene, a landscape, gave her some comfort. She had almost decided to paint the pasture behind her house, with the ponies out to graze after the day's plowing. But that would have been hopelessly sentimental. And the picture would have been static; in a painting, the powerful creatures, twenty-four hands high, massing two metric tons apiece, would never prick up their ears, toss their manes, and gallop to the far fence kicking their heels like a group of foals. That was how she liked to remember them, not frozen in time. She needed a painting she could pretend might be reality.

The door to her cabin swung open. She heard it, but did not turn. Besides Jenniver, only Snnanagfashtalli could open the door, and she was glad she would to able to see her friend one last time. Not to say goodbye, though. If she said goodbye, Fashtall would try to stop her. She reached out quickly and concealed the remains of the crushed medical sensor. She had promised only that if she needed help, it would signal. It would never signal anything now, and she did not need any help for what she had to do.

"Ensign Aristeides." The voice was not Fashtall's; it belonged to the science officer, the first officer—the captain. "May I enter?"

Snnanagfashtalli came up behind her and rubbed her cheek against Jenniver's temple in the greeting-to-friends. The cream and maroon fur slid smoothly across Jenniver's short, coarse brown hair.

"If you wish," she said. It was not an invitation; it bound her to nothing, not even, strictly, to courtesy. She should stand, salute, make some acknowledgment at least of his presence, if not his superior rank. But she could not even summon the trivial effort required to move in earth-normal gravity. She did not want to offend Spock. On the contrary, he was one of the few people on board she truly admired.

Though Mandala Flynn had treated her kindly, not with the contempt of the previous security commander, Jenniver had feared her for the repressed violence in her, and, paradoxically, for her comparative physical fragility. As a duty, Jenniver had respected Captain Kirk, in the detached way she employed to separate herself from the majority of human-type people who looked through her, tried and failed to conceal their revulsion for her, and felt profoundly uncomfortable in her presence. Snnanagfash-talli, she felt about as she had never felt about another being in her life. Perhaps it was gratitude for friendship and consideration; perhaps it was love. But she had never experienced love, as giver or receiver, so she did not know. She could not ask Fashtall, and she knew no one else well enough to ask. If she asked and they laughed at her, the humiliation would overwhelm her.

But Spock she admired. She always felt she might turn clumsily around—though she was not, in fact, clumsy—and inadvertently crush any other human or human-type on the ship: but about Spock was a resilient strength that reassured her. She never worried about hurting him by mistake with some not-well-thought-out step. And he was the only humanlike creature on the ship who was not repelled by her form. He was indifferent to it, and that reaction was such a relief to her that she could feel comfortable in his presence.

"Do you feel well now?"

She hesitated, but answered. It did not matter what she said; he could not stop her. She hoped he would show her the courtesy of not trying.

"No." She would not lie to a direct question. "I feel ashamed and dishonored. I have failed, just as I have always failed at everything."

"Ensign Aristeides, do you realize that you almost died? That any other member of the crew surely would have died, too quickly to sound the alarm?"

"The result was the same. I fainted—I must have fainted, otherwise how could the prisoner have escaped? The captain and my commander are dead. I should not have become ill. My people do not contract illnesses. It would have been better if I had died."

Fashtall growled. "I tell you again that your people expect too much of themselves."

Jenniver patted Fashtall's long-fingered hand, which lay curled and relaxed on her shoulder.

"They ask no more than all the others can give. Only I cannot answer."

Spock came around and sat down facing her.

"I do not understand what you are saying."

"Mr. Spock, the crops my people grow are so laden with heavy metals that a single bite of our bread would kill a member of any natural species we know about. We are immune to every human plague, and nearly every toxin. And the doctor tells me I contracted *food poisoning?*" She laughed bitterly. "It is nothing but more evidence that I am a useless throwback, suspended somewhere between true humanity and true Changed."

"Suicide does not appear to me to be a creative way of solving your difficulties."

"I left my home because I was inadequate to live there. The reasons are different here, but I am still not adequate. I am half-human and the worlds hold no place for me." She looked away. "You cannot understand."

"Do you think not?" Spock asked. "I, too, am half human."

Jenniver laughed again. "Ah," she said, "truly, you see no differences between us?"

He had the manners not to make things worse by answering.

"I do not doubt you have been made to feel uncomfortable at times, or that you have been the target of hatred," Jenniver said. "But on this ship, I have seen how the others look at you, and how they look at me. I have seen that you need no friends, but if you chose to reach out, friends would be there for you. I admire your independence, but I cannot mimic it. I yearn for friends, but my own species flees from me. I would have gone mad if not for Snnanagfashtalli." She sighed. "I did my best to perform a job for which I was not suited. I knew I would, inevitably, fail. But do you think I can endure the shame of failing because of an illness whose epidemic included only me?"

"It was no epidemic," Spock said. "Strictly speaking it was not even an illness."

"No use to humor me, Mr. Spock. I'm tired of that, too."

"I suspected it when Nurse Chapel said you alone of all the crew were stricken. Despite the virulence of the toxin of hypermorphic *Clostridium botulinum,* you would have had to ingest a massive dose to be affected—a dose too large to be administered in any but its purified form. An analysis of the test results confirmed my suspicion."

"What are you saying?"

"You were poisoned."

Snnanagfashtalli growled low in her throat.

"Someone tried to kill you, very nearly succeeded, and would have succeeded with any other being on this ship, including me. I believe this same being also poisoned two citizens of Aleph Prime, in the same manner, and arranged the death of Captain Kirk. I cannot yet make assumptions about whether Commander Flynn was a planned target."

"My gods." Jenniver blinked slowly several times, her thick brown eyelashes brushing her cheeks. Fashtall patted her gently.

"Who has done this?" The diagonal pupils of Fashtall's maroon eyes dilated at the prospect of the hunt.

"And why?" Jenniver asked.

"I do not know," Spock said. "I do not know the answer to either question. Dr. Mordreaux was thoroughly scanned when he came on board, and he carried nothing —certainly no gun or poison capsule."

"I'd hardly let a prisoner give me a poison capsule, anyway," Jenniver said. "I'm that competent, at least."

"Indeed," Spock said. "Ensign, when you were on duty, or shortly before, did you experience any sharp, jabbing sensation?"

"Like a dart, you mean? No, but I wouldn't. My nervous system wasn't designed to respond to that sort of stimulus." Severe physical trauma was the only injury that ought to be life-threatening to one of her breed, and that was the only kind of pain she would feel.

"I see." Spock considered what she had said, then looked her in the eyes again. "Do you *remember* losing consciousness?"

"No," she said quickly, then looked away. "But I must have."

"According to Mr. al Auriga you were found, barely

conscious, braced against the door. This would seem to indicate that even if you did faint, Dr. Mordreaux would have had serious difficulty getting past you."

"That was the idea. But obviously I was wrong. He *did* get out. You saw him yourself."

"I believed that to be true. But if he could not have escaped from his cabin, some other explanation must exist."

"I wish you'd tell me what it was."

Spock stood up. "Do you understand now that you are not responsible for what happened? Whatever did happen, you cannot be blamed."

Jenniver tried desperately to believe that, but it was hard, so hard . . . "I should not have become ill," she said, for that still was true.

Snnanagfashtalli snarled, a howl of frustration. "She will not hurt herself now!" she said. "If she tries I will tear out her throat!"

Jenniver and Spock both looked at Snnanagfashtalli, who glared back with no awareness of irony. With a sudden feeling of release, Jenniver burst out laughing and hugged her friend.

"It's all right. I'll be all right now."

Spock went to the door and opened it, then turned briefly back.

"Ensign," he said, "please satisfy my curiosity. You did not apply for the position in security?"

"No," she said. "I tried to transfer out. I kept getting turned down before, and I hadn't got up the nerve to ask Commander Flynn."

"What post did you wish?"

"Botany. It wouldn't be quite the same as plowing rock with a four-hitch of ponies. But it's the closest I can get without going home." She paused. "I don't want to go home."

Spock nodded. He understood.

Once the crisis had passed, he would initiate her transfer himself. He closed the door behind him and left the friends alone.

Chapter 5

Dr. McCoy awoke with the worst hangover he had ever had in his life. He should have taken something for it last night, but he had been too drunk, too distracted—and he preserved the anachronistic morality that one should pay for one's excesses. But when he arose, he had to flee immediately into the washroom; sickness took him till his stomach was empty, his eyes were running, and his throat was sore from the taste of bile. Giving up the attempt to discipline himself, he took an anti-nausea pill and two aspirin, and drank a glass of isotonic solution that would help him rehydrate. The taste was so vile that he nearly got sick again.

McCoy sighed, and washed his face. His eyes were red-rimmed and bloodshot; he looked like he still was crying.

Maybe I'll get to be an old alky lying in a back street on some godforsaken out-of-the-way frontier planet, he thought. All I need is a three-day growth of beard—

At that point he noticed, to his disgust, that the brand of beard repressor he used had worn off: he had not kept track of the reapplication schedule. While the whiskers had not yet grown so long that they made him look even more dissolute, the stubble was scratchy and irritating.

He tramped from the cubicle where he had slept—be accurate, he thought: where he had lain unconscious— back to his own quarters. Failing to keep his gaze averted, he saw that the quarantine unit was empty, the machines shut down and pushed back against the wall. Someone— Spock, perhaps, or more likely Christine Chapel—had kept their wits about them, last night, far better than he. Jim's body had been taken to the stasis room.

McCoy washed, shaved, applied more whisker repressor, and put on clean clothes. He was embarrassed about the way he had acted since Jim's death—no, since well before, since refusing to believe the evidence of his machines as well as his own medical training and experience. The moment Uhura relayed the horrible information about the spiderweb, McCoy had known he could not save Jim, but some overwhelming impulse had forced him to try to pull off a superhuman feat. Had his motivation been love, or merely stubbornness and pride? No matter now; he had failed.

He was ashamed, as well, of the way he had treated Spock. The worst thing was that even if he apologized— which he intended to do—he would never be sure Spock understood how sorry he was, any more than he would ever know if he had caused him any distress in the first place.

Their conversation was vivid in his mind. He would almost have preferred a memory blackout. As it was he recalled last night with the surreal clarity of a dream.

What he had insisted that they do was absurd. In the daytime, sober, with the first shock of grief and incomprehension fading to a dull throb of loss and sorrow, McCoy knew his idea was impossible. He had seen it in a dream because it *was* a dream.

Spock knew it. His excuses, his explanations, were all so much technological claptrap, a disguise for the real reason he refused to do anything. He knew, deep in his gut, what McCoy now understood: that playing with fate was wrong. Perhaps he actually had been less affected by Jim's death than McCoy—perhaps his unemotional acceptance of circumstance permitted him to see more clearly. But what it came down to was that death was not an unnatural state; it could be delayed, but never denied; they could not go back, like children telling a story, and fix things so it was all all right, so everyone lived happily ever after, ever after.

McCoy sighed again. He had work to do that he had neglected for too long, but as soon as he was finished he would go find Spock and admit that the Vulcan had been right.

A knock on the door woke Sulu. He lay staring upward for several seconds, wondering where he was. Not on the *Enterprise*—

Now he remembered. He glanced across the cabin; Ilya's bunk was rumpled and empty.

The door opened silently and light from the corridor spilled in through the narrow crack.

"Mr. Sulu?"

He pushed himself up on his elbows, blinking. He could see nothing but shadows beyond the strip of light.

"Yes . . . ? What . . . ? Who is it?" He felt so tired and groggy that his head spun.

"It's Hunter. I have to talk to you." Her voice sounded rough and strained.

Sulu pushed the screen back against the wall, where it obediently dimmed to black. He fumbled for the light switch, and raised the illumination of the cabin as he pulled his blankets a little farther up his chest.

"Yes, ma'am? Come in."

She walked slowly, reluctantly, to the foot of his bunk. Her hair hung down, unbraided.

"I just got a subspace transmission," she said. "From the *Enterprise*. It's . . . extremely bad news." She passed her hand across her eyes, as if she could wipe away pain.

Sulu found himself clenching his fist so hard that Mandala's ring dug into his hand.

"What is it? What's happened?"

She sat down on the end of the bed. "There's no easy way to tell you this. Jim Kirk has been murdered."

Stunned, he listened to her tell him what had happened, though the words were little more than random sounds. Captain Kirk, dead? It was not possible. A whirl of images engulfed him, of the kindnesses James Kirk had shown him, of all the captain had taught him, of the several times Kirk had saved his life.

I would have been there, Sulu thought. I would have

been on the bridge when it happened, I might have been able to do something. I might have been able to stop it.

"I'm the highest ranking Starfleet officer in the sector," Hunter said. Her voice nearly failed her; she stopped, took a deep breath, and put herself under control again. "It's my duty to investigate Jim Kirk and Mandala Flynn's deaths. I'm going to—"

Sulu raised his head, unbelieving, cold grief slowly swelling over him.

"Mandala?" he whispered. "Mandala is dead?"

Captain Hunter's voice trailed off. Sulu stared at her, shaking deep down, his face gray with the second, even more devastating shock.

"Oh, gods," Hunter said. "Oh, gods, I'm sorry. I didn't realize . . ."

"You couldn't know," Sulu said. "Hardly anybody knew." He gazed down at his hands, which could do nothing, now. The ruby ring seemed dull as stone. Now, he was helpless. "We only just figured it out ourselves." If he had been there, he might have done something. "It wasn't your fault." But maybe it was mine, he thought. Maybe it was mine.

"I'm leaving for the Enterprise in an hour," Captain Hunter said. "I've got a two-seat courier. The other place is yours if you want it." She got up quickly and left. Afterwards, Sulu never knew whether she went away because she was going to cry, or because he was.

Max Arrunja unlocked Dr. Mordreaux's cabin for Mr. Spock, with no more comment than bare civility required; the second member of the doubled guard simply stood by the doorway and stared straight ahead. Spock did not try to talk to her, or require her to speak to him. The security division had lost a respected commander, one with far more direct effect on their lives than Captain Kirk had had, someone who had replaced an unsatisfactory superior not with mere competence but with leadership that earned admiration. To a certain extent they blamed Spock for her death, and he had very little evidence that they were wrong.

He knocked on the door, and took the muttered reply as permission to enter. In the dimness beyond, the professor lay curled on his bunk, hunched up under a blanket.

"Professor Mordreaux?"

A pause. "What do you want, Mr. Spock?"

"I told you, sir, that I would return when you had had time to recover from the effects of the drugs you were given on Aleph Prime."

"I'm not sure drugs are such a bad idea just now."

"Dr. Mordreaux, there is no time for self-pity. I must know what happened, both here and at the station."

"I did it," Mordreaux said. He sat up slowly and turned toward the Vulcan, waving the lights to a higher level.

Spock sat down facing him, waiting for him to continue. The science officer did not trust himself to speak; he realized he had been hoping for a denial he could believe, and some other explanation than that the teacher he had respected most in his lifelong quest for knowledge had murdered Jim Kirk.

"I must have, I think," Mordreaux said. "I wonder what caused me to do it?"

A ray of hope, there. "Professor, if you were in a fugue state—"

"I didn't do it *now*, Mr. Spock. They haven't driven me crazy yet. And despite that joke of a trial, I've never murdered anyone."

"Sir, you have just said you committed the crime."

Mordreaux looked at him, then laughed. His laugh contained some of the life it had had before, but it held self-deprecation as well.

"I'm sorry," he said. "I assumed you kept up with my papers, even the last ones. They were too outrageous even for you, I suppose."

"On the contrary, Dr. Mordreaux, my information terminal is programmed to flag your name. I have found your work most fascinating." He shook his head. "You never should have left the Makropyrios; your research would have withstood its critics."

Dr. Mordreaux chuckled. "It already *has* withstood its critics. It's made believers of them, the few who know. They believe so hard, they're suppressing the work. They're suppressing me, for that matter."

Spock stared at him, the meaning coming slowly clear. Dr. Mordreaux had said twice that he worked to fulfill his friends' dreams; he said he must have murdered Captain Kirk, but he did not do it *now* . . .

"You cannot mean you have put your theoretical work on temporal physics into practical use!" Despite himself, the Vulcan was shocked.

"Of course I did. Why not?"

"Ethical considerations, not to mention the danger. The paradoxes—"

"Theoretical proofs weren't enough—I had to demonstrate the principles. I could keep on publishing papers all my life, but the *Journal* wouldn't take them anymore, and without its imprimatur, my monographs got no more attention than those of some self-serving pseudoscientist. I might as well have joined an offworld branch of the Flat Earth Society."

"You would have been better to do so," Spock said. "At least there, the danger is only to your own sanity."

"I don't understand your objections," Dr. Mordreaux said. "No one was hurt. The friends I made on Aleph Prime *begged* me for the practical applications."

"So you complied. You sent them back in time, and that is why you were convicted of unethical experimentation."

Dr. Mordreaux shrugged. "Yes. I'd been working on displacement, just to prove it was possible. I'm a little tired of being laughed at. But my friends didn't laugh at me. On the contrary, they were intrigued. Several of them even helped me, one in particular who realized that my transmission beam was essentially a retooled transporter —and retooled a transporter for me. That speeded up my work by a year or more."

"Dr. Mordreaux, there is a qualitative difference between a small demonstration with inanimate objects, and sending human beings to other times to stay!"

"Yes, I suppose you're right. It's more spectacular. But I think I would have got in the same amount of trouble whether I'd worked with people or not."

"Why did you do it?"

"Because the people were my friends, and they were very persuasive. Mr. Spock—isn't there some other time and place you'd like to live, that you think would be better than now?"

"No, Professor."

"Tell the truth!"

"Dr. Mordreaux, as you are aware, I am a hybrid. The techniques for intercrossing highly-evolved species of different evolutionary origin were only perfected a few years before my birth. I would not even exist in an earlier time."

"Don't split Vulcan hairs with me, you know what I mean. Never mind. The present may seem Utopian to you, but I assure you that virtually any human being who learns to trust you enough to discuss their hopes and dreams will reveal a deeply-rooted desire to live in some other time, a conviction that they somehow are out of place, and belong somewhere they are unable to reach."

"Very romantic," Spock said drily, recalling Mr. Sulu's fascination for a long-extinct culture of Earth that would, if he appeared in it, more likely than not consider him a heathen freak, and in which he would have the statistical choice of dying of blood poisoning from a sword cut received in a duel, or of the Black Plague.

"The people I sent back were the first people to believe in me for a long, long time, Mr. Spock. I could hardly tell them I had the one thing in the universe they wanted, then refuse to give it to them."

"You must go back and retrieve them."

"Absolutely not!"

"I respect your loyalty to your friends, Professor, but your future—essentially your life—is at stake. If they are in fact your friends, they would not abandon you to a punishment that they could stop."

"Maybe not," Dr. Mordreaux replied, "on the other hand, you're putting even friendship to a fairly severe test with that statement. Besides, bringing them back still wouldn't do *me* any good. I wasn't tried for doing experiments on intelligent subjects, not really, though that was what I was convicted of. My demonstration threw someone into a panic, someone high up in the Federation: the authorities would still find some way or other to silence me."

"But the other factors—"

"I did take historical changes into consideration, of course. But my friends went so far back that the danger is minimal."

"How far?" The equations did show that one's ability to alter events in the past was inversely proportional to the square of the distance in time one traveled.

"I won't answer that, I won't give you any clues to finding them. But their chances of making any significant change approach zero, beyond the seventh decimal place."

"But sir, if you brought your friends back to their own time, you would prevent yourself from coming to the attention of the authorities, and none of this would happen."

Dr. Mordreaux laughed again. "Now *you're* talking about changing events in the past. You're not talking about retrieving my friends, you're talking about going back and preventing their leaving in the first place. What happened to your high ethical principles?"

"Professor, the contradiction you are trying to point out is completely specious."

"I *won't* bring them back. That's all they ever asked of me, not to bring them back!"

Spock could see that Dr. Mordreaux would lose his temper soon if the conversation continued in the same direction, so, for the moment, he stopped attempting to persuade him to change the course of his own actions.

"The past aside," Spock said, "your assumption is that a future version of you was the murderer of Captain Kirk."

"I don't know why I'd do it, but that's the only explanation I can think of. It troubles me that I could change so much. I was under the impression that rehabilitation made one completely non-violent. But, yes, I don't see any other explanation. Unless of course you think I turned into a fog and slipped out of this cell through molecular interstices."

"The security officer guarding you was poisoned. Due to her metabolism she was not fatally susceptible to the toxin. But she was obviously meant to die. If she had, it would be assumed you had escaped, then returned. You were meant to be blamed for the captain's death."

"Why would I frame myself?" Dr. Mordreaux said, speaking more to himself than to Spock.

"The more basic question is why you would want to murder Captain Kirk."

Dr. Mordreaux shook his head. "I never met him before yesterday, so it must be something that happens in the future."

"Captain Kirk is dead, Dr. Mordreaux. He will not affect anyone's future."

"Something he did in a future in which he wasn't killed . . ." The professor's voice trailed off.

"I have had empirical experience with time travel," Spock said. "This ship has been involved in several inci-

dents that could have disrupted the future of our civiliza-
tion at the very least—and there is evidence that the
potential damage is far more basic. In each previous case
we were able to prevent the disruption. Professor, this is
another such incident. I believe we must repair the damage to the continuum, or suffer the consequences."

Mordreaux gazed at him in silence for some time.

"You want to prevent my future self from killing Jim
Kirk."

"That would be the effect, yes. But—" Spock stopped.
Perhaps it was better, for the moment, that Dr. Mordreaux believe Spock's motives to be essentially selfish.

"I can't say I like the idea of myself—even a self that
doesn't exist yet—killing anyone, Mr. Spock."

"Then we must work together to gain our ends."

Dr. Mordreaux laughed suddenly. "Mr. Spock—do you
realize that this conversation in itself might be enough to
change my actions in the future? Maybe . . ."

They stared at each other for several seconds.

Nothing changed.

Spock's memories were unaltered; the captain was still
dead.

Dr. Mordreaux shrugged. "Well, it was just a thought."
He looked at Spock with sudden suspicion. "I want a
promise from you before I agree to help."

"What sort of promise?"

"You mustn't try to prevent my friends' going back or
staying back."

Spock considered the offer for some moments. Would
repairing this break in the time-stream without dealing
with the other be sufficient? Or would it simply be unfin-
ished effort, ultimately futile? He doubted he would be
able to reconcile his analysis of the effects with Dr.
Mordreaux's. In the upper levels of any branch of science,
however precise, there was room for doubt, conflict, and
contradictory philosophies; obviously, Dr. Mordreaux
disagreed that time displacement had a lasting, damaging
effect.

But Spock believed that it did, and he had to try to stop
the damage.

"I will offer you a compromise, Professor."

"Such as?"

"I reserve the right to try to convince you that your actions must be undone, if only to rescue you from the fate to which you have been condemned."

"You want me to deliberately suppress my own work!"

"I would hope you might persuade yourself to use it more responsibly."

"If I use it at all I'll find myself right back on my way to a rehab colony! It isn't what I do with it that's frightening, it's that it exists at all. Its potential as a weapon is almost unimaginable. I have the choice of this fate, and vindication of my work with a few people, or living out my life as a discredited fool in the minds of everyone. You see which I've chosen! Do you accept my conditions or shall we forget the whole thing?"

Spock took a deep breath: he was offering his honor against very high stakes. "I will comply with your wishes."

"There are damned few beings in the universe that I'd trust this far, you know. Especially now."

"I value your trust, sir," Spock said, quite sincerely.

Dr. Mordreaux nodded.

Spock spent another half hour in the V.I.P. cabin while the professor described the general workings of the time-changing unit. As Spock began to understand just how simple the device really was in principle, he grew more and more intrigued with it, and with the fact that no one had ever discovered it before, if only by pure chance.

Then again, perhaps someone had—and simply used it with far more secrecy.

Ian Braithewaite entered the engine room of the *Enterprise*. He had been born on Aleph Prime; he had never been anywhere else. He raced sail-ships as a hobby: he could match techniques with anyone from Aleph, tacking between magnetic field and solar wind or running free before an ion storm toward interstellar space. But the racers he handled, the swiftest, frailest, most dangerous and exhilarating ones, lacked any engine at all. Nothing he had ever experienced compared with the *Enterprise*.

Only the impulse engines were running—imagine how it would feel with warp drive on full force! The power vibrated at a frequency far too low to hear, but he felt it. It pounded up and through his legs, into his body, all the way to the tips of his fingers. It lent itself to his determination. He did not intend to let such a ship fall into the hands of traitors.

"Are ye lost?"

Montgomery Scott had seen more than one sleepless night recently, and the stress of the previous day overlaid even his exhaustion. Here was someone, Ian felt certain, who had been loyal to his captain.

"I need to talk to you, Mr. Scott."

"Abou' what?" Scott asked.

"This is a magnificent ship!" Ian said abruptly, unable to contain his admiration any longer.

"Aye," Scott said listlessly. "That it is."

"Mr. Scott—"

"Sir . . . it's been a bad time. Technically you should no' be here—I'm no' one to stand on silly rules, but right now I canna show you around."

"Mr. Scott, I'm not so insensitive that I'd ask for a grand tour after what's happened. It's about what's happened that I must talk to you."

Scott frowned. Finally, he said, "Come wi' me, we can talk in my office."

Mr. Scott came very close to telling Ian Braithewaite that if not for him none of this would have happened at all. But the prosecutor sounded so serious, so unsettlingly intense, that Scott decided he should acquiesce, if only to find out—for a change—what was going on. For he had tried to sort out the last twenty-four hours and failed utterly; the only explanations he could think of came to conclusions he could neither accept nor believe.

The engineer's office, barely a cubicle, had room for a couple of chairs and a computer terminal and that was about all. Scott transferred a thick untidy stack of readout flimsies from the extra chair to the floor so Braithewaite could sit down, and turned the second chair away from the keyboard so he could sit down himself.

"It's no' usually so messy," he said apologetically.

"That's of no account," Braithewaite said. "Mr. Scott— I'm trained as an investigator and I'm determined to apprehend the people who killed James Kirk."

" 'People'!" Scott said. "But the ship was searched. They found no one who could have helped Dr. Mordreaux—no accomplice."

"They found no one on the ship who wasn't on the crew."

Scott stared at him coldly. "You're saying one of us

helped murder the captain. Is this to mean I'm under suspicion?"

"What—? No, on the contrary! I'm here because it looks to me like you're one of the few people on the ship I can trust absolutely."

"Why?"

"Mr. Scott . . . like you, I saw Mr. Spock where he was not supposed to be. I saw him where he *could not* be."

"I dinna understand."

"Somehow, he was on Aleph Prime, before the *Enterprise* arrived. Don't ask me how, but he was. I saw him. He denies it."

"But that's—"

"Impossible? As it was impossible yesterday for him to be in the transporter room and on the bridge at the same time?"

"Surely—ye dinna think Mr. Spock is involved in the captain's death!"

"I think something extremely peculiar is going on. You encountered it, and so did I. If Captain Kirk had paid attention to you yesterday, it's possible he'd still be alive. Mr. Scott, I don't pretend to understand what's happened, not yet. All I've got is suppositions, which I don't want to throw around. Without proof, they're slander, for one thing, but more important, suspicion's hard to take back once you've cast it."

"Aye, that's true," Scott said, impressed despite himself, for he had been unable to talk over his worries with anyone—even in the hopes that they would show him some simple, undeniable reason why he was wrong—for just that reason. "And hard to take it out of one's own mind . . ." He stopped, not wanting to say any more, wishing he had not said as much.

The trailed-off phrase tantalized Ian, but it was too soon to follow it up directly. He asked a question that seemed to change the subject but actually did not.

"Mr. Scott, did Mr. Spock ever offer *any* explanation for his being in the transporter room? Any reason at all?"

"Ye heard all he ha' said to me on the subject. And right after that, Captain Kirk . . ."

"Yes, of course." Ian rubbed his temples: the headache had never really gone away, and now it had begun to intensify.

"Are ye all right? Do ye need some water?"

"Yes, please." Braithewaite blinked to try to dispel the double vision. He closed his eyes tight for a moment; that was better. He wondered what the early symptoms of hypermorphic botulism were. Scott handed him a glass of water and he drank it gratefully.

"Ye dinna look at all well," Scott said.

"I'm not feeling too well, but I'm upset and I'm angry and that's making it worse. Mr. Scott, could a person be beamed from some spot on the *Enterprise* to some other spot?"

"Well . . . one could beam from one place, to the transporter room, then to another place. Ye'd have to materialize on the platform in between. 'Twould be a most lazy and energy-intensive thing to do. Verra wasteful."

"But it could be done."

"Aye."

"Mr. Scott, suppose someone beamed Dr. Mordreaux out of his cell to the transporter . . ."

The engineer did not alter his expression as Ian spoke, but involuntarily he turned dead white.

"The possibility does exist," Ian said.

"Well . . ."

"Your objections are—?"

"The cabin was shielded, alarms were set. If someone tried it, we'd know. And it shouldna be possible to push a transporter beam through the energy-field."

"The shields must have been put in place around the cabin specifically for this trip. They might not be completely secure. Or perhaps the beam was boosted, and the alarms turned off."

"That would be a verra complicated business."

"But it could be done?"

"Perhaps. But only by a few people."

Ian waited.

"I could ha' done it."

"Only you?"

"Mr. Spock . . ."

Braithewaite started to speak, but Scott was shaking his head.

"Nae," Scott said. "This is all wrong. It isna possible."

Braithewaite rubbed his knuckles in frustration. It had seemed so workable: beam Mordreaux out of his cell, then beam him to the empty turbo lift waiting at the bridge; he would get out, fire at the captain, and enter the lift again. His accomplice would beam him back to the transporter room, thence to his cell. But unless Scott were covering for someone—and Ian did not believe he was—his expertise would have to be a guide away from a tempting but inaccurate path.

"Nay," Scott said. "That isna quite what happened." He paused, and drew a deep breath. "The shields are designed to scramble any transporter beam, it's no' possible to power through them whatever the strength." He looked at Ian, resignation and betrayal in his expression. "Someone who knows the security systems of this ship verra well, who knows how they all interrelate, cut the alarm webs and the shields for an instant, and then, before either could reform—they take a few seconds—that was when the beaming could be done. It could be done several times, and no one would be likely to notice."

"Who would be able to arrange it?"

"The captain could ha' done it, or the security commander. I could ha' done it."

"The security commander. That's interesting." Ian had been told Flynn was ambitious, but she was poorly educated and she was stateless as well; it did not seem to him that she had much chance of advancing any farther. His suspicions intensified. "Anyone else, Mr. Scott?"

"Or . . . Mr. Spock." Scott said the last reluctantly, all too aware of what that meant in terms of his altercation with the science officer.

"Someone else could ha' learned, somehow," he said abruptly.

"But you saw Mr. Spock in the transporter room only a few minutes before the attack. And he denied being there."

"Aye," Scott said miserably. "I canna believe it . . . I couldna believe it if I hadna seen Mr. Spock wi' my verra own eyes, and talked wi' him." As always under severe stress, his accent grew stronger. "I *canna* believe it. There must be another explanation. There must be."

Ian Braithewaite gazed down at his long-fingered hands. Not quite enough: better to get more evidence, more witnesses.

"Mr. Scott, we'd best not speak of this to anyone else, for the time being. It's all circumstantial, and of course you're right. There could be another explanation. It could be some dreadful accident." He stood up.

"Ye dinna believe that, do ye?"

"I wish I did." He clapped Scott gently on the shoulder and started away.

"Mr. Braithewaite," Scott said, a little too loudly.

Braithewaite turned back.

"There is another explanation, ye know."

"Please tell me."

"I'm making it all up, about Mr. Spock. To protect myself and divert suspicion to him."

Braithewaite looked at him for several seconds. "Mr. Scott, I hope that if I'm ever in an uncomfortable position, I have a friend around who's half as loyal as you."

In the records office, Dr. McCoy requested from the computer the wills of James T. Kirk and Mandala Flynn.

Flynn's will was a cold, impersonal document, written, not even audio-taped, and stored in the ship's memory in facsimile. It said no more than to use whatever pay she might have accrued for a wake—McCoy managed to smile a little, at that, for his own will reserved a small portion of his estate for the same purpose—and to bury her on a world, it did not matter which one, so long as it was living.

Flynn's will was unusual, for she had bequeathed nothing and mentioned no one. Half by accident, most ship people acquired souvenirs of the places they had visited, exotic, alien artifacts to keep or to give to friends and family back home. But according to boarding records the security commander had arrived with very few possessions, and according to her personnel file she not only had no living relatives, she had no official home world, either. She had been born in deep space, in transit between two out-of-the-way star systems; neither of her parents was a native of either. They had been members of a trading vessel, *Mitra*, which sailed under a flag of convenience; Flynn's mother had been evacuated as a child from a world now deserted, part of a buffer zone between Federation and Romulan space, and her father was born in an artificial colony that went bankrupt and disbanded. A few years after Flynn joined Starfleet, the trading ship and all its crew, all her family, were lost, victims of accident or treachery, and no trace of them was ever found.

One would have to go at least two generations farther back in Mandala Flynn's genealogy to find a world that might claim her, relatives who might acknowledge her; she herself had not cared to do so. Even if she had, her classification would have remained that of a stateless person: a citizen of nowhere, with all the attendant prejudice and suspicion offered one with no real home, and—some would say—no real loyalties either.

Most ship people preferred cremation or space burial, but given Flynn's background McCoy did not find it so surprising that she wished to return to the earth, any earth.

McCoy let Flynn's will fade from the screen, and steeled himself to look at Jim's.

Like most people, Jim Kirk had recorded his will directly onto a permanent memory cell. It could be amended by codicil or destroyed, but the main text could not be altered.

Jim appeared on the screen. McCoy's eyes stung and he blinked rapidly, for it was as if his friend were merely in the next room, speaking to him, not cold and dead.

Reading from a sheaf of papers, Jim spoke legal formalities and proofs of identity, and a straightforward distribution of his estate. He left his assets in trust for his orphaned nephew Peter, his brother's child. Then he looked up, straight at the memory-recorder, straight into McCoy's eyes, and grinned.

"Hello, Bones," he said. "If you're watching this, I'm either dead or so close to it as makes no difference to me anymore. You know I don't believe in heroic intervention to preserve life after the brain is gone, but I'm repeating it so you'll have a legal record of my preference for dying as gracefully as possible."

The smile faded abruptly, and he gazed more intently at the recorder, strengthening McCoy's eerie feeling that Jim really was just at the other end of a communications fiber.

"Leonard," Jim said, "up till now I've never come right out and told you how much I value you as a friend. If I've gone from now till my death without telling you, I apologize. I hope you can forgive me; I hope you understand how difficult saying such things is for me." He smiled again. "And I tease Spock about being emotionless—at least he admits that's his ideal.

"Thank you for your friendship," Jim Kirk said simply. He paused a moment, then finished giving the instructions required in a will. McCoy hardly heard the last few lines; he could hardly see Jim's face. Unashamed, he let the tears run down his cheeks.

"I prefer cremation to burial in space," Jim said. "I'm not much attracted by the idea of floating mummified by vacuum for the next few thousand millennia. I'd rather be burned, by the heat of my ship's engines."

"I thought he would choose fire," Spock said as the screen faded to gray.

McCoy spun around, startled, wiping his face on his sleeve.

"How long have *you* been there?" he asked angrily, forgetting he owed Spock an apology.

"Merely a few seconds," Spock said mildly. "I have been looking for you for a considerably longer time, Dr. McCoy. I must speak with you in absolute confidence. I have discovered something very important. I would like to resume last night's conversation. Do you recall it?"

"Yes," McCoy said, calming his irritation. "I have to apologize. I was wrong in the suggestions I made and I was wrong about the other things I said to you. I'm sorry, Mr. Spock."

"No apology is necessary, Dr. McCoy."

"Dammit, Spock!" McCoy said. "At least give me the chance to excuse myself gracefully, even if it doesn't make any difference to you how big a fool I've made of myself!"

"On the contrary, Dr. McCoy. While it is true that your impulses were the result of overemotionality, it is also true that they were correct. They indicated the right course to take—indeed, they indicated a course which is absolutely essential. We must prevent Dr. Mordreaux from murdering Captain Kirk."

McCoy searched Spock's face for any clue to madness. His expression was as controlled as always. But was there a certain haunted glitter in his eyes?

Perhaps Vulcans went mad the same way they did everything else, with serenity and an absolute lack of emotion. Bring Jim back to life? McCoy encountered the blank expanse of loss created in his mind by the death of his friend. It would always hurt when he brushed up against those knife-edges of despair, but the empty places beyond were filling with memories. McCoy had begun to accept Jim's death. But completing the process would be a long and arduous task, and he did not think he could bear being dragged back and forth over the threshold of acceptance and denial by the mad plans of Mr. Spock. That McCoy had suggested them himself to begin with made them less tolerable, not more.

"Mr. Spock, I went a little crazy last night. If I didn't hurt you I'm glad of it, because I certainly tried. I'm ashamed of myself because of it. I couldn't accept having failed so completely when the person I failed was my closest friend."

"I do not understand the connection between your emotional state of last night and the task we have to do."

"We have no task, Spock, except to bury our dead and mourn them."

"Dr. McCoy—"

"No! If I can admit that I went off my rocker last night then you can admit the possibility that your judgment just might be a little untrustworthy right now."

"My judgment is unimpaired. I am unaffected by these events, which have caused you so much distress."

McCoy did not want to fight with Spock; he did not even feel up to trying to force him to admit he cared that Jim was dead. His irritation was not great enough to overcome the tremendous lethargy he felt. He turned his back.

"Please go away, Spock," he said. Leave me alone, he thought. Leave me alone to grieve.

He hugged himself, as if he were cold: he did feel cold; a chill had descended with the silence. Spock did not reply for so long that McCoy believed he had gone, leaving as quietly and stealthily as he had arrived. The doctor turned around.

He started violently. Spock had not moved; the Vulcan gazed patiently down at him.

"Are you willing to listen to me now, Dr. McCoy?"

McCoy sighed, realizing he would have no peace till he heard what Spock had to say. He shrugged with resignation.

Spock accepted the gesture as acquiescence.

"Dr. Mordreaux should not have killed the captain," Spock said.

McCoy went on the defensive. "I'm well aware of that." He had rubbed his nerves raw trying to think of things he

could have done differently, any procedure that would
have saved Jim's life. He had come up with nothing. Perhaps now Spock would tell him of some obscure paper he
should have read, some untranslated monograph on the
emergency treatment of spiderweb . . .

"I mean no criticism, Dr. McCoy. I mean that in the
normal course of probability, unaffected by anachronistic
events, yesterday, James Kirk would not have died. Indeed, Dr. Mordreaux would not even have been on the
bridge."

McCoy's scowl deepened. "What the devil are you trying to say? What do you mean, 'anachronistic events'?"

"The drugs that were given to Dr. Mordreaux to keep
him manageable and incoherent have worn off. I spoke to
him this morning. I now know what he was working on,
all alone on Aleph Prime. I know why his work was suppressed."

Annoyed by the apparent change of subject, McCoy
did not reply. He would sit here till Spock was finished,
but he had no intention of expressing enthusiasm for a
lecture on weapons research.

"He has taken his monographs on temporal displacement, the ones that caused such controversy, and attempted to bring his theories into practice. He has
succeeded."

McCoy, who had been listening halfheartedly at best,
suddenly straightened up and went back over what Spock
had said, sorting through the technicalities.

"Temporal displacement. Motion through time. You
mean—time travel?"

"I have just said so."

"So you intend to use his realized theories to go back to
yesterday and save Jim's life? I don't see why your plan
is any different—or any more ethical—than the one I
suggested."

"It is very little different in effect, only in means and
motive. Your motive was to save the captain's life. Mine
is to stop Dr. Mordreaux."

"Forgive me, Spock, if I fail to appreciate such subtle
shades of ethics." McCoy's tone grew sarcastic.

"No subtlety is involved. But I have not provided you
with sufficient information to understand my logic."

McCoy set himself unwillingly for a long discourse, but
as Spock related what he had learned in the past few

hours, the doctor grew interested despite himself. He could not deny that Jenniver Aristeides might have been deliberately poisoned, and he could understand Spock's reasons for deciding that Mordreaux could not have escaped from his cell in the first place, much less returned to it, despite the general chaos. McCoy was less convinced that the gun presented a mystery: however thoroughly the ship was searched, with whatever sensitive instruments, however tight the security net, someone clever enough could hide the weapon or dispose of it.

McCoy kept listening, and finally he realized where the explanation was leading.

"Spock," he said, "you're telling me that Jim wasn't killed by the Georges Mordreaux we have in custody on the *Enterprise* at all—that it was some *other* Georges Mordreaux. One from the future!"

"Precisely, Dr. McCoy. It is the only explanation that fits all the parameters of the incident. It is what Dr. Mordreaux himself believes. Given that he had access to the information he would need to go back—come back—in time, it is also the simplest explanation."

"Simplest!"

"Indeed."

"Simpler than an accomplice?"

"An accomplice who appeared from nowhere, looked exactly like Dr. Mordreaux, referred to an incident that has not occurred—yet—and vanished again?"

"Someone on the ship who had some reason to hate Jim—someone who understands hologrammatic disguise . . ." His voice trailed off at Spock's look.

"Hologrammatic disguise is easily detectable," Spock said. "It was not such a disguise."

"An actor, then. Someone experienced in transformation—"

"Who also managed to hide long enough to change back to normal and dispose of the weapon, with everyone on board searching for someone resembling Dr. Mordreaux?"

"It's possible," McCoy said belligerently.

"Indeed it is. It is also possible that the *Enterprise* is playing host to a shape-changer."

"That's easier to believe than a time-travelling assassin!"

"My theory possesses one unique factor, which may persuade you to help me."

"What?"

"If this hypothesis is correct, then these events are a serious perturbation in the time-stream. They must be put right. Captain Kirk need not die. He *must* not die."

McCoy rubbed his eyes, sorting through Spock's barrage of reasoning. It made a certain amount of absurd sense; at the very least it explained the pervasive feeling he, and Jim, and half the other people on the ship had had: that everything was going wrong, in some weird, implacable, uncontrollable way.

"All right, Spock," he said. "What do you want me to do? I'll help you, if I can."

Did a flicker of relief, even of gratitude, pass over the Vulcan's face? McCoy chose to believe so.

"Technically, I am in command of the *Enterprise* until Starfleet can assess the situation and assign another captain," Spock said.

"Or promote you into the rank permanently."

"Out of the question. I would not accept it, but in any event it will not be offered. That has no relevance to our concerns. I cannot perform the duties of captain and carry out this task as well: Dr. Mordreaux and I will have to build the hardware to take me back to yesterday. It will take some time and it would be better if we were not disturbed."

"Why can't we just whiplash back?"

"For the same reason that we will not attempt to calibrate the singularity and use it to travel back: because it would result in our taking the entire ship into the past, including the captain's body; we would be forced to confront ourselves, to try to persuade ourselves—"

"Never mind," McCoy said quickly. "What do you want me to do? Say I've taken you off duty on medical orders?"

"Not an unreasonable suggestion," Spock said thoughtfully. "You may do as you think best, whether you wish to dissemble or simply refuse to answer queries at all."

"Under normal conditions you'd have to go to sleep pretty soon," McCoy said, for he knew the schedule Spock had put himself on. "Come to think of it—how are you going to stay awake?"

"I can delay the compulsion."

McCoy frowned. "Is that wise, Mr. Spock?" Spock so often pushed himself beyond all limits, though no doubt he would deny that he tried to prove himself more than the equal of any full Vulcan.

"It is of no account," Spock said. "I will simply require a few minutes later on today to stabilize my metabolic state. It will not affect my work."

"But that's absurd! Why don't you just go to sleep? We've got plenty of time!"

"But we do not. The effort required to change an event is proportional to the square of its distance in the past. The curve of a power function approaches infinity rather quickly."

"The longer you wait, the harder it will be?"

"Precisely. In addition, we are still proceeding toward the rehabilitation colony, and if we cannot complete the hardware before I am forced to relinquish Dr. Mordreaux to the authorities it may never be completed at all."

"Wait. I thought you believed he was wrongfully convicted. I thought you were going to try to prove him innocent."

"Unfortunately, that is impossible."

"Why?"

"Because even if he were innocent, which technically he is not, he is not being rehabilitated for that crime. His work is perceived as such a threat that a high-level decision has been made, somewhere in the Federation, to eliminate it."

"That's paranoid, Mr. Spock!"

"Their actions, or Dr. Mordreaux's belief that this is what is happening? I doubted the proposition myself. However, the trial records are lost from the public archives. The professor's name has been eliminated from the news indices of Aleph Prime. And, most important, his monographs are being systematically eradicated from Federation memory banks. The Aleph Prime computer infected the computer on the *Enterprise* with a virus program. It seeks out and destroys Dr. Mordreaux's work; it replicates itself and transfers itself to any computer with which it has contact. It had already done its work on the *Enterprise* when I discovered it, and it is only because my own computer is protected, immunized, if you will, against such infection that I retain copies of the papers."

McCoy slowly began to understand how frightening the

implications of Mordreaux's theories were. Anyone who could put them to use could change the time-stream: history itself. Even now they might all be changing, being changed, without their consent or even their knowledge. He shivered.

"No argument I or anyone else could make would prevent the authorities from sending Dr. Mordreaux through rehabilitation," Spock said.

McCoy folded his arms across his chest. "I have no reason to feel any sympathy at all for this man, Spock, but it does sound to me like he's being thrown to the wolves."

"Thrown to—? Oh . . . I recall the reference. On the contrary, doctor. There are several ways to prevent his being imprisoned, but he will not accept my help. He prefers that a very small number of people appreciate the validity of his work. The alternative is for his theories to remain discredited, and that, he cannot accept."

"You're going to let them 'rehabilitate' him?"

"I have no choice. I have given my word not to try to undo his past actions, however self-destructive they may be."

"Mr. Spock—"

"Dr. McCoy, I cannot take the time to argue with you now. I do not disagree with your position, but for now we must be satisfied with Dr. Mordreaux's help in saving Captain Kirk. Do you wish a formal assignment of captain's duties?"

"Don't see that it's necessary," McCoy said.

Spock nodded and started away.

"Spock—wait."

The Vulcan turned back.

"Why the secrecy, my covering for you and all that? Let's just announce what happened and what we plan to do, and we'll have every member of the crew on our side."

"That is quite possibly the worst course of action you could imagine."

"You aren't making any sense."

"This work is perceived as threatening, not only to the Federation but to the history of the universe itself. If we are detected using it—by, for example, Ian Braithewaite —we would undoubtedly find ourselves court-martialed and on our way to the same rehabilitation colony that awaits Dr. Mordreaux."

"Oh."

Spock addressed McCoy gravely. "Dr. McCoy, what we are attempting to do is not without its perils, and a rehabilitation colony is not the greatest of the possible dangers. I may fail. I could conceivably make things worse. Would you prefer that I proceed without your involvement?"

McCoy took a deep breath and let it out slowly. "No, Mr. Spock, I can't stand on the sidelines even if it means taking the chance of going down with you. I'll help you as much as I can."

"That is a mixed image at best, Dr. McCoy, but I appreciate your intent."

Spock felt sleep creeping up over him, fogging his perceptions and distorting his vision. It was too early, too early: he should have had at least until this evening before the need grew compelling. The past twenty-four hours had put him under so much stress that he had been forced to divert attention from controlling his sleep patterns to controlling emotions that under normal circumstances were so thoroughly repressed as to be essentially nonexistent.

He hurried toward his own quarters instead of Dr. Mordreaux's, hoping he had not left making the changes until too late.

The warmth in his cabin, closer to Vulcan normal temperatures, surrounded him, and the whole texture of the light changed. He closed the door and stood for a moment, making the transition from the human world to his own.

But he had no more time to wait. He lay down on a long, polished slab of Vulcan granite, a meditation stone, one of the very few luxuries he permitted himself. He closed his eyes, and relaxed slowly. He could not relax as completely as he would have liked: if he did he would fall immediately asleep. Yet if he remained tense he would not be able to control his body enough to give himself the few more days, the few more hours, that he needed.

There was no help for it. He had to take the chance. The ironic thing was that the level of concentration he required was so deep that he could not pay attention to staying awake.

Gradually he grew aware of every bone, every organ, every muscle and sinew in his body. He breathed deeply, forcing cells to degrade the molecules that were the products of fatigue. He went deep into his own mind to restrain a biological response already compressed to the danger point. He had to struggle with himself; he required every bit of determination left in him. But when he progressed back through the layers of his mind, he was rewarded by renewed clarity of intellect.

For now, he had succeeded.

Dr. McCoy stepped off the turbo lift onto the bridge. He was about to toss a cheery greeting toward Uhura, but one glance at the strain and grief in her beautiful, elegant face, at her eyes red-rimmed from tears, reminded him that as far as everyone else was concerned, they had lost a respected officer or a friend. Already McCoy had begun to think of Jim as just gone away for a short vacation; McCoy's own despair had vanished. But it was essential that he conceal his hope. Spock's assessment was no doubt accurate: if they fell under suspicion they would be stopped.

Near Uhura, he paused. She took his outstretched hand, and he squeezed her fingers gently, comfortingly. He wanted to pull her to her feet and swing her around and hug her and tell her everything would be all right soon; he wanted to tell everyone on the bridge, on the ship, that it was all a mistake, all, practically, a joke.

"Dr. McCoy . . ."

"Uhura . . ."

"Are you all right?"

"So far," he said, feeling brutal, feeling dishonest. "And you?"

"So far." She smiled, a little shakily.

McCoy started toward the lower level of the bridge.

"Dr. McCoy?"

"Yes?"

"Doctor, communications on the ship are . . . muddled. I don't mean the machinery." She gestured toward her station. "I mean people talking to each other. Rumors. Suspicions. I suppose Mr. Spock can't tell us, if we all *are* under suspicion. But if we're not, just a few words from him—"

"Suspicion! Uhura, what are you talking about?"

"I've gone through tough security interviews—you know my clearance level—but I've never been through an interrogation anything like the one this morning."

McCoy frowned, very surprised. "I'd've thought Barry al Auriga would have more tact." Mandala Flynn had gone through al Auriga's files with McCoy and recommended him for promotion to her second in command soon after she came on board. One of the reasons she had chosen him over several other officers of comparable seniority was that his psychological profile, and his service record, indicated that he behaved gently and gracefully under pressure.

"I don't mean Barry. He's taken my statement, of course. It's Ian Braithewaite. Dr. McCoy, the rumor is that the prisoner couldn't have got out of his cell by himself so there must be a conspiracy. That's what Mr. Braithewaite's looking for, anyway. He as much as accused Mandala of being involved. I felt like scratching his eyes out when he said that."

McCoy scowled. "I never heard such a load of tripe. Besides, Ian Braithewaite hasn't got any jurisdiction on the *Enterprise*. Even if he did, it wouldn't give him the right to browbeat you—or slander someone who can't defend herself anymore." Braithewaite was far from unique in believing that a stateless person was a security risk, almost by definition. McCoy sighed. "Uhura, page Mr Braithewaite, would you? Hunt him up and tell him to get to the bridge, on the double."

"Yes, Doctor."

He slid into Jim Kirk's seat and spent the next few minutes gazing at the viewscreen, paying little attention to the spectacular starfield. He wondered what would happen when Spock carried out his plans. Would anyone have any memory of what had really occurred, or would the events simply vanish from their perception? If so, what did that do to the beings who were here, now?

Will we vanish, too? he wondered.

The more he thought about it, the more he became entrapped in the paradoxes and confused by them.

The lift doors swept open and Ian Braithewaite came onto the bridge, his manic energy confined by the belligerent hunch of his shoulders. He descended the steps in one stride and faced McCoy.

"I assume you'd like to talk to me," McCoy said. "Since you've been so aggressive about talking to the rest of the crew."

"I'd rather talk to the new captain, but he's avoiding me."

"Look here, son," McCoy said, not feeling nearly as much the kindly old doctor as he made out, "you're the one who vanished out of sick bay without my say-so. You've got a bad concussion—you ought to be in bed."

"Don't try to change the subject!"

"What exactly *is* the subject? From what I hear you've got some bees that need chasin' out of your bonnet."

Braithewaite's expression was for all the world like Spock's when he did not comprehend some colorful human metaphor.

"What's a bee? For that matter, what's a bonnet?"

"Oh, never mind. Deliver me from people who've never walked on the surface of a planet. Braithewaite, what the devil do you mean harassing the crew? We've all gone through a hell of a lot in the last day, thanks to you and your damned prisoner. We've lost someone we admired very much and I won't have you putting anyone under any more strain."

"I don't see that you have anything to say about it. The crime occurred in my jurisdiction and I'm investigating it."

"You don't have any jurisdiction over a Starfleet vessel."

"Oh, you're an expert in system law as well as a doctor, are you? I'm impressed."

"Mr. Braithewaite, what's with you? Everyone saw your prisoner murder the captain, and unless you've let Mordreaux loose yourself he's safely in custody."

"I don't intend to discuss what I know with you."

"Oh, you don't, don't you?" You young twerp, McCoy added, coming within a hairsbreadth of saying it aloud.

"Where's Mr. Spock—or should I say, 'Captain' Spock?"

"I think he'd object in the strongest possible terms if you called him that to his face. He and Jim were real close for a long time, and while he'd rather have his nails pulled out than admit it, Jim's death hit him hard."

"Really? I suppose he's off somewhere prostrate with grief."

"Look here, I don't understand your belligerence at all. What's the matter with you? If you have something to say, say it—don't keep flying off the handle at everything I say to you."

"I want to talk to the commanding officer."

"I'll have to do, then."

"Spock has turned over command to you?"

"For the moment."

"Where is he?"

"He's—asleep," McCoy said. The lie was badly prepared. He tried to explain about the singularity observations and the Vulcan ability to put off sleep, until he realized Braithewaite doubted every word.

"Even though the formal hierarchy calls for Montgomery Scott to assume command, you've been given the position."

"The choice between us is up to the commanding officer," McCoy said. Then he tried a more conciliatory tone. "Besides, Scotty's working on the engines—he hasn't got time to be in command, he's too important right where he is."

At Braithewaite's expression, McCoy was immediately sorry he had tried to jolly the prosecutor along.

"I've got better things to do than trade clever lines with you," Braithewaite said, and turned to leave.

"Ian," McCoy said, in the softest southern drawl, the tone he found himself using only in times of deepest fury.

Braithewaite stopped, but did not turn around again.

"Ian," McCoy said, "whether you like it or not, I'm in command here till Mr. Spock comes back on duty. And if you keep harassing the crew—if you keep harassing my people I'll have you confined to quarters."

Now Braithewaite did swing around, fists clenched. "You think you can do that, do you?"

McCoy smiled his kindliest old country doctor smile, but his voice was still very soft, very low.

"Try me," he said.

Spock looked over Dr. Mordreaux's shoulder at the schematics the professor had been re-creating for the past several hours. They flicked past, one after another, glowing on the video screen. The device possessed the simplicity of an elegant mathematical proof; it was as streamlined and deadly as a crystal knife.

"With both of us working on it we ought to be able to finish it in a couple of hours," Dr. Mordreaux said.

"How powerful is the unit, Professor?"

"You mean how far back can you go? That doesn't

depend on the changer itself, it depends on how much current you can draw. The *Enterprise* could probably deliver enough power to send you back about a week if you diverted the warp drive. Much farther and you'd begin stressing the systems beyond their inherent resiliency."

"I see," Spock said.

Dr. Mordreaux glanced up at him. "That's farther than you need to go. Unless you lied to me about what you intend to do."

"Vulcans do not lie, Professor. I will keep my word to you, however illogical I believe your position to be, unless you release me from my promise."

"Good," Dr. Mordreaux said. "Go back and save your captain, and be satisfied with that."

Spock had no new arguments to offer Dr. Mordreaux to make him change his mind, so the science officer kept his silence.

"It's a happy coincidence you picked up those bioelectronics on Aleph," Dr. Mordreaux said. "Without them the changer would be about the size of a shuttlecraft and twice the mass."

"I do not believe in coincidence," Spock said absently, making a mental list of the other tools and materials they would need. "Any coincidence observed carefully and logically enough will prove explicable."

"You be sure and let me know what the explanation is, when you figure it out," the professor said.

For a concept Spock did not believe in, coincidence certainly had occurred to him frequently in the last few days. But he did not have time for careful and logical observation of the various phenomena right now. He bent over the video screen again.

The door to Dr. Mordreaux's cabin opened behind them. Spock turned.

Ian Braithewaite glared at him from the doorway. "Asleep indeed," he said. "I hope you're having sweet dreams, Mr. Spock."

"My sleeping habits are none of your affair, Mr. Braithewaite."

"They are when they form the basis of a fabrication meant to mislead me."

"Did you wish to speak to me, Mr. Braithewaite, or are you merely checking on Dr. Mordreaux? As you can see, he is confined."

Braithewaite came closer, squinting to see the screen better. "Locking Dr. Mordreaux up with access to the computer is like giving anyone else the front door key. What are you—"

Mordreaux hit CLEAR on the terminal's board.

"What was that?"

"Nothing you'd be interested in," Mordreaux said, but his bravado faltered with his voice.

"Dr. Mordreaux has offered invaluable help with the interpretation of the observations that your orders interrupted," Spock said. "This could be his last opportunity to contribute to scientific knowledge, a fact even you should be able to appreciate."

Braithewaite glared at him with unrelenting hostility. "I find it very difficult to be impressed with his contribution to the universal pool of knowledge." He reached toward the terminal.

"Do not tamper with the computer on the *Enterprise,* Mr. Braithewaite," Spock said.

"What!"

Spock did not acknowledge any need to repeat himself.

Braithewaite stopped, fists clenched at his sides. Then, slowly, he relaxed. He nodded, thoughtfully, and without another word he left the cabin.

Spock turned back to Dr. Mordreaux.

"He knows you lied, Mr. Spock. He doesn't threaten— he waits till he had enough evidence, and then he goes in for the kill." Dr. Mordreaux returned their calculations from the computer's memory to the screen.

"I did not lie, sir." Spock gazed at the convoluted equations twisting across the screen. "Working on the changer has given me valuable insight into the design of my observational apparatus. You have given me the aid I hoped for."

"A technicality. If I have it was purely inadvertent. Or —another coincidence?"

"Most unusual," Spock said, and went back to work.

Dr. McCoy started at the sound of his name, jerking upright with the sudden moment of wild alertness that prepared him for emergencies. After all these years he had not ever really got used to it.

"What is it? I'm awake!"

He looked around and realized he was still on the

bridge. Everyone was looking at him, with odd expressions: he could not blame them. His face reddening, he settled back in the command seat, not quite pretending he had not fallen asleep but not inviting anyone to comment on the subject, either.

It was Chekov who had spoken to him, to bring his attention to the fact that Mr. Scott was calling the bridge.

"Yes, Scotty?" McCoy said. "Is everything all right?"

There was a short pause. "Dr. McCoy . . . is that you?"

"None other."

"I need to report to Mr. Spock on the state o' the warp drive. Can ye tell me where he is?"

"He's probably sound asleep by now," McCoy said, regretting the untruth that came more easily the second time he spoke it. "I guess you'd better report to me, for the time being."

Another pause. McCoy began to wonder if the intercom were on the fritz, too, like the engines and half the other equipment seemed to be these days.

"T'ye, Dr. McCoy?" Scott said.

"Well, yes, I'm more or less in charge till Spock comes back on duty."

"He ha' made ye his second in command, then." The hurt in Scott's voice came through very clearly. His feelings were injured: he had been bypassed, no way around that. The chief engineer had no way of knowing it was for his own protection, and McCoy could not tell him.

"Not exactly, Scotty," McCoy said lamely, hoping to salve the bruised ego. "It's just till everything gets sorted out. I suppose he feels you're essential where you are."

"Aye," Scott said, then, coldly, " 'sir.' I dinna doubt he knows what he's doing."

The intercom clicked off. McCoy sighed. He had managed Scott no better than he had managed Braithewaite earlier.

As Montgomery Scott turned off the intercom in his office, he slowly met Ian Braithewaite's gaze. Scott felt stunned and betrayed.

"I'm very sorry," Braithewaite said, quite sincerely.

"Dr. McCoy is right," Scotty said. "I dinna have time for administration. The work's only half done on the engines—"

"Dammit, man!" Braithewaite cried, leaping to his feet.

"Either McCoy is working under duress, or he and Spock together have betrayed you and everyone else on this ship! How can you keep making excuses for them?"

"I've known them both for a verra long time and I've never had reason to distrust either of them," Scott said. His feeling of betrayal was mixed with anger; he was not sure if the anger was directed at McCoy and Spock or at Braithewaite. Perhaps it was at all of them; perhaps it did not matter.

"It's hard," Braithewaite agreed, recalling one time, in particular, when he had offered his trust and found it used against him. "But Spock, at least, has exhausted his opportunities for being given the benefit of the doubt. It's of no practical interest anymore whether Mandala Flynn was an instigator or merely a follower. McCoy *may* be less guilty—but there's no way to make either of them out to be completely innocent."

Scott said nothing; he stared at a schematic design pinned to his bulletin board.

"Is there, Mr. Scott?" Ian asked gently. "If you can tell me any other possible explanation for what's been going on here, I'd be very grateful to hear it. I don't like the idea that three Starfleet officers have conspired to take over a ship, to free a dangerous criminal, and to murder their captain—"

"Stop!" Scott said. "Please . . . dinna recite the litany again." He paused to collect himself. "Everything ye say is true, aye . . . But I canna see the *why* of it. Maybe Starfleet will give Mr. Spock the *Enterprise* and maybe they won't. It's a terrible chance to take. He would ha' got a command of his own had he wished, eventually. And why should Dr. McCoy agree to such a scheme? He canna gae any higher and still practice medicine, and he's said any number of times he dinna want to give that up."

Ian sighed. He did not want to let Scott in on all his suspicions, not so much because he would find them impossible to believe, or even because revealing the knowledge would put Ian in breach of his own orders, as because the information itself would endanger the engineer.

"I haven't got absolute proof that Dr. McCoy is a willing member of the plan. I hope he isn't—if he isn't we still have the chance of bringing him back over to our side. I can make some assumptions, but you won't like them any more than my suspicions. I hope what happened was that a plan to free Dr. Mordreaux got so far out of hand that nobody had any choice what to do anymore. The worst it could be . . . well, Mr. Spock has control of the ship right now, he has no need to wait for Starfleet to turn command over to him."

"That's crazy!" Scott said. "And forby, the crew wouldna stand for it!"

"That's what I'm counting on, Mr. Scott. That's why I confided in you in the first place."

"Oh," Scott said.

"I can count on you to help me?"

"Ye can count on me to try to help to find the truth," Scott said, and that was all he would promise.

Chapter 6

That evening, ship's time, Dr. McCoy walked nervously toward the transporter room, where Spock had said to meet him.

The whole day had been dreadful. Spock had been squirrelled away working on the time changer. Scott's bruised ego had put him into an unholy snit; he replied to nothing but the most direct questions and then only in monosyllables. Ian Braithewaite was skulking around giving the third degree to everyone he came in contact with and inventing heaven alone only knew what sorts of fantastical conspiracies. McCoy chuckled to think what the young prosecutor would do if he managed to stumble onto the truth, but his chuckle carried a certain rueful air. Barry al Auriga was infuriated because in trying to debrief the witnesses to Jim's murder he kept running into people who had already had their observations overlaid by Ian Braithewaite's preconceptions. And one of the preconceptions was that Commander Flynn, despite having died trying to protect Jim Kirk, had somehow planned his assassination.

McCoy had a suspicion that al Auriga had had more than a subordinate's respect for his commander: that he had some feelings he had managed to keep well-concealed till now. But Barry's nerves were clearly stretched almost to the breaking point. He was trying to stay in control of himself; so far he had succeeded, but McCoy had a feeling the lieutenant was not too far from flinging caution and his temper to the wind, if Braithewaite got in his way one more time.

Apparently McCoy's warning to the prosecutor had had very little if any effect. McCoy did not want to carry out his threat to confine Ian to quarters, but he was going to have to do it. Morale on the *Enterprise* was so low it probably could not even be measured; McCoy could not let matters go on unchanged, with rumors and suspicions flying, for much longer.

But Spock had finished the time-changer, so perhaps all McCoy's worries were for nothing. The doctor stopped in the doorway to the transporter room and there the science officer was, altering a module from the transporter's innards.

If what he planned succeeded, McCoy would not have to do anything at all. If Spock succeeded, none of this ever would have happened in the first place.

Spock acknowledged his presence. "Dr. McCoy." He picked up the smaller of two peculiarly organic-looking devices and attached it to the module of the transporter.

"Spock," McCoy said, "Spock . . . what happens to *us?*"

"I do not understand what you mean."

"If you go back in time and change things around, we won't exist anymore."

"Of course we will, Dr. McCoy."

"Not here, not now—not doing what we're doing. What happens to . . . to this probability-version of all of us? Do we just fade out of existence?"

"No, Dr. McCoy, I do not believe that is what will occur."

"What, then?"

"Nothing." Spock closed the panel and opened it again, checking that the addition could be concealed in the available space.

McCoy snorted with frustration.

"You see," Spock said, "if I succeed, this probability-version of us will never have occurred. We will not fade out of existence because we never will have existed in the first place. It is quite simple and logical."

"Sure." McCoy gave up. He could feel his pulse accelerating with nervousness, and even fear; he did not even want to think about what his blood pressure must be just now. "Let's do it and be done."

"Very well." Spock picked up the larger device and slung it over his shoulder. It dangled from its strap, glimmering like a cluster of large amber beads.

"Spock, wait—how will you get *back?*"

"As you so astutely pointed out," the Vulcan said, "if I succeed I will not need to come back. But if I should be forced to return, the energy required is far less. In fact, after achieving threshold energy, one is virtually dragged back to one's own time. One sets up a strain that must eventually be relieved. The changer's power-pack will be sufficient."

"Should I wait for you here?—Will you come back immediately after you go? Or—" McCoy could not resist. "Or before?"

"I will endeavor not to return before I leave," Spock said with perfect seriousness. "Though it would be an intriguing experiment . . ." He paused, then returned his attention to the business at hand. "The calculations are far less complex if one remains away as long as one spends in the past. I expect to be gone no more than an hour."

"I'll do my best to be here."

"Dr. McCoy . . . if I am gone for an unconscionably long time, it is essential that I, or whatever remains of me, be brought back here, to my own time. Otherwise the conflict between where I am and where I should be could create difficulties; there is also the possibility of a damaging paradox." He showed McCoy a control on the unit he had attached to the transporter. "The auxiliary changer will pull me back. All you need do is activate it. But this signal cannot be accurately aimed. It is not likely that I would survive if you were forced to use it."

"Then I won't."

"You *must*. If I am gone more than . . . one day, you must."

"All right, Mr. Spock."

Spock stepped up onto the transporter platform.

"Goodbye, Mr. Spock. Good luck."

Spock touched a control on his unit of the time-changer. The transporter hummed to life, but instead of the usual stable beam surrounding the figure on the platform, there was a tremendous flash, like rainbow lightning.

The lights went out. More frightening, the soft sound of the ventilation fans ceased, and the ship lay in a moment of darkness and silence so complete that McCoy thought the explosion had deafened and blinded him.

The *Enterprise* had lost all power.

Ian Braithewaite suspected instantly what was happening when the power went out: the same thing had happened on Aleph Prime when Dr. Mordreaux began playing around with his time-travel device. That was what had first alerted Braithewaite to the peculiar activities, and what had drawn him into this horrible complicated matter of conspiracy, treachery, terror, and murder. He cursed himself for underestimating Spock and Mordreaux; he cursed himself particularly for being too timid to run the investigation aggressively. He should have called in civilian police from Aleph long before now; he should have called in Starfleet as well. But he had been trying desperately to keep the time-travel capability as secret as possible, as he had been ordered; there was no point in suppressing the work if it were publicized all over the Federation.

Emergency generators brought the ship back slowly to an eerie half-light. Ian flung himself out of his cabin and pounded down the corridor toward Mordreaux's cabin, fearing that the device had been used to take the professor out of even the absurd semblance of custody he had been in on the *Enterprise*. He wondered how long it would take before the ship was diverted from its course toward Rehab Seven—Ian suddenly realized that he had no way of knowing it already had not, except that surely Mr. Scott would know and tell him.

And how long will it be before we're all told our fate? he wondered. To be sold to the Klingons, or to the Romulans, as hostages, and the starship peddled to the enemy; or were the plans for starship and crew more direct, more private? Ian Braithewaite knew that if he ever had such a creation as the *Enterprise* in his own hands, he would not let it go for any amount of treasure.

At the junction of two corridors, he stopped. What point to going to Mordreaux's cabin? He would not be there: Spock had just freed him! But the science officer would have had to use the transporter in tandem with the changer. Ian might be able to catch him, at least. If he hurried.

He changed direction, and ran.

Still dazzled by the sudden flash of the transporter/changer, McCoy blinked. In the darkness, he wondered if this was what it was like never to have existed at all.

"Mr. Spock?"

He received no answer.

He gradually became aware of the self-luminous dials on the transporter, casting a strange silver glow over his hands. He drew away, into the shadows, and stood quietly waiting for something, anything, to happen.

The darkness crept away in the dim illumination of emergency power. He waited: but nothing changed.

McCoy began to hear the shouts of consternation from nearby crew members: it was always traumatic, on the rare occasions when the power failed in a starship. Everyone was frightened.

McCoy did not blame them. He was frightened, too, and he knew what was going on.

McCoy glanced at the transporter platform, but decided it would be better to return in an hour than to wait for Spock here.

Starting out the doorway, he nearly ran into Ian Braithewaite.

"Damn," Braithewaite said. "I hoped . . ."

He blocked the door. Aside from being more than a head taller than the doctor, he was twenty years younger.

"It isn't too late, Dr. McCoy," he said earnestly. "I know what happened last night—I know what kind of stress you were working under. I know you weren't yourself."

"What are you talking about?"

"I was awake, when Captain Kirk . . . died. I saw you arguing with Mr. Spock. I know you didn't want to comply with his demands."

McCoy stared at Braithewaite, dumbfounded.

"I can't promise you immunity, not after last night." He grasped McCoy by the shoulders. "But I know how much pressure can be brought to bear on someone. I've seen what it can do. If you help me I swear I'll do everything in my power to have this reduced from a capital crime."

McCoy went cold. He realized—Finally you realize! he thought, it's *you* he's after, you and Spock, not just Commander Flynn or some faceless nameless phantom conspiracy.

Spock was not being so paranoid after all.

"Are you sayin'—" McCoy heard the soft threat again in his own voice. "Are you sayin' you think Jim Kirk— Just exactly what *are* you saying?"

"Captain Kirk was still alive. I saw you disconnect the life-support systems."

"He was dead, Ian. His brain was dead before I took him off the bridge, only I wouldn't admit it. That's what Spock and I were arguing about. I couldn't admit that I couldn't do anything to save Jim, I couldn't admit that he was dead."

Braithewaite hesitated. "You were so drunk you didn't know what you were doing, how could you know if he was dead or not?"

"Even blind drunk I could have heard the brain-wave sensors. Hear them! My god, I'd been listening to them for hours."

Braithewaite gazed down at him thoughtfully. "I'd like to believe you," he said. "But why did you do it in the middle of the night, without contacting his family, or even his executor?"

"The only family he has is a young nephew. *I'm* Jim's executor. You can look at his will if you want to. He asked not to be kept alive if there were no hope of recovery. I'd been keeping his body alive for hours, against his wishes, trying to pretend to myself that he might get well. It wasn't fair, not to anybody, particularly not to Jim."

Some of the tension left Braithewaite's stance, and he stepped aside, but he followed McCoy down the corridor.

"The power failure—it was the result of using the time-travel device."

McCoy did not reply.

"Dr. McCoy, I want to believe your story about Captain Kirk, please believe me. But you've got to tell me where—and when—you sent Spock and Mordreaux."

"I didn't send them anywhere. What do you mean, 'when'? Time travel? That's the craziest thing I ever heard. I told you you can't talk to Spock till he's gotten some sleep. But Mordreaux is still in his cabin. Why don't you go check?"

McCoy was too preoccupied to notice the fury that spread over Ian Braithewaite's expression when he was confronted again with the pathetic fabrication of Spock's hibernation, or estivation, or afternoon nap if they wanted to call it that. The falsehood of it had been blatantly demonstrated to him. But Ian knew his own flaws. He was out of his depth in this case, and had been from the beginning, trying to balance his passion for justice against a threat so devastating it was almost incomprehensible, trying to weigh suspicion against his own good faith.

You're being naive, Ian, he thought. Again.

But it was possible that McCoy himself was being deceived.

"All right," he said. "I'll check on Dr. Mordreaux. But you've got to come with me." He was not so naive that he would trust McCoy till he had some proof of the doctor's innocence.

McCoy sighed. "Whatever you want, Ian," he said. His voice was uneven. He was shaking, from being forced to relive Jim's death. He went with Braithewaite toward Mordreaux's cabin, getting angrier and angrier at the attorney. He doubted that seeing the professor would allay the young busybody's suspicions, and suppose Ian discovered that it was Spock, not Mordreaux, who was missing? The only safe thing to do was to get him out of the way long enough for Spock to do his work.

At Mordreaux's cabin, Barry al Auriga stood talking to the two guards on duty. All three security officers looked up.

"We've come to see Dr. Mordreaux—if he's still here," Ian said.

al Auriga frowned, but kept his temper. "He's here."

"Unlock the door."

"No, Barry," McCoy said. "Don't."

Everyone stared at Dr. McCoy; Ian Braithewaite turned pale.

"I *was* right," he whispered. "You *are* . . ."

"That's enough out of you," McCoy said. "Barry, would you please take Mr. Braithewaite into custody, and lock him in his room till he learns some manners?"

"Dr. McCoy," al Auriga said, "it will be a pure pleasure."

"Gently, please."

"I'll handle him with gloves of softest silk."

Ian tried to back away from the huge, massive security officer, but he was trapped between him and McCoy, and the two other guards stood at ready.

"You don't understand! Mordreaux is *gone!* McCoy and Spock helped him escape!" He had to look *up* to meet al Auriga's glare: it was years since he had encountered anyone taller than he was, and the effect of al Auriga, looming over him, was terrifying. He pressed his hands flat against the cool bulkhead behind him.

"They killed Jim Kirk!" Ian said. "The security commander helped plan it, but she wanted too much so they killed her, too—"

al Auriga reached out and grabbed Braithewaite by the throat.

"Barry—" McCoy said.

"I won't hurt him," al Auriga said. "I won't—" His voice broke. "Unless he says another word." He bent down and looked at Braithewaite straight on, pinning him with the glare of his incredible scarlet eyes. "If you say another word against Mandala, I'll kill you."

Braithewaite set his jaw and met al Auriga's gaze, in silence, but without flinching.

Well, McCoy thought, he's got some backbone, I'll say that for him.

al Auriga marched him down the hall, around the corner toward his cabin, and out of sight.

McCoy appreciated the fact that Barry had refrained from saying, "I told you so."

Spock materialized on the transporter platform in a blaze of rainbow light. He paused for a moment before stepping down, for the transfer had wrested him through time and space, twisting the continuum and brutalizing him as well. Every muscle in his body felt wrenched.

It took him a moment to dispel the pain, a moment longer than he thought it should. When he moved he felt stiff; he tried to hurry but found it nearly impossible.

"Mr. Spock?"

Spock froze for no more than a second, then turned

calmly toward the chief engineer, pushing the changer back behind him on its strap so Scott could not see it.

"Mr. Scott. I should have . . . expected you."

"Did ye page me? Are ye all right? Is something wrong wi' the transporter?"

Spock said the first thing that came to mind, realizing, after he spoke, that he was telling Scott what Scott claimed Spock had said in the transporter room.

"I simply noticed some minor power fluctuations, Mr. Scott," Spock said. "They could become reason for complaint."

"I can come back and help you," Scott said, "as soon as I've reported to Captain Kirk about the engines." He frowned.

"That is unnecessary," Spock said. "The work is almost complete." He did not move. Scott remained in the doorway a moment longer, then turned on his heel and left Spock alone.

Spock waited until he knew the chief engineer was out of sight of the transporter room. Scott would enter the turbo lift with Ian Braithewaite and the captain, and then a few minutes later Scott would come back down again. After that it should be possible for Spock to enter the lift unobserved—no one else had come into the bridge before Dr. Mordreaux appeared—and wait inside to intercept the professor's deranged future self. Spock touched his phaser. He would prefer not to be forced to use it, but he did not quite see any other way of stopping Mordreaux permanently. Stopping him now would be useless if he were simply to return in time again, somewhere else, and murder the captain there.

Spock concealed himself near the lift, around a corner and in shadows.

"Ah, Spock, I *thought* you came after me."

The Vulcan spun around: and came face to face with Dr. Mordreaux, the same, slightly older Georges Mordreaux who had appeared on the bridge of the *Enterprise*, dressed in the drab gray prison uniform his other self wore, carrying the same vicious-looking gun he planned to use in a few moments.

"I should have known better than to involve you at all, but I had to get you away from that damned singularity, you caused me more trouble than Braithewaite and Kirk and the whole Federation put together."

"I do not understand what you mean, Dr. Mordreaux."
Spock let his hand move slowly toward his phaser.

Dr. Mordreaux gestured with the muzzle of his pistol.
"Please don't do that. I never meant to hurt anyone, I was
only trying to keep myself out of more trouble. But you
have no idea how complicated things can get. You make
one change, it sets in motion a whole series of others that
you couldn't predict . . ."

"Professor, you are seriously disturbed. You must not
carry out the action you plan. It is exactly as you say: it
will start a whole chain of events that you do not wish to
happen."

"No, no, this one will fix it."

He gazed at Spock a moment longer, and the science
officer realized neither of them had any choice anymore.
If Spock could not stop the professor, the professor was
going to kill him. And Jim Kirk.

Throwing himself to one side, Spock drew his phaser.
As he aimed it he heard the pistol go off, and he felt the
impact of the bullet. It slammed him against the bulkhead and he slumped to the deck, still trying to aim the
phaser.

He failed.

Spock's vision clouded over as he opened his eyes. He
knew it as a symptom of spiderweb. He tried to ignore
the prospect of his own death, he tried to do something,
anything, perhaps he still had time to save Jim's life, to
stop Professor Mordreaux . . .

He saw and felt the tendril reaching out toward his outflung hand, tickling his palm. He jerked away, rolling to
escape it, and ended up on his knees, panting, blood running down his face and into his eyes from the bullet graze
at his temple. He wiped his eyes on his sleeve, and his
vision cleared.

The spiderweb bullet had imbedded itself in the bulkhead, not in his body. It had begun to grow downward,
seeking warmth and nerve cells. As he watched the mass
of fibers still reaching toward him, they shivered, glimmering in the light like a skein of silver thread. All of a sudden the fibrils contracted, pulling themselves up into the
main body of the growth, and then they relaxed again and
the sheen and movement faded.

The spiderweb was dead, and this one had lost its prey.

Spock wiped the blood from his face and eyes and concentrated for a moment on stopping the flow from the bullet wound. He was drenched with sweat.

Dr. Mordreaux was on his way to the bridge.

Already running, Spock grabbed up his phaser from where it had fallen and headed toward the turbo lift, no longer caring if anyone saw him and wondered where he had come from. The lift seemed to take hours to arrive. He plunged inside.

After an eternity, the lift slowed and stopped at the bridge. The doors slid open.

Spock took one step forward, and halted.

He could smell the human blood, and hear the labored breathing of his mortally wounded friend.

Dr. McCoy worked frantically. No one looked toward the open lift.

Again, Spock felt caught up by the chaos; again, he felt the medical team trying to save the captain.

He felt the tubes and needles enter him, and damped down the fresh surge of scarlet pain as oxygen flooded his body. But all the physical manifestations of the world were peripheral. Despite Spock's strength, Jim was slipping away. Spock's mind and Jim Kirk's were melded together, but all the force of Spock's will could not prevent the dissolution of his friend's consciousness. It was being crushed out of existence, and he could not hold it together against the destructive force.

"Spock?"

"I am here, Jim." He did not know if he heard the words or sensed them directly; he did not know if he spoke or thought his answer. He felt himself slipping away with Jim.

"Spock . . ." Jim said, "take good care . . . of my ship."

"Jim—"

With a final, agonizing effort, nearly too late, Jim Kirk dragged himself away from Spock, breaking off the terror and despair.

The physical resonance of emotional force flung Spock back against the railing. He slumped to the deck.

He and Jim Kirk were both alone.

When the lift doors automatically closed, shutting Spock off from the scene he had hoped to stop, he realized he actually had fallen backwards. His body trembled uncontrollably. The turbo lift waited patiently to be told which deck to take him to. But there was nothing to be done here, nothing at all that he could do.

His hand shaking, he touched the changer control that would rebound him back to where he belonged; he vanished from this time-stream.

Jim Kirk was dead.

Rebound dragged Spock back through the continuum with the same muscle-wrenching force as he had left it. He materialized on the transporter platform and fought to keep his balance. When he staggered, McCoy caught and steadied him.

"Good lord, Spock, what happened?"

"I failed," he said. His voice was hoarse. "I watched Jim die again."

McCoy hesitated for a moment, trying to think of something to say. He fell back on practicality.

"Come on. Let's get you cleaned up."

He pulled Spock's arm over his shoulder and helped him out of the transporter room.

"Mr. Spock!"

The sight of Spock, his face and shirt covered with half-dried green blood, startled Christine Chapel. "What happened?"

"He fell out of bed," McCoy said shortly, and immediately regretted his tone. "I'm sorry, nurse. I didn't mean to snap. Please get me a tray and see if you can find that hybrid skin synthetic I mixed up."

He made Spock sit down. Chapel brought the instrument tray and left it without a word.

Well, McCoy thought, I deserve a cold shoulder.

He slipped the changer's strap free and laid the device aside, then started to clean the blood from Spock's face.

"What *did* happen? This looks like a bullet graze."

"It is," Spock said without meeting McCoy's glance. "I encountered the future Dr. Mordreaux. I failed to stop him."

"It looks like he nearly stopped you." McCoy suddenly realized what must have happened. "Spock—he didn't shoot at you with the same gun—?"

Spock nodded.

McCoy whistled softly. "You were lucky. But you *did* see him?"

"Yes."

"You're sure . . ."

"That he was from the future? Yes, Dr. McCoy. I had more opportunity to observe him on this occasion. He was . . . a different Dr. Mordreaux." He glanced at McCoy quizzically. "Did you doubt that was what I would find?"

"Well, it's nice to have some confirmation."

Spock fell silent for a few moments while McCoy cleaned the bullet wound.

"I must go back again."

McCoy started to protest, but nothing he could say, from pointing out that Spock had probably lost nearly a liter of blood to telling him they were both under suspicion of murder, treason, and proscribed weapons research, would be likely to delay him long enough for him to fully recover. Besides, at this point probably their only chance *was* for him to go back and try again. McCoy would have to stay here, cover Spock's tracks, and—under different circumstances McCoy would have been able to laugh at this—give him time.

"Are you going back to the same place again?"

Spock considered his choices, a limited number.

"No," he said finally. "The future Dr. Mordreaux said something which leads me to believe that he is responsible for calling the *Enterprise* to Aleph Prime. My observations on the singularity correlate with his work, somehow, apparently to his disadvantage."

"You mean it wasn't Braithewaite or Starfleet after all who diverted us—but Dr. Mordreaux?"

"The future Dr. Mordreaux. Yes. I believe that to be true."

"Can you go that far? It's quite a distance, besides being a long time. When you left before, you blacked out the ship."

"If I cannot draw power from the warp engines, I will have to turn the *Enterprise* around and return to Aleph Prime—that is, to the position in Aleph's orbit from which the signal came."

Christine Chapel came in and put down the packet of skin synthetic; McCoy and Spock fell abruptly silent. She gave them a strange look and went away again.

"Scotty isn't going to be thrilled when he hears you want the warp drive back on line. And we're going to have a hard time explaining why we want to backtrack."

"I do not intend to inform Mr. Scott of my plans; if he has finished repairing even one of the warp engines it will not be necessary to obtain his permission to tap its power. Nor do I see any reason why I should explain a change in the ship's course except to say that it is necessary."

McCoy opened the packet and drew out the skin synthetic with sterile tweezers. This was the first time he had had a chance to try it, and he was anxious to see if it worked. If the cells had fused properly Spock's body would not reject the skin, as it did skin synthetic for either humans or Vulcans. Since Spock was the only Vulcan/human cross around—at least the only one McCoy knew of—null grafting tissue for his unique immunological system was not exactly common. He covered the long graze and sprayed on a transparent bandage.

"Hardly shows," he said, rather pleased. "I'll want to check it every day or so . . ." His voice trailed off as Spock raised his eyebrow again.

"Right," McCoy said. "You won't be here. *I* won't be here. I hope."

Spock rose. "I must find out about the warp engines—"

"You're asleep, remember? Spock, this is an order. You lie down, right here, and stay here till I get back. I'll find out about the warp drive and I'll get you some clean clothes. Do me a favor and tell the computer to let me into your cabin so I don't have to figure out the override procedure for the lock."

"The computer does not lock my cabin, Dr. McCoy."

"What?"

"My cabin is not locked. Vulcans do not use locks."

"You're not *on* Vulcan."

"I am aware of that. But I see no reason to behave differently in the matter of locks, any more than I see any reason to change my behavior in other respects."

McCoy looked at him incredulously. "Most everybody on the *Enterprise* is fairly honest, but it seems to me you're pushing your luck."

"Luck is not involved. I have observed that human beings behave as they are expected to."

"Most of us, maybe, but—"

"Doctor, do we have time for a philosophical discussion?"

"No, probably not." McCoy gave up the argument reluctantly, intending to begin it again at the first opportunity—then reminding himself that if all went well it never would have occurred to start with. "All right, never mind. You rest for a few minutes, hear? I'll be right back."

After McCoy left sick bay, Spock lay down on the bunk in the cubicle. He still had to be careful not to sleep, but he needed the physical rest desperately. He would not admit pain. But he could ignore it only so long; it was a physiological sign of danger.

As he rested his body and tried to keep his mind alert, he thought about coincidences, the coincidences that had begun to show their causes. The *Enterprise* had not been called to Aleph Prime at random; Dr. Mordreaux had devised a way to order it to the station. There was some strong significant relation between the professor's work, and the entropy effect Spock had discovered as a by-product of his observations of the singularity.

A flash of insight took him, like an electric shock, and he saw how his new factor applied to Dr. Mordreaux's work. It was a direct result of travel through the fourth dimension, not a by-product at all. The singularity that had been created was merely the spectacular physical manifestation of the one-way trip Dr. Mordreaux's friends had taken through time. Spock could not see why he had not understood it before. Perhaps he had been too willing to accept the human view of coincidence; or perhaps the connection was too simple to be easy to see. The theoretical connection between naked singularities and the possibility of time-travel, and, conversely, time-travel and the creation of singularities, was centuries old. Discovery of that interrelation appeared to precede the discovery of the principles behind interstellar travel, in virtually all technological societies.

But the entropy effect was something new, and it was the far more disastrous consequence of temporal displacement.

Dr. Mordreaux's friends *must* be returned to their own time, to repair the rip through the continuum that their journey had caused.

Spock had no way to estimate how Dr. Mordreaux would take this new information, or even whether he would believe it. He might refuse to accept it, and see it as nothing more than another attempt by Spock to try to make him betray his friends.

The Vulcan began to realize just how high were the stakes against which he had placed his honor.

McCoy stopped just inside the engine room. The air was full of the smell of ozone, singed insulation, and melted semiconductors. Scott sat in his office, bent over his computer console: if things were so bad he could not set to work fixing them immediately—practically by instinct as far as McCoy had ever been able to see—then things were bad indeed.

"Hello, Scotty," McCoy said. "What a—"

He cut off his flippant remark as Scott went rigid in his chair. McCoy knew the chief engineer was enraged even before he turned around, which he did, slowly, still seated in the swivel chair, pushing with his left hand, which was clamped so tight around the edge of the console that his whole forearm trembled.

"Scotty," McCoy said gently, "what's wrong?"

"Nae a thing."

"Come on. Is it this blasted command business? I don't want it—I'm sure Mr. Spock didn't even think about how you'd feel, he just chose the arrangement he thought would be most efficient."

"There's nae a thing wrong," Scott said again. "Nae a thing at all. What do ye want? I canna take time to chat."

All right, you stubborn Scot, McCoy thought, if you want to play at being official, I've got years more experience at this game than you do.

"I can see that, Mr. Scott," McCoy said. "I certainly don't want to waste your valuable time. Just give me an update on the engines, impulse and warp."

Scott looked taken aback by McCoy's response, as if he had been bluffing somehow, and never expected McCoy either to call him on it or take the offensive. McCoy had the feeling, as well, that even so he had not acted as Scott hoped he would, but he was at a complete loss about what Scott did want just now, and as Scott could not take the time to chat, McCoy could not take the time to play armchair psychiatrist, or even have another try at patching up the engineer's ego.

"The impulse engines are just barely functioning," Scott said. "If my people work round the clock we'll be able to decelerate by the time we reach turn-around for Rehab

Seven. But the engine room crew ha' already been working round the clock for days, and they're exhausted."

"Do you know what caused the blackout?" McCoy asked, because he thought that was the question he would be expected to ask.

"A power drain. 'Tis as if someone fed the current into the transporter and beamed tremendous amounts of electrical energy out into space."

"Well, it couldn't be that," McCoy said quickly, hoping to divert Scott from information the engineer would be better off not knowing. "That doesn't make sense."

"Nae, it dinna make sense."

"What about the warp engines?" McCoy asked quickly, before the other subject could go any farther.

"Canna decelerate in normal space with the warp engines."

"That isn't what I asked. If I go up to the bridge and ask for warp factor four toward—toward Arcturus, would I get it?"

Scott opened his mouth, but no words came. Finally he managed a halfhearted murmur. "Aye," he said. "Aye, ye would."

"Thank you, Mr. Scott. That's all I need to know."

McCoy realized that Spock would be more than a little conspicuous on Aleph Prime in a Starfleet uniform with *Enterprise* insignia: he would arrive at the station before the ship was even ordered there. It would be inconvenient at best if Spock were taken into custody and charged with being absent without official leave.

McCoy felt uncomfortable, rooting around in Spock's wardrobe, and the high temperature in Spock's cabin made him perspire. But he took a moment to look for a garment of less military cut. Behind the uniform shirts, and the formal jacket, he found several tunics of a more casual style.

He returned to sick bay carrying the fresh shirt bundled up under one arm, hoping no one would ask him about it.

"Spock?"

Spock sat up smoothly in the dimness of the cubicle, wide awake and alert, looking not quite so haggard as when McCoy kept him from falling off the transporter platform. McCoy glanced at Spock's temple: the skin synthetic was holding well.

"Here's a fetching outfit for you," McCoy said, handing him the dark brown tunic. "Less noticeable than starship-officer blue."

Spock took the shirt, with a quizzical expression, but he did not object to McCoy's choice.

"Are the warp engines in operating condition?"

"Mr. Scott says they are."

The clean shirt was made of some silken material, gathered at the cuffs, with a restrained design of gold at wrists and collar. Spock put it on.

"Haven't seen you wear that before," McCoy said.

"Wearing it on the *Enterprise* would not be appropriate."

"Very becoming. Matches your eyes."

Spock picked up the time-changer and got to his feet. "I would not want to frustrate your curiosity, Doctor. My mother gave me the tunic." He walked past McCoy out of sick bay.

After a moment McCoy followed.

"It is not necessary for you to accompany me, Dr. McCoy," Spock said when the doctor caught up to him. The science officer began setting the changer's controls without checking his stride.

"How long will you be gone this time?"

Spock stopped. "I cannot say," he said slowly. "I had not—It is impossible to estimate."

"Paging Dr. McCoy," the ship's computer said. "Vessel approaching. Dr. McCoy to the bridge, please."

"Oh, not *now*," McCoy said.

"Best that you reply, Doctor. There will be another blackout of the ship's power, more serious than the last, and your presence will be required elsewhere. I do not need . . . a going-away party."

"All right," McCoy said, realizing that his wish to accompany Spock to the transporter had no real logical reason. "But if I have to bring you back, how long should I wait this time?"

"At least twelve hours. But no longer than fourteen, or the time-changer will not provide enough power to return me through the distance the ship will have traveled."

"Good lord—you mean you'll materialize somewhere out in deep space?"

"Possibly. It is more likely, however, that the return beam would be spread out over a considerable volume of intervening space and time—"

"Never mind," McCoy said quickly. "No longer than fourteen hours."

"Dr. McCoy to the bridge," the computer said again. "Dr. McCoy, please reply."

"Is it my imagination, or do I detect a certain hysterical tone?"

"The integrity of the computer's data-base has been severely compromised," Spock said. "And unfortunately I have had no opportunity to repair the damage done by the sudden power failure."

"Sluffing off on your duties, eh?" McCoy said, and then, before Spock could reply to him seriously, "I didn't mean it, I'm sorry, I think I'm getting a little hysterical myself."

"Report to the bridge, Doctor." The Vulcan turned on his heel and walked away.

"Unidentified vessel approaching," the computer said. "Phasers on ready."

"Oh, good grief," McCoy said, and hurried toward the lift.

Before he reached the transporter, Spock paused to think for a moment. He could go back to Aleph Prime and prevent the *Enterprise*'s being diverted; or he could speak to Dr. Mordreaux once more and show him the proof that might persuade him to release Spock from his promise. That was without doubt the most logical action.

By the time Dr. McCoy cancelled the automatic aiming of the phasers, the unknown craft that had alerted the sensors had approached close enough to be seen on the viewscreen unmagnified. It was small and fast, a moving silver speck against the starfield.

"Who is it? Where is it from?" McCoy wondered if Braithewaite had managed to send a message to Aleph Prime to call in reinforcements for his troublemaking.

Both Chekov and Uhura were off duty and McCoy could not remember the names of the younger ensigns who sat in their places.

"We're receiving a transmission, Dr. McCoy," the second shift communications officer said.

"Put it on the screen."

Hunter flickered into being before him. At the edge of the image, McCoy could see Mr. Sulu, silent and grim, a glazed expression of grief in his eyes. Hunter did not look much better. McCoy knew exactly how she and Sulu must feel: the way he had felt the night Jim died. He had a sudden impulse to say to them, to everyone, It's going to be all right, we're going to make it all right again. Somehow.

But nothing had happened, nothing had changed. The power had not even gone out again. Where was Spock?

Perhaps nothing ever *would* change. Perhaps this time track would continue unaltered, with Jim Kirk and Mandala Flynn dead, and if Spock succeeded in doing anything it would be no more than beginning some alternate version of reality. McCoy's eyes stung with sudden tears, with a suspicion of hopelessness brought on by uncertainty.

"Captain Hunter," he said sadly. "Hello, Mr. Sulu."

"Hello, Dr. McCoy," Hunter said. Mr. Sulu nodded, as if he could not trust himself to speak.

"I'm sorry to have to see you again under such circumstances."

"It isn't what I'd hoped for. Permission to beam aboard?"

"Of course," McCoy said—then realized his mistake. Aside from Spock's not having left yet, McCoy had no idea whether the transporter was still suited for normal use.

"Captain," he said quickly, "on second thought you'd better dock with the *Enterprise*. We just had a massive power failure, and I'd rather not use the transporter till we get things sorted out."

"As you prefer," Hunter said.

Hunter rotated her stocky little courier, bringing it in back-to-back with the *Enterprise*, to join the docking ports smoothly. McCoy was waiting for her when she climbed from her ship into the larger craft's gravity field. She jumped to the deck.

Sulu followed, more slowly.

"Captain," McCoy said. "Mr. Sulu."

"Oh, gods, Doctor," Hunter said, "I can't stand that military crap right now. Can we be a little more informal? Hunter. Do people call you Leonard?"

"Sometimes. That's fine."

"Thank you. What happened?"

McCoy sighed. "That will take some explaining, Hunter. Let's go in and sit down to talk."

"All right."

Neither noticed when Sulu left them, long before they reached the officers' lounge.

Sulu did not think he could stand to listen to explanations. All he knew, all he needed to know, was that Mandala was dead. He stopped at the door of the stasis room, gathering up enough nerve to go inside.

Finally he stepped close enough for the door to sense him, and it opened.

Inside, two of the stasis units glowed softly, their energy fields stabilizing the bodies within them. They were marked, coldly, officially, KIRK, JAMES T., CAPTAIN, and FLYNN, MANDALA, LIEUTENANT COMMANDER. Sulu paid his respects to his former captain silently, brushing his fingertips across the name. Finally, with great reluctance, he opened the unit where Mandala's body lay.

A shroud of blue light glowed around her.

Spiderweb gave no easy death, and no easy memories to the people left behind. Sulu could see the struggle she had gone through, even in her blank-eyed face. She had fought: to the end of her life she had never given up.

Her hair had come down; it curled in a tangled mass around her face and shoulders.

Sulu pushed his hand through the protective energy field to touch her cheek, to brush back a lock of her hair. Her ruby ring, on his finger, glowed black through the blue light, and its gold highlights flashed.

He wished he could close her eyes. He knew he could not.

Sinking to the floor, pulling his knees to his chest, with his arms wrapped around them, Sulu hid his face.

A long time later, immersed in dreams and memories, he felt a touch on his shoulder. Startled, he looked up.

Barry al Auriga crouched down beside him, gazing at him in silence.

"I should have been there," Sulu said. "On the bridge."

"To die with her? She would not want that."

"What do you know about it?" The vehemence of his reaction startled him, and he tried to turn away.

Barry's hand tightened on his shoulder.

"I grieve, too," he said.

Sulu faced him again.

"It is not proper to fall in love with the commander of one's section," Barry said. "And I could see that you . . . I could see she wanted you . . . I could say nothing. But I grieve with you."

Sulu grasped Barry al Auriga's forearm. "I'm sorry. I didn't know . . ."

al Auriga shook his head. "Nor did she. It does not matter now." He got to his feet, drawing Sulu up with him. "Come away. This is not the place to remember her."

Sulu pushed the stasis unit back into place. It was the one last thing too much for him. He stood with his back to al Auriga, both hands pressed hard against the wall, trying to control his silent tears.

"Come away," Barry said again. He put his arm around Sulu, like a brother: he was crying, too.

Chapter 7

Hunter listened, her face a mask. McCoy could not tell what she thought or how much she believed of the tale he was telling her, she was so unresponsive. But he was all too aware of the frazzled edges of his story, the loose ends and dissembling. He finished, and took a long gulp of his drink.

Hunter toyed with her feather-tipped black braid.

"All right, Leonard," she said. "Now, please, the truth."

He blinked in surprise. He could not think what to say; her disbelief was too direct.

"You're a very lousy liar."

Still he could not reply.

Hunter leaned forward, resting her elbows on her knees, and spoke with angry sincerity.

"I could pilot this ship through the holes in that story. Mysterious accomplices and a disappearing gun and a Changeling with food poisoning? Do you expect me to believe Mandala Flynn would have put up with a second in command who can't find a single bit of useful information in twenty-four hours? She was far too ambitious to pick an incompetent second—that would make *her* look like a fool. I assume you've been giving al Auriga the same run-around you've given me. But there's a difference, now: you may be his superior, but you aren't mine. Where's Mr. Spock? Where's Ian Braithewaite, for that matter?"

"Well, until Spock gets some rest—"

"Don't! Not again! His captain's *dead,* the crime's unsolved, he's in command, and you want me to believe he went off to sleep for three days? Even if he did, there's been a complete power failure, you've got computers crashing all around you—and you want me to believe a Vulcan science officer stayed asleep? Come on!"

"After so long—"

"Dr. McCoy," she said, and her voice chilled him, "Dr. McCoy, there's nothing mystical about catch-up sleep. I know the techniques. You could probably learn them yourself. Spock isn't catatonic, he's not in some kind of trance that would damage him to come out of. He can wake up—and he *would* wake up, given the circumstances you've described."

McCoy's hands felt cold, and a drop of sweat ran down his side. If he told her the truth . . . She knew too much about the ship and the people on it to be fooled as long as Braithewaite had been, and he could not confine Hunter to quarters.

But he did not think she would believe him, and he could not take the chance of trying to convince her he was telling the truth. In desperation, he tried once more to mislead her. All he needed to do was give Spock more time. But what was the science officer *doing?* With every second that passed, every random noise, McCoy expected the power to fail as Spock departed again. Why was he still on the ship?

"Hunter," McCoy said gently, "none of us has been acting very rational since Jim died. I know how you feel, truly I do, but I think you're getting a little bit overemotional—"

Hunter stood up.

McCoy kept on speaking, recklessly.

"I know how close you and Jim were. He told me . . . the last thing he ever said to me was about you."

Her expression did not change. She gazed at him directly.

"He knew he made a mistake, refusing your partnership's invitation. He wanted to tell you himself, but when he got hurt, he knew he was dying. He knew he'd never see you again. He asked me—"

"Shut up."

"He wanted you to know."

"I don't believe you," she said, her tone completely flat.

The Entropy Effect   175

"It's true!"

"You haven't said a true word to me since I came on board," Hunter said. "Jim trusted you—he trusted you more than he trusted anyone else, including me. But I swear I don't know why." She started out of the officers' lounge.

McCoy jumped up and grabbed her arm. Startled, she spun away and into an attack position so quickly she nearly struck him, but she held back in time, lowered her hands, and turned away from him again.

"Where are you going?"

She did not answer, but McCoy followed. Soon he realized she intended to go to Mordreaux's cabin.

"There's no point in trying to talk to Mordreaux." He spoke all in a rush; his voice sounded even less convincing than the ragged words themselves. "He's completely incoherent. He's—"

"Don't lie to me anymore, Leonard," Hunter said. "Either tell me the truth, or just be quiet."

Ian Braithewaite tried again to force open the door of his cabin, and again he failed. The lock no longer responded to his voice. The blocked communications terminal kept him from talking to anyone; he could not contact Mr. Scott. In frustration and fury, he pounded on the door. He had already made himself hoarse by shouting every time he heard someone pass.

McCoy had really got to him, all right, with that sentimental tripe about carrying out his good friend's last wishes. The man was a consummate actor. Ian supposed that was a talent most doctors cultivated anyway, and McCoy had used the ability magnificently. In a strange way, Ian could hardly help but admire him. He carried out his aims with a certain flair. The prosecutor realized now that McCoy could not be forgiven or excused any of his actions: however upset the doctor had been at the time of Kirk's death, he had become well reconciled to it. No doubt the potential profits from the hijacking of the *Enterprise* and the use of the time-changer had soothed his grief and his conscience.

Ian felt completely helpless, as helpless as he had been in al Auriga's grasp. The security officer had not hurt him, but Ian was at the mercy of McCoy and Spock and Mordreaux. The precariousness of his own position began to grow clear. Until now he had been too angry to worry very much about his own safety. This was the first time since coming on board the *Enterprise* that he had not had too many other things to think about.

He was not frightened. He considered his possible fate with a certain resignation, a fatalistic attitude. Perhaps they *had* beaten him. It certainly looked like it now. But if he got one more chance, just one stroke of luck, he would not be so fussy about absolute proof of their guilt.

As far as he was concerned, the only question left to be answered was whether they planned to use the ship and the time-changer for their own benefit, directly, or to take it and the *Enterprise*, the most advanced example of Federation technology in existence, and auction them off between the Federation's enemies.

He flung himself down on his bunk and threw one arm across his eyes. His stomach churned; he felt nauseated by tension and anger. He lived his life on the verge of ulcers, a fact he denied. He was convinced that if he could just sort out the events of the last day properly and deduce what would happen next, then he could somehow stop the progression of disaster. But all he could do was think, over and over again, I shouldn't have trusted McCoy. After everything I've seen I should have known better, I shouldn't have trusted McCoy.

He heard the door open; he lay very still, pretending to be asleep. Light crept past the folds of his sleeve. He wondered if McCoy had come to dispatch him, as he had got rid of the captain, or if Spock had come to poison him, as he had somehow poisoned Lee, and Judge Desmoulins, and the security guard. Footsteps approached. He prepared himself to fight, trying to tense his muscles without appearing to move.

"Mr. Braithewaite?"

The tension went out of Ian in a rush. He pulled his arm away from his eyes and sat up quickly.

"Mr. Scott—thank god!"

"I had to override the lock," Scott said. "I tried to reach ye on the communicator, but I couldna get through."

"They've cut me off," Braithewaite said. He sprang to his feet. "I tried to give McCoy another chance, and he had me arrested."

"Aye," Scott said dully.

Ian took Scott by the shoulders. The engineer did not meet his gaze.

"I knew I could trust you," Ian said. "I knew there had to be somebody on this ship who would make a difference. My god, if you weren't here—"

"Dinna remind me," Scott said. "Dinna tell me compliments. There's naught but shame in all of this."

"We've got to try to recapture Spock and Mordreaux. They've both left the ship but they might have overlooked some kind of clue. They were working in Mordreaux's room—come on!"

He plunged out into the corridor, oblivious to being seen or recaptured. Scott followed.

Dr. Mordreaux hunched down in a chair, his arms crossed over his chest. He glowered at Spock.

"Dammit, no!" he said again. "I knew this would happen if I helped you, I *knew* it. You'll never be satisfied till you manage to impose your own will and your own ethics on mine!"

"I assure you, Dr. Mordreaux—"

"Shut up! Get out! Do whatever you want, I don't care."

"Do you release me from my bond?"

"No! Your actions are on your own head. If you do this, I'll expose you for the liar you are."

Spock gazed down at the time-changer. Dr. Mordreaux's threat was trivial enough: If Spock broke his promise and kept the professor from being arrested, the promise technically would never have been made; if Spock failed, the professor would be taken to the rehabilitation colony, and no one would pay attention to what he said. But even if the threat were a compelling one, it would not control the Vulcan's actions. Spock alone had to decide whether he must break his word, and whether he could live with himself afterward if he did.

The door to Dr. Mordreaux's stateroom slid open.

"Ye said they'd escaped!" Mr. Scott said to Ian Braithewaite.

Braithewaite stared at Spock and Mordreaux, his stunned expression changing to relief and triumph. "It doesn't matter, we've caught up to them. Get that thing away from Spock. It's—it's a weapon!"

"Mr. Scott," Spock said, "have you been looking for me?"

"Mr. Spock . . . Mr. Braithewaite has made some serious accusations against you, and against Dr. McCoy. I ha' some questions I canna work out in my mind. I think we must talk."

Braithewaite snorted in disgust.

"Are you giving me an order, Mr. Scott?" Spock asked.

"I dinna wish to put in a formal charge of unfitness against ye, but I will if ye force me to it."

"You will be charged with mutiny."

"Will ye no' just explain?" Scott cried. "Ye willna answer my questions, ye've lied to me—"

"For gods' sakes, Mr. Scott!" Braithewaite yelled. "This is no time to argue over your hurt feelings!" He lunged toward Spock. "Give me that—"

As Braithewaite grabbed for the time-changer, Spock pushed him aside and fled. He shouldered his way past the two security officers at Dr. Mordreaux's door, but Scott and Braithewaite followed him on the run, and the taller man closed the distance quickly.

"Stop him!" Scott shouted, and the sounds of confused voices and running footsteps intensified into chaos.

Spock raced through the corridors of the *Enterprise*. He spun around a corner and ran headlong into Dr. McCoy and Captain Hunter. But Hunter had no reason to try to stop him; he escaped again and abandoned McCoy to the confusion as Scott and Braithewaite caught up to them. He could hear everyone shouting at each other, cursing, yelling conflicting orders and explanations, with McCoy doing his best to complicate matters further. But after a moment the muddle broke up into a string of pursuers again. As Spock plunged into the transporter room, Ian Braithewaite put on a final sprint, launched himself at Spock, and rammed into the Vulcan's knees. They went down in a tangle, Ian clutching at the time-changer and trying to drag it away.

Spock clamped his fingers around the muscle at the base of Ian's neck, seeking out the vulnerable nerve. The prosecutor collapsed in an angular heap. Spock freed himself and lurched to his feet. Without taking the time to double-check the settings of the changer, without stopping to think whether he should try to go farther back than he originally planned, all the way to the beginning, Spock leaped onto the transporter platform. Hunter appeared in the doorway, her energy-pistol drawn. She aimed it: it would not stun; it was a killing weapon.

Struggling halfway to consciousness, Braithewaite groaned. "Stop him," he said. "Stop him, he murdered Jim Kirk."

But she hesitated. As Mr. Scott and two bewildered-looking security officers rushed into the transporter room, followed a moment later by Dr. McCoy, Spock pressed the controls and felt the rainbow light engulf him, crush him, and rip him away into the continuum.

Dr. McCoy felt the warp engines shudder into unwilling resurrection, feeding their power through the time-changer. The drain was too great. As the lights faded, the doctor watched Hunter lower her energy-pistol.

She had plenty of time to fire, McCoy thought.

"What the hell did he do?" Hunter said.

"He made a fine botch of my repairs again, for one thing," Scott said from the darkness, his old self for a moment.

"Emergency power should come on line in a minute or so," McCoy said. "Like I told you, we've been having some problems—"

"You've got more than problems," Hunter said, in a tone that silenced him.

The quiet movement of the air returned, and the lights glowed dimly back to life around them. The voices of frightened crew members jumbled together in an erratic crescendo. The computer began to babble, then lapsed into fuzzy white noise.

Mr. Scott helped Ian Braithewaite to his feet. Dazed, the prosecutor almost fell again. McCoy hurried forward, but Ian jerked away from his help.

"Keep your hands off me." He sat down on the transporter platform and buried his face in his hands.

"All right, Ian," McCoy said mildly. He turned to the security officers. "Is anyone guarding Dr. Mordreaux?"

"I—I guess not, Doctor."

"You better get back there then, both of you. Everything's under control here."

They looked skeptical. McCoy did not blame them.

"Out!" he yelled.

They left, reluctantly, to return to their post. McCoy folded his arms and regarded Braithewaite.

"You're supposed to be in your quarters, Ian," he said. "What are you doing out?"

"I freed him, Dr. McCoy," Scott said. "I dinna ken what's happened to this ship, I dinna ken what's happened t'ye and Mr. Spock since all this started. But Mr. Braithewaite has asked questions that need answering, and you willna answer them."

"Scotty, you disobeyed my direct orders—"

"Your orders! Ye are no' a command officer! What business had he leaving ye in command?"

"Spock left the doctor in command because it was the only way he could carry out his plans," Braithewaite said. "He had to keep you out of the way."

"Now just a minute," McCoy said.

"Stop it, all of you."

The three men fell silent, recognizing the tone of someone who had earned obedience and respect.

"I outrank all of you, including Spock," Hunter said, "and if I have to pull rank to find out what's going on, then consider it pulled. Dr. McCoy, do you have anything to say now?"

He started to answer her—but Spock had got away, and perhaps he needed only a few minutes to put everything right, but if he failed again and returned, he would be stopped if his plans were known. McCoy could not take the chance of revealing what they were trying to do. He shook his head in defeat.

"Mr. Scott?" Hunter asked.

"I dinna ken what has happened. Dr. McCoy said Mr. Spock was deep asleep. He isna asleep, you saw that for yourself. That didna look like any transporter beam I ever saw before, either—and where could he go? I canna make his actions come out to make any sense in my mind. Unless Mr. Braithewaite's suspicions are correct. I dinna want to believe them—but if they're no' true, why does Dr. McCoy want to go to Arcturus?"

"Arcturus!" Hunter said.

"Where'd you get the idea I wanted to go to Arcturus?" McCoy asked, baffled.

"Ye told me ye did," Scott said, and then, when McCoy shook his head, "Ye said, if ye asked for warp four to Arcturus, would ye get it."

"I didn't mean it," McCoy said. "I just picked the first example I could think of. But so what if I *did* want to go to Arcturus? What possible difference could that make?"

"Leonard," Hunter said, "Arcturus is almost exactly equidistant from Federation, Romulan, and Klingon space. It's neutral—most of the time, anyway. People go to Arcturus to make deals."

"I don't *want* to go to Arcturus," McCoy said again. "I only wanted to know if the warp drive was on line."

"He doesn't even make up decent excuses!" Ian said.

"No, Mr. Braithewaite," Hunter said, and she looked as if she were about to burst into laughter. "You're right about that, Dr. McCoy doesn't make up good excuses. But what do you have to say?"

"Spock's been trying to free Mordreaux," Braithewaite told her. "He was on Aleph right after the trial, I saw him. And he was monkeying around with the transporter just before Kirk was murdered. But Spock couldn't get Mordreaux away, so he settled for escaping himself once things began to fall apart on him. He'd already drawn Dr. McCoy into his scheme. The security commander was involved, but they got rid of her—"

"The security commander? You can't mean Mandala Flynn!"

"Yes—She wanted to command a ship like this so badly she could taste it. It was no secret, she even told Kirk. But he laughed at her. He must have known that a stateless person had no chance of advancing that far in Starfleet."

"You've got some pretty strange ideas, Mr. Braithewaite."

"But that's what happened! Spock probably offered her the *Enterprise* in return for her help. They had to get rid of Kirk first. Dr. Mordreaux tried to kill him but failed, so Spock pressured McCoy into letting Kirk die."

"Dammit, Braithewaite, he was dead! He was already dead!" McCoy's voice broke and he turned away. In the following silence he managed to collect himself again. "I carried out his wishes. I followed the terms of his will. You can look at it if you want."

"I intend to," Hunter said. "Whatever you did or didn't do afterwards, that doesn't change the fact that Jim was assaulted."

"You could have stopped them!" Ian cried. "Why didn't you shoot Spock when you had the chance?"

Hunter glanced down at the pistol still in her hand, and

slowly holstered it. "Do you think I'd kill a person on your say-so?"

Ian stood up and started toward the transporter console. "It still isn't too late! We can still—" He halted just as McCoy was about to leap at him to prevent his revealing the time-changer's auxiliary unit. Ian swayed, a lost, confused look on his face.

"What's the matter?" Scott said. "Ian—"

The prosecutor collapsed, his body completely limp.

"The nerve-pinch—" Scott said.

"It isn't that," McCoy said, on his knees on the floor beside Braithewaite. He recognized the symptoms immediately, this second time in as many days. "It's hypermorphic botulism! Help me with him, there isn't time to wait for a stretcher!"

In the grip of the changer, Spock felt time pass. The sensation was very different from that of the transporter alone, which was nothing more than a brief moment of dislocation at the end of the process. This felt as if he were falling through space, through hard vacuum, buffeted by every eddy of the solar wind, every current of each magnetic field, tossed by gravity waves, by light itself.

He materialized two meters above the ground, in Aleph Prime's core park, and fell the rest of the way. He landed hard enough to knock the wind out of him, and he had to fight to keep from losing consciousness.

It could have been worse. He knew he could not calibrate the device with total precision—getting from a moving starship to the place where Aleph had been several days before was accomplishment enough—so he had chosen to appear in open space. That way he had a better chance of not reincorporating inside a wall. He would have preferred to appear in the emergency transmitter room, but felt the chances against succeeding were too large to challenge. He got up, brushing himself off, glancing around to discover whether or not he had been seen.

He had chosen darkness as well as open space: the park mimicked a diurnal cycle, and right now it imitated night. An artificial moon hung in the dull black starless sky.

Leaving the park behind, Spock entered one of the maze of corridors that formed Aleph Prime. He passed a public information terminal and requested the time: he had arrived, as he intended, approximately an hour before the emergency message to the *Enterprise* had been transmitted.

In the pre-dawn hours, even revelers on leave from the ships and transports and mining operations centered around Aleph had mostly gone to their beds, but the few beings Spock did pass paid him no attention. McCoy had been right about the uniform; it would have made him more conspicuous. He was well aware of the human penchant for comparing assignments, ships, commanders: had he been in uniform it would not have been long before some overfriendly inebriated human raised more questions than he could answer.

The small government sector was even quieter than the rest of the station. He knew where the emergency transmitter was, but it was inaccessible to anyone without the proper code. He walked slowly down a hallway lined with glass-walled offices, all dark and deserted: customs, security, Federation, Starfleet, the public defender's office, the prosecutor's office—

The lights flicked on; Ian Braithewaite left an inner chamber and entered the main room. Spock froze, but it was too late to get out of sight. Clutching briefcase, portable reader, and a handful of transcript flimsies, Braithewaite came into the hall. The lights faded out when he closed the door. He noticed Spock only when he nearly ran into him; he glanced down distractedly.

"Sorry," he said. "Can I help you? Are you looking for somebody?"

Of course, Spock thought. He has not met me yet; he does not know who I am, and he has no suspicions about me. Tomorrow, when the *Enterprise* arrives, he will remember that he has seen me.

Does this mean I fail here, too?

"Where is the Vulcan consulate?" Spock asked.

Braithewaite pinched the bridge of his nose between thumb and forefinger. "Oh. Right. You're in the wrong sector, all the consulates are in a higher-class part of the station entirely." He gave directions to an area in Aleph Prime's north polar region. Spock thanked him, and Braithewaite left, reading one of the transcripts as he walked. It was no wonder it took him time to recall where he had seen Spock before.

Once the prosecutor was out of sight, Spock tried the door to the emergency transmitter. It was, of course, locked, and the computer that guarded it demanded identifications. He was careful not to speak to it or palm the sensor; he did not want it to have legally admissible proof of his presence.

For a moment he thought about returning to the public information cubicle, accessing the computer, and breaking through its guards to open the transmitter room. He had deceived the Aleph Prime systems before, or, more accurately, he would do it in the future; he could do it now.

But that was exactly what Dr. Mordreaux would do. It was the simplest, most direct way of getting to the transmitter, which the professor had to do if he were to order the *Enterprise* to Aleph. All Spock had to do was find a place of concealment, wait, and capture him when he arrived.

Cautiously, Spock tried each door along the corridor. Somewhat to his surprise, one of them opened. Inside it was dark but he did not wave up the lights. He could see well enough: it was a small, empty courtroom, perhaps the one in which Dr. Mordreaux had been convicted, sentenced, and denied any appeal.

Tout comprendre c'est tout pardonner, Spock thought: a philosophy difficult to express in Vulcan. He could understand why the humans faced with Dr. Mordreaux's research had been so terrified of it, so determined to suppress it that they would subvert justice to succeed. It was hardly his place to forgive them, though; he could only wish they were not so utterly certain to misuse what the professor had discovered. Had he been on Vulcan, had Vulcans been the only beings involved, they would have studied the principles and honored the discoverer; and they would have agreed, by ethical consensus, never to put the principles into use.

He knew it. He was certain of it. Almost certain.

Concealing himself inside the small darkened courtroom, where he could look out but not be seen, he waited.

His logic did not disappoint him this time. After only a few minutes, Dr. Mordreaux skulked down the hall toward the emergency transmitter, glancing nervously over his shoulder at every other step, stopping short at every faint noise. Over his shoulder he carried a time-changer almost identical to Spock's.

He placed his hand against the locking panel: he had succeeded in breaking the security circuits, just as Spock would have done. The door slid open. Spock drew his phaser and stepped into the hall.

"Dr. Mordreaux," he said softly.

The professor spun, panic in his face. He grabbed for his own weapon.

"No, wait!" he cried.

Spock fired.

He caught Mordreaux before he fell. His phaser had, of course, been set only to stun. He did not wish to kill if he could possibly avoid it. He lifted the elderly man easily and carried him into the courtroom, secured the door from the inside, opaqued the glass walls, and raised the light level so the professor would be able to see when he came to. Spock sat down to wait.

In sick bay, Dr. McCoy worked frantically, afraid too much time had passed, afraid he would fail again, afraid he would have to watch Ian Braithewaite, too, die under his hands.

Spock, he thought, where the devil *are* you, why don't you *do* something? The world's coming apart at the seams and there's nothing I can do to stop it.

Outside the intensive care unit, Scott and Hunter waited. The erratic tones of the life-support systems could not quite obscure Scott's voice.

"He was afraid he'd be killed," he said, his voice strained, and tortured. "He was afraid . . ."

The poison was overwhelming Ian's body despite the support of the critical care machines. His heart trembled into fibrillation and his body convulsed with the shock that restored the beat again.

Fight, you stupid headstrong busybody, McCoy shouted in his mind.

He barely noticed when Hunter left.

Chapter 8

Hikaru Sulu sat crosslegged on the floor of Mandala Flynn's cabin, his hands relaxed on his knees, his eyes closed. He tried to recapture any of the feeling he had had in the room when she was alive. But it was as if she had never been here: she had left behind nothing of the sort that makes one's room into a reflection of one's own personality. She had put Hikaru's antique sabre up on the wall, but it hung alone on the bare expanse. Her ring, warm on the inner surface, cool on the outer, circled his finger.

Mandala's individuality had not been a function of anything she owned. She was gone, and there was no retrieving her except in memory. She lived strong and clear in his mind—he thought for an instant he caught the soft bright scent of her hair—and he began to understand her disinclination to gather possessions. He could not lose his memories of her, and they could not be taken from him.

The bed was still rumpled from their lovemaking.

The power failure startled him from his reverie, and prodded his guilt. Wandering through the *Enterprise* in a haze of grief, he was no use to Hunter, no use in finding out what had happened. From what Barry al Auriga had told him, every possible explanation dissolved in a mire of peculiar occurrences. Hikaru felt as stunned and angry as Barry, that Mandala was under suspicion.

He stood up slowly, rising all in one motion from the crosslegged position; in the silence the returning hum of the ventilators sounded very loud. Like a ghost passing through the dim illumination of half-power, Sulu left his lover's cabin.

In the transporter room, Hunter touched the peculiar addition to the console, being careful not to disturb any of its connections or controls. Spock had no place to beam to, not with a normal transporter, but, as Ian Braithewaite had tried to say, this machine was definitely not a normal transporter anymore.

"What is that thing?" Mr. Sulu asked. He had rejoined her as she left sick bay. Hunter was glad of his company, not only because he could be of use to her with his knowledge of ship and crew, but because she had worried about him all alone with his grief. They had talked about Mandala and Jim on the way from Aleph to the *Enterprise;* she knew how badly he was hurting.

She returned her attention to the construct in the transporter. "I'm not quite sure." She itched to open it up and see what its innards looked like. "I think I'll give Dr. McCoy one more chance to tell us what's going on, and what that thing does, before I start playing around with it."

She closed the amber crystals back into the transporter, and she and Sulu headed back toward sick bay.

"How are you holding up?" she asked quietly.

"Better than a little while ago," he said. "And you?"

"When I find out why they had to die I'll be able to tell you," she said. "I don't want it to be for nothing."

"It isn't nothing," Sulu said. "Nobody is acting like I'd expect them to, not Dr. McCoy or Mr. Spock or Mr. Scott, and people don't just change like that for no reason at all."

She knew he meant it as a defense, but it could equally be used to accuse them. She did not say so.

In sick bay, Ian Braithewaite lay unconscious and surrounded by the critical care machines. The sensors showed his life signs stable, Hunter noted with some relief: she had expected him to die.

McCoy and Scott sat in silence in McCoy's office, neither glancing toward the other. Hunter sat on a corner of the doctor's desk, and Mr. Sulu stood just inside the door-way.

"Is Mr. Braithewaite going to be all right?"

"I don't know," McCoy said.

"He was afraid he'd be poisoned," Scott said.

"Will you stop saying that? He wasn't poisoned here! Somebody fed him the toxin encapsulated. The matrix has been dissolving for a couple of days. Since before he came on board."

"Since he saw Mr. Spock on Aleph, before the *Enterprise* ever reached it, just as I saw Mr. Spock where he couldna have been!"

"Braithewaite was probably already hallucinating—"

"Are ye saying I'm hallucinating, too? D'ye meant I've been poisoned, too?"

Hunter was willing to let them argue if the result was some useful information, but this was ridiculous. "Dr. McCoy," she said, "I just found something very strange in the transporter. A bioelectronic addition."

Scott glanced sharply at her. "Bioelectronic! So was the gizmo Mr. Spock had wi' him when he disappeared—some kind o' weapon, Mr. Braithewaite said. Nae thing like that should be in the transporter!" He stood up.

"Stay here, Mr. Scott," Hunter said, without looking at him, keeping her gaze fixed on Leonard McCoy. The doctor lied with his expression no better than with words. His face turning slowly very pale, he stared at her. "I don't want to take it apart, Mr. Scott. Not yet. Leonard, do you want to tell me what it is?"

"Not very much, no."

"Then I'll tell you something about it. It boosts the beam. And it alters it into . . . something else. The most interesting thing about it is the return control."

"You didn't touch it—!"

"No. Not so far. But if I engage it, and Mr. Spock still has the gadget's mate with him, it will bring him back. From wherever he is. Isn't that right?"

"Maybe."

"Damn it! Will you just tell me what the hell is going on!"

"Give Spock a little more time," McCoy said. "Please."

"How much more time?"

"He said he'd try to come back within twelve hours. He's been gone almost two."

"Do you really expect me to do nothing for twelve hours? Without a reasonable explanation? Or even an unreasonable one?"

McCoy shook his head. "If you didn't believe me before, there's just no chance you'd believe what I'd tell you now."

"Leonard," she said, "what have you got to lose?"

"Everything."

In the uncomfortable pause, Mr. Sulu stepped forward. "Dr. McCoy," he said, "please trust her. How can she trust you if you don't give her a chance?"

McCoy looked up at the helm officer, buried his face in his hands with a groan, and, finally, raised his head again.

"If you turn on the thing in the transporter," he said slowly, "you might bring Spock back. But more likely you'd kill him."

"Why don't you start at the beginning?"

He drew in a deep breath, let it out, laced his fingers together and pressed his palms against his closed eyes, and started to tell a story so much more preposterous than even the one Ian Braithewaite had constructed that Hunter listened, fascinated despite herself.

When he finished, Hunter and Scott and Sulu all stared at him.

"I've no' heard a crazier story in my life!" Scott said.

"Scotty, you *know* time-travel is possible," McCoy said.

"Aye . . ." The engineer withdrew into himself.

"Either Dr. Mordreaux wasn't as loony as I thought," Hunter said, "or *you* have gone stark staring mad."

McCoy sighed. "I know how it sounds, especially now after I've spent so much time trying to mislead you. I kept hoping Spock would succeed, if I just gave him the chance."

"And now you want *me* to give him the chance."

"Hunter—you could have stopped him, before. You didn't."

"I wouldn't kill Spock because you lied to me any more than I'd do it because Ian Braithewaite wanted me to."

"Don't kill him now. Just give him a little more time. It's all the truth, I swear to you."

Hunter leaned back against the wall and stared at the ceiling. "I couldn't do anything for Jim anymore, but he was Jim's friend, and that is the real reason I didn't stop him."

"Hunter," Sulu said intensely, "it's a little time—against the chance that Mandala and the captain won't be—wouldn't be—killed after all. It's a risk worth taking!"

She laughed softly. "Not if we're wrong, it isn't." She shook her head, surprised at herself. "I think I'll spend the next ten years hanging by my thumbs in a military prison for this, but Spock can have his damned twelve hours."

Lying on the bench in the courtroom, Professor Mordreaux groaned. Spock went to his side, and, when his former teacher had fully regained consciousness, gently helped him sit up.

"Spock? Mr. Spock, what are you doing here? How . . . ?" He glanced beyond the Vulcan to the time-changers. "Oh, no," he said, and began to laugh.

Spock had expected as much, though he had hoped for some semblance of rationality. He would no more be able to reason with this version of Dr. Mordreaux than the last.

The professor jumped to his feet. "How long have I been unconscious? Maybe there's still time!" He rushed toward the door but Spock caught and stopped him before he had gone three steps.

"Mr. Spock, you don't understand! There's no time to lose!"

"I understand perfectly, sir. If we wait a few more moments, at least one event in this time-stream will have changed, and perhaps the *Enterprise* will not be diverted."

"But that isn't me! I mean I'm not him!" He made an inarticulate noise of pure frustration and drew a deep breath. He closed his eyes and opened them, and began again.

"You're stopping the wrong person," he said. "I've come here to try to stop myself—my mad self—from calling you away from the singularity. I know everything that's happened. You're here to keep Jim Kirk from being murdered. I've been chasing myself through the time-streams for . . ." He stopped, and laughed again, still on the edge of hysteria. "Of course duration is meaningless.

Don't you understand, Mr. Spock? I'm trying to stop myself, to save myself—"

Spock rushed past him, out of the courtroom and across the hall. The door to the transmitter room stood wide open. Spock plunged through it, Dr. Mordreaux right behind him.

A second Dr. Mordreaux turned away from the subspace transmitter. The tape spun through the machine with a high-speed whine.

"Too late!" Dr. Mordreaux, in front of him, cried with glee.

"Too late," Dr. Mordreaux, behind him, said softly. "Too late."

The professor by the transmitter touched his time-changer. Spock's hands passed through his insubstantial form, and then he was gone.

The future Dr. Mordreaux and Mr. Spock stared at the transmitter. They both knew the message could not be countermanded or overridden. That was part of its fail-safe system.

"Damn," Mordreaux whispered. And then, "Let's get out of here before somebody comes along. If they recognize me they'll probably shoot me on sight."

They retrieved the time-changers from the courtroom, left the government sector of Aleph Prime, and walked together in silence to the core park. It was deserted now, at dawn, and probably the safest place Dr. Mordreaux could be. They sat down on a bench. Mordreaux buried his face in his hands.

"Are you all right, Professor?"

After a bit, he nodded. "As well as can be expected, considering that the universe keeps proving to me how much easier it is to create chaos than order."

"One can prove easily enough that chaos is the primary result of all that has occurred."

Mordreaux looked up at him. "Ah. You've seen the connection between your work and mine. We aren't fighting me, we really are fighting chaos. Entropy."

"I believed at first that I had made some error in my observations," Spock said.

"No, they were all too accurate. Ever since I started to use the time-changer, the increase of entropy really *has* been accelerating."

"I found the destructive potential difficult to accept."

"Yes. I find it so, too. For a million years human beings

have done their best to discover the ultimate weapon. It was left to me to invent the one that really can destroy our universe."

He ran his hands through his hair, a habit that had not altered through all the years.

"It's getting very bad by my time, Mr. Spock. The universe is simply . . . running down. Well. You can imagine."

"Indeed."

The false moon vanished behind a painted hillside on the far wall, and streaks of incandescent scarlet sunlight streamed out of the wall behind them.

"Why did you let it go so far, professor? Or have you been attempting to change things back for a long time?"

"A long time, yes. But I couldn't even begin until I re-created my work. The virus program was very efficient, Mr. Spock. All my papers dissolved away. One could search memory bank and library and seldom even find a reference to my name."

"You could have contacted me. You must know of my respect for your work. You must have known I would keep copies safe."

Mordreaux reached out to pat Spock's hand, and the Vulcan did not flinch from his touch. All the emotions he received from his old teacher were of sympathy and appreciation, and to his shame Spock felt himself in serious need of the unwanted feelings.

"Ah, my friend, but you did not survive the accusations made against you. You were sent to rehabilitation, though the authorities must have known what that would mean for you. I'm sure they did know you would resist their efforts to reprogram your mind. . . ."

Spock nodded. Many humans had been sent to rehabilitation and come out obedient, complacent, but living; only a few Vulcans had ever received such a sentence, and all of them had died. Knowing he was that much closer to Vulcan than human gave Spock a peculiar sort of comfort.

"What about Dr. McCoy? And Captain Hunter?"

"Starfleet forced Hunter to accept a dishonorable discharge. She divorced her family to protect the children from shame, and she joined the free commandoes. She was killed on the border a few months later. One of her officers committed suicide in protest at the treatment Hunter received—"

"Mr. Sulu!" Despite himself, Spock was surprised. Sulu had never seemed the type to go quite as far as *hara-kiri*.

"Sulu . . . ? No, the name was Russian. I forget exactly what it was. I think Mr. Sulu entered the free commandoes as well." Dr. Mordreaux shrugged. "Little difference, only a slower method of suicide. As for Dr. McCoy . . ." The professor shook his head. "I tried to keep track of him. But after they released him he disappeared. Even before they began the sentence he had lost heart. He was convicted of murdering Jim Kirk, you see."

"Yet you came out with your mind intact, that is clear."

"They had second thoughts about me," he said. "They realized how valuable I could be, doing exactly what I was convicted of."

"How did you escape?"

"After I went mad I was of very little use to them, and they stopped watching me quite so carefully. It took me some time to bring myself back to sanity . . . thence here."

"I cannot understand why your other self murdered Captain Kirk. You said—on the bridge, yesterday, tomorrow—that he had destroyed you. But all he had done was respond to the orders you sent yourself."

"I know. But in the time-track in which he didn't die, he defended your proposal—that I was too valuable to destroy—all too well. After I went mad, I thought it would have been better if I *had* been sent through rehabilitation. I would have been docile and happy and no one would have persecuted me. So I decided to go back and prevent him from saving me."

"How many time-tracks are there?"

"They multiply, Mr. Spock, like lemmings. The main track split several ways when I sent my friends back in time; it split again, after my trial, when a particularly murderous future version of me came back and started a campaign of revenge—"

"The defense counsel? And the judge?"

Dr. Mordreaux nodded. "And Ian Braithewaite, but he came last."

The imitation sun had risen high enough to cast shadows, and their silhouetted images stretched far down the hillside.

"Another track just split off, when I sent that message. There's the one in which you finish your observations and the change is traced back to me and I'm persecuted for it, and the one in which I prevent your finishing, and realize the entropy effect myself in several years." He glanced quizzically at Spock. "You see how complicated it gets."

"And they all evolve from your first use of the time-changer."

"Yes. I'm afraid so."

"What happened when you tried to alter those events?"

"I've tried once so far. I went back to persuade myself not to demonstrate time-travel. I stayed only a moment. Because I saw one of my friends kill me—another me, I mean, one from *my* future, or another time-track . . . I've been afraid to try again. I know I must, eventually, but . . ."

"Your chances of altering events from so far in the future are negligible."

"I have to try."

"I am not so far removed."

"You'd go back again—and try to stop me?"

"I promised you not to interfere with your friends." Spock looked away. "My oath seems . . . a trivial matter, compared to what will occur if I do not break it."

"I doubt your oath is ever trivial to you, Mr. Spock," Dr. Mordreaux said. "May I release you from your promise?"

"I cannot say. Are you the same being I gave it to?"

"I think I must have been. So much has happened, and my memories of the time before I went mad have grown foggy. But it sounds familiar, and it's certainly something I would have demanded of you, when I was younger and more foolish. Mr. Spock, I beg of you to let me release you from your promise. I swear to you that to the best of my knowledge, I have the right."

"I must go back to the start of the unravelling," Spock said, "whether you have the right to permit me to do so or not. I am grateful for your oath, and I will try to accept it."

"Thank you, Mr. Spock." Dr. Mordreaux hesitated. "There's something else I have to tell you, though. It wouldn't be fair not to."

"What is it?"

"The farther you go, the more often, the more damaging it is to your system. It isn't only the continuum that's thrown into disarray. You've noticed the effects of time-travel on your body?"

"I have experienced . . . some discomfort."

"Discomfort, hm? Well, everyone knows Vulcans are hardier than humans. Still, it *is* dangerous and it *is* cumulative. It's only fair to tell you that, before you decide what to do."

Spock did not even pause. "The choice is between travelling farther back in time, or returning to my own time to face dishonor, shame for my family, and death. I do not see that that is a particularly difficult decision to make." He picked up his changer.

Mordreaux picked up his, too. "Maybe I should go with you."

"That is both unnecessary and irrational. You would be jeopardizing your life, though your chances of accomplishing anything approach zero."

Mordreaux rubbed his fingers over the amber-bauble surface of his changer. "Thank you, Mr. Spock. The more often I've moved through time, the more frightened I've gotten of it. I don't look forward to dying."

Dr. Mordreaux led Spock to his own rooms in Aleph Prime: the rooms of the earlier Dr. Mordreaux, the one now in the hospital awaiting transfer to the *Enterprise*. He had lived in an older section of the space station, midway between the core park and the glimmering outer shell. Asteroids formed the substructure of the city: here the corridors resembled tunnels, the rooms, caves.

Dr. Mordreaux's possessions lay in a shambles. Books and papers littered the floor, and the screen of the computer terminal blinked in the way self-aware machines have when their memories are ripped out or scrambled. The furniture had been overturned, and shards of crockery covered all the floors.

"It appears you objected strenuously to your arrest."

"Maybe I'm not in the same track I thought I was," Mordreaux said. "But I don't remember any where I didn't go quietly."

He shuffled through the destruction, to the back room, the laboratory, where the disorder was less extensive. The transporter did not appear damaged. Mordreaux glanced into its workings.

"They've taken the changers, of course," he said, "but the rest of it looks all right."

He tightened a few connections while Spock worked

out the coordinates he would need to use to go back before the track of maximum probability began to split into multiple disintegrating lines.

"The transporter's set," Dr. Mordreaux said. "How about you?"

"I am ready," Spock replied. "What will you do, sir?"

"As soon as you leave, I'll return to my own time. If I can."

Spock stepped up on the transporter platform, holding his time-changer in both hands.

"Goodbye, Dr. Mordreaux."

"Goodbye, Mr. Spock. And thank you."

Spock replied by touching the controls of the changer. The two energy fields interacted in a rage of light, and Spock vanished.

From Spock's viewpoint, the cavern-like back room of Dr. Mordreaux's apartment faded out through spectral colors, red-orange-yellow-green-blue-purple to blazing ultra-violet as the energy increased; Spock felt himself being pulled through a void, then thrust back across the ultra-violet energy barrier, through the rainbow, into normal space. He felt himself materialize again, one molecule at a time, as the beam wrenched him back into existence.

He staggered, lost his balance completely, and crashed to the stone floor, falling hard, barely managing to curl himself around the time-changer so it was not damaged. He rolled over on his back, staring upward, momentarily blinded. He started to get up, but froze with an involuntary gasp of pure flaming agony.

Startled voices surrounded him, then shadows: he was still dazzled by the assault of ultra-violet light. He flattened his palms against the cool floor and shut his eyes tight. The pain had become too great to ignore or put aside.

He tried and failed to free any single voice from the tangle around him. He could hear and sense consternation, surprise, outrage. The Aleph Prime authorities must have followed him and Dr. Mordreaux, or kept the room under surveillance: now they had come to arrest them, more important, to stop them, and nothing would ever convince anyone that he and Dr. Mordreaux were attempting something utterly essential.

One voice threaded through the mass of noise.

"Mr. Spock? Are you all right?"

He blinked slowly several times and his vision gradually returned. The professor bent over him, frowning with concern.

"How did you get here? What are you doing here?"

Spock pushed himself upright, a lurching, graceless motion. Cramps reverberated up and down all the long muscles of his body and he felt as though the room were spinning around him. He refused to accept that perception; he forced his eyes to focus on Dr. Mordreaux, sitting on his heels beside him.

It was not the Dr. Mordreaux he had just left: it was a far younger man, a man who looked nearly the same as he had years before, when Spock knew him at the Makropyrios. In a month he would have aged ten years, after the stress of accusation, trial, and sentencing.

"May I help you up?" Mordreaux asked courteously. He extended a hand but did not touch Spock, and Spock shook his head.

"No. Thank you." He got to his feet, awkwardly but under his own power. The time-changer thumped against his side.

"Where in heaven's name did you get that?" Mordreaux asked. "And where did *you* come from?"

"What's wrong?" someone called from the other room, and one of the two people standing in the doorway turned back to answer.

"Somebody just materialized on the changer platform."

"Well, Mr. Spock, it's been a long time." Dr. Mordreaux gestured toward the changer. "Longer for you than me, I think, if we count from the Makropyrios."

"I came to warn you, Dr. Mordreaux," Spock said. His voice sounded weak and he could not halt the shaking of his knees and hands. He straightened up, forcing away the pain, confronting it directly. Several of the people from the sitting room crowded in at the doorway: Dr. Mordreaux's friends, the people whose dreams had sent him on a fatal course. Spock had hoped to arrive when Dr. Mordreaux was alone.

"Come sit down," the professor said. "You look like death."

Even for Spock there came a point where he had to admit his limits. He limped into the adjacent room and took the chair Dr. Mordreaux offered.

The people in the doorway moved aside for him, and stood together in a suspicious circle: six adults, four children.

"What does he want, Georges?"

"Well, Perim, I don't know yet." He motioned for everyone to sit.

"Are you a Vulcan?" one of the children asked.

"This is Mr. Spock," Dr. Mordreaux said. "He was one of my very best students when I was a physics teacher, and now he works on a starship. At least I believe he does *now*—but he may have begun to do something else by the time he comes to us from."

"No," Spock said. "I still serve on the *Enterprise*."

One of the younger people, no more than student age himself, handed Spock a glass of water. He sipped from it.

"That's about enough of old times and afternoon tea," said Perim. He took the hand of the child who had spoken and drew her away from Spock and Mordreaux. "What's he doing here? It's a damned inconvenient time to visit. Unless he's come to stop us."

"Is that why you're here, Mr. Spock?"

"Yes, sir, it is." He glanced from one face to another, wondering which person had reacted—would react—with such fear and violence when the future Dr. Mordreaux attempted what Spock was about to try now. The group of time-travelers drew together, and Spock felt their rising anger and apprehension.

"Sir," Spock said, "within a month, you will be accused of murdering all these people. The charge will be proven against you, as will the charge of unethical experimentation upon intelligent beings. Your work will not be vindicated; it will not even be classified and controlled. It will be suppressed. It engenders such apprehension among judicial and executive officials that they will see no other way to restrain what you have created. You will be sentenced to rehabilitation. The *Enterprise* is assigned to transport you. During the voyage, you cause the deaths of the commander of security and of Captain James T. Kirk."

"That's preposterous!"

"It is true. You must not continue this experiment. It leads only to disaster."

"Wait a minute," said one of the time-travelers.

"You're saying we shouldn't go. You want us to stay here."

"You must."

"We can leave a record of our plans so Georges won't get into trouble—we've all agreed to try out his theories."

"Agreed, hell," said a middle-aged woman perched on the back of a couch. "We talked him into letting us do it."

"Several of you do leave records," Spock said. "They are used as evidence of his persuasive abilities. Of his power over you, if you wish."

Dr. Mordreaux flung himself into a chair. "I thought I had taken enough precautions to avoid that difficulty," he said. "But certainly I can take other measures."

"They will not be sufficient," Spock said. "Or, rather, perhaps they would be, but you must not carry out this plan. Your fate, the fate of these few people—that is relatively trivial compared to the wider implications of the work. The displacement of your friends permanently into the wrong continuum creates a strain that space-time cannot withstand."

"Good lord," Perim said. "You sound like you're talking about the end of the universe."

"In time, that is what it amounts to."

"In time that's what everything amounts to!" said the middle-aged woman.

"Not in less than one hundred Earth-standard years."

Silence.

"What a load of crap," the woman said sharply. "Listen, Mr. Spock, whoever you are, wherever, whenever, you've come from, I don't care how terrific a physics student you used to be, I've been through those equations myself and I don't see any opportunity at all for the creation of torsion in the continuum."

"You have erred. The error was inevitable, but you have erred nonetheless."

"Georges, dammit—" She turned toward Mordreaux.

"It's true, Mr. Spock. I worried that the transfer might cause some distortion. But it just doesn't happen. Nothing in the equations shows it."

"You have erred," Spock repeated. "Your plans distort reality to such an extent that the increase of entropy accelerates. The effect is not large at first, of course—but within twenty years larger stars have begun to nova. Precarious ecosystems have begun to fail."

"Prove it," said Perim.

Spock glanced toward the computer terminal in the corner of the room. "I will show you the derivation," he said.

He worked at the keyboard for half an hour. The children played games in another corner. After a few minutes most of the other adults drew back, unable to follow the progression of a proof far out of any of their specialties, but the middle-aged woman, Mree, and Dr. Mordreaux watched carefully. Perim, the young girl's father, loomed, arms crossed over his chest, at Spock's left shoulder.

Spock gave himself some clear space in the middle of the screen and typed in a new equation.

"What the bleeding hell is that?" Mree said.

"Profanity is not necessary," Spock said. "I will explain anything you find beyond your comprehension."

"It isn't beyond my comprehension," she said angrily. "It's a correction factor, that's obvious enough. You can prove any damned thing you please if you throw in correction factors."

"Mree," Dr. Mordreaux said, "please let him finish before you get angry. And Mr. Spock, Mree built the time-changer in the first place. If you could hold down the sarcasm a bit I think we'd all be happier."

"I intended no sarcasm," Spock said.

"All right. But it's safe to assume that both Mree and I can follow whatever you put on the screen, as long as you don't pull anything out of thin air, which as far as I can tell is exactly where you got that."

Spock sat back, resting his hands on his knees and gazing at the video screen. "That is the equation I derived from observations I am, in this time-stream, preparing to begin. As you can see, the current numerical value is extremely small, but as you can also see, it is dependent on the value of t minus t_1, squared. In short, its value not only increases, its increase accelerates." He bent over the keyboard again and showed how the correction factor fit into the original equations.

Dr. Mordreaux whistled softly.

"Georges," Mree said, "there isn't a shred of evidence for that factor!"

"That's quite true," Mordreaux said. "What about it, Mr. Spock?"

"There is no evidence for its existence because it does not yet exist. The value of t is dependent upon the mo-

ment at which you begin to distort the temporal continuum by sending people back in time, and leaving them
there."

Mree muttered something profane and disbelieving.
"That's the stupidest argument I ever heard. It's completely circular."

"Dr. Mordreaux has created the circle," Spock said.

"You're trying to save James Kirk's life, aren't you?"
Mordreaux glared at Spock, his mood changing from
calmness to the first time. "Of course, it's obvious. He
must be an exceptional person. I admire your loyalty,
Mr. Spock, but it isn't any reason to ruin the plans of all
my friends. You've warned me and that's sufficient—I
won't allow myself to be arrested after I've sent Mree and
the others back. I'll go back myself if necessary."

"Been trying to persuade you to do that all along,"
Mree said.

Spock stood and faced his old teacher. "Dr. Mordreaux, Vulcans do not lie. The entropy effect caused me
considerable . . . distress—" It took a great deal of effort
for him to admit that, true as it was—"when I discovered
it. I believed I had made a mistake. But you—a future
version of you, who has been trying to repair the continuum even as I have tried—assured me I had not. He
comes from the time when the effects are having serious
consequences."

Mordreaux scowled at him. "Vulcans *say* they don't
lie, but for one thing the statement isn't necessarily true
and for another you aren't a Vulcan. Not entirely. And
human beings are the best liars in the universe."

"I . . . I have endeavored to enhance the Vulcan ele-
ments of my background, and suppress the human char-
acteristics."

"Why won't you just accept my compromise? You
won't be involved in what I'm doing, your ship will never
be called to Aleph Prime, and your captain will be safe."

"The fate of James Kirk is not involved with what I
have told you. Whether he lives or dies has nothing to do
with what will occur if you go through with your plans."

"Where's this fabled version of me, then? Why doesn't
he come back and tell me all this himself?"

Spock started to answer. But behind him, Perim suddenly grabbed him, catching him in a headlock and drag-
ging him off-balance.

"We can't let him stop us! Help me tie him up and let's go—"

Spock let himself be pulled back until Perim himself was off-balance, then the Vulcan ducked down and around and threw the larger man over his shoulder, to the floor. Perim lay stunned, no longer a danger, and Spock turned back toward Dr. Mordreaux, satisfied that he had discovered which of the professor's friends had a quick temper.

"You tried," Spock said. "You tried at least twice. The second time—"

An instant too late, he felt the hand grip his shoulder. The fingers dug in, seeking and finding the vulnerable nerve before he could react. All feeling left him. He stayed on his feet another moment, swaying, then collapsed.

Through a haze of paralysis, Spock saw Mree bend over him.

"He'll be okay, Georges," she said. "But Perim's right—Let's get out of here before it's too late."

Spock struggled to regain control of his body, but Mree's understanding of the aggressive move was thorough, and she had incapacitated him just short of unconsciousness. He could not help but admire her for mastering the technique: humans who tried it usually either failed to produce any effect at all, or used it so aggressively that it proved fatal. Only an unusually proficient student could produce immobility with consciousness.

Dr. Mordreaux hesitated. Spock could see him at the edge of his vision, but he could neither turn his head nor speak.

"All right," Mordreaux said abruptly.

They filed into the laboratory. Spock struggled unsuccessfully to regain some feeling, some power of movement.

A wash of rainbow light, a dazzle of ultraviolet energy, told him he had failed again. They were fleeing, to some place he would never find, and he could come back again and again and again, earlier and earlier, further fragmenting the very substance of the universe as he attempted futilely to repair the damage being done. But he would *always* fail, he knew it now, something would al-

ways happen to cause him to fail. Entropy would always
win.

As it must.

He cried out in despair.

Fighting the hopelessness that washed over him, somehow he flung himself over onto his chest. Every nerve
and muscle in his body shrieked as he reached to drag
himself along the floor like the crippled creature he was,
like the first primordial amphibian struggling for breath
on the shores of a vanishing lake, knowing instinctively
in the most primitive interconnections of his brain that he
would probably die, if he continued, that he would surely
die, if he stayed, that his only chance was to keep going,
to *try*.

Hunter wandered into sick bay, wishing she were almost anywhere else in the universe. She stopped in the
doorway of McCoy's office.

"Leonard," she said, "Mr. Spock's twelve hours are
nearly up."

"I know," McCoy said miserably. "Hunter, he told me
he had an outer limit of fourteen hours—"

"Oh, gods," Hunter said, exasperated. "Leonard—"

"Wait—" McCoy looked up. "Did you hear—it's the
sensors!" He jumped up and ran past her into the main
sick bay.

In the critical care unit the signals had fallen to zero,
but not because the toxin had finally overwhelmed Ian
Braithewaite's life. Hunter took one look at the empty
bed and ran out into the corridor. She caught a glimpse
of Ian disappearing around the corner.

"He's trying to get to the transporter!" McCoy said.

Hunter raced after Ian. He was still very weak and she
narrowed the gap between them, but he stumbled into
the lift. Hunter launched herself toward him and crashed
against the closed doors, an instant too late.

"Damn!" She waited seething; McCoy caught up to her
as the lift returned. They piled inside, and as soon as it
stopped again Hunter rushed out and after the prosecutor.
He had already reached the transporter room, already
opened the console: he stared down at the bioelectronic
construct that bulged up out of the module like a glimmering malignant growth.

"Don't, Ian! Gods, don't!"

"It's the only way," he whispered.

Supporting himself on his elbows in the doorway of the laboratory, Spock whispered, "Dr. Mordreaux . . ."

The small group of time-travelers parted, turning to look at him, all of them startled to hear his voice. And all of them *were* there.

Spock could not force his eyes to focus properly: he thought he was seeing double. But then the second Dr. Mordreaux stumbled off the transporter platform and fell, as Spock had, and the first Dr. Mordreaux, the one who belonged in this time, this place, knelt beside him and turned him over. The older professor groaned.

Using the doorjamb for support, Spock dragged himself to his feet. Mree looked from one Mordreaux to the other, then back at Spock.

"Sir—" Spock said.

"Nothing changed," Mordreaux said. "Nothing . . . changed . . ." His voice was like sand on stone, skittering, dry, ephemeral. "I waited, but the chaos . . ."

Spock forced himself across the few meters of space between him and the professor, and fell to his knees. The present Dr. Mordreaux stared down at himself.

"They are determined to go, sir," Spock said. "I tried to show them what would happen—"

Mordreaux's hand clamped around his wrist. "I don't want to die like this," he said. He looked back at himself. "Believe him. Please believe him." He sighed, and his eyes closed, his hand fell limp beside him, and the life flowed slowly from his body.

The present Dr. Mordreaux sat back on his heels.

"My god," Mree whispered. "My god, look."

The future Dr. Mordreaux faded gradually to dust, and the dust dissolved toward nothingness. As it collapsed into subatomic particles, Spock snatched up the time-changer, reset it, and flung it into the dust. Attuned to the molecules that had formed Dr. Mordreaux's body, it pulled them with it as it quivered and vanished back to its own time. Spock wondered why he had bothered to make the repair in space-time, since it appeared that he would fail to prevent the more serious damage that was about to occur.

He stood up slowly, aching with fatigue. "Do you believe me now?" His façade of control and emotionlessness began to crack. "He knew he would die if he came back this far again. He knew it! He feared it. By his time, the changes you have caused have become so intolerable that he deliberately chose death, to try to stop you!"

"What about us?" Perim cried. "That's years in the future! Our hopes—"

"And the hopes of your children?" Spock glanced at the curious little girl who had asked if he were a Vulcan —he realized that no one had adequately answered her question—and she gazed solemnly at him, as if she understood everything that had happened. Perhaps she did, better than he or anyone else. "Far in the future, when your child is grown, and the universe is nothing but chaos —what then? You will go back, you will be safe." He looked at each member of the group, adults and children alike. "Your children will take the consequences."

The present Dr. Mordreaux rose. "Mr. Spock . . ." His voice shook. "Perhaps—"

"Georges!" Perim took one step forward, his fists clenched. "You can't—"

Mree clasped his arm, gently, it seemed, but he stopped and fell silent.

"I think we're going to have to find other hopes," she said.

"No!"

"Perim," Mree said, "Spock is right. We've been selfish—we knew that all along, but now we know what the results of our selfishness will be."

"I'm sorry," Dr. Mordreaux said. He looked around at his friends, Mree and Perim and the others who had watched, unbelieving.

The young student who had given Spock water had tears streaming down his face. "It would have been—" He could not finish.

"My friends, I'm sorry," Mordreaux said. He went to the transporter and began to disconnect the additions. Perim and one of the others tried to stop him, but Mree and the other three adults prevented them from interfering. Mordreaux finished the dismantling, then, tears running down his face, too, he hugged each of the other people. "I can never make this up to you," he said when he got to Perim. "I know it."

Perim pulled back from the embrace. "You're right,"

he said, his tone nearer a growl than any human sound. "You can't." He picked up his child, and fled.

Ian Braithewaite stabbed at the control button on the time-changer. Hunter and McCoy reached him at the same time, but too late: they pulled him away from the transporter control as the strained warp engines rumbled into operation, so out of sync that the *Enterprise* itself shuddered. The light spilling across the transporter started its rainbow flux, red-orange-yellow—

McCoy groaned in grief and despair.

—green-blue-violet—

The ship went dark; the beam faded, and McCoy found himself lying sprawled on the floor. When he opened his eyes the lighting was perfectly normal, and he was all alone. He pushed himself to his feet; he was as stiff as if he had been lying there for hours. Something terrible had happened, but it was like a dream that he grasped for as it slipped through his fingers. Something had happened: but he did not know what.

"What am I doin' here?" he muttered. He looked around the empty room one last time, shrugged, and returned to sick bay.

In the sitting room, after the others had left, Dr. Mordreaux looked ruefully at Spock, then at Mree. "I suppose I'd better not publish my last paper," he said.

Despite all that had happened, Spock felt more than a twinge of guilt and unease at the idea of suppressing knowledge. Again he wished for a society as settled as that on Vulcan.

"I guess not," Mree said. "I sure won't mention it. Damn. The idea was great while it lasted."

"Might any of the others try to force one of you to re-build the time changer?" Spock asked.

Mordreaux shrugged. "They might. Who knows? What's ever certain? But I think that's our problem, not yours, Mr. Spock."

"I hope I didn't hurt you," Mree said. "I'm sorry."

"Your technique is flawless," Spock said. "I congratulate you."

"Thanks," she said.

Mordreaux glanced toward the doorway into the laboratory, where his other self had collapsed to dust.

"Will you be all right, Mr. Spock? Can you get back to your own time, without . . ."

"Your other self had made many more trips than I."

"The physiologies are different."

"I have no choice, Dr. Mordreaux. I can no more stay here than you can send your friends back to the times they would prefer to live in. I am aware of the risks." He stood up. It was pointless to remain, pointless, and, quite possibly, dangerous. Every moment he remained increased the chances that he would inadvertently commit some act whose effects would cascade into disaster somewhere in the future. "I must go back," he said. He picked up the time-changer. It was smooth and cool in his hands.

"Mr. Spock—"

"I must go back," Spock repeated. "I must go back now." His fingers tightened convulsively on the time-changer, because he wanted nothing more than to throw it as far away from him as he could, and never touch it again. He did not want to travel through time again. He was so tired, and he did not want to fight the pain anymore . . .

He was afraid.

"Goodbye," he said, and touched the controls.

He heard their voices bidding him goodbye as the changer's power pack built up threshold energy around him, and then all sound faded as he was dragged into a drowning riptide. Ultraviolet lanced into his vision.

For all his assurances to Dr. McCoy, he was not certain within himself that *he*, this time-stream's self-aware version of himself, would continue to exist once the journey ended.

The *Enterprise* materialized around him: he had only a moment to be sure of that, before he slipped down into such pure agony that it was the only sensation his mind could perceive.

The rainbow light faded, and Mr. Spock was gone. Georges looked at Mree; she gazed at the transporter platform and shook her head.

"Do you suppose he'll be all right?"

"I hope so. We'll have to wait a few weeks until he gets home again. Then I can put in a call to the *Enterprise*. If he doesn't remember what happened, I can just say hello."

"Are you going to call him from here?"

Georges frowned. "What do you mean?"

Mree took his hand. "If Perim is angry enough, he might easily start threatening you. You could be in a lot of danger."

Georges thought about that for a few moments, and then said quizzically, "*I* could be in danger?"

Mree shrugged.

"I suppose I could put the changer together by myself," Georges said. "But Perim knows as well as I do who actually built it."

"Yes," she said. "But I've been planning to leave Aleph anyway. I don't guess it makes that much difference whether I travel through the fourth dimension, or the normal three."

"You think I should leave, too."

"That's right."

"Run away?"

"Like a jackrabbit," she said. She paused, and then, more seriously, she said, "Georges, what do you have here to stay for?"

"Not very much," he admitted. The seconds stretched out as Mree and Georges looked at each other, remembering other conversations very much like this one.

"I asked you to come with me enough times before," she said. "Shall I ask you again, or are you wishing I wouldn't?"

"No," he said. "You don't have to ask me again. Wherever it is that you're going . . . do you suppose they'd have any use for a mad scientist?"

"Sure," she said. "As long as you're teamed up with a mad inventor." She gestured toward the time-changer. "Think of the projects we can handle. Why, we can't go wrong."

They laughed together, ruefully, and hugged each other very tight for a long time.

Shouting incoherently, Jim Kirk sat up in his bunk. He clutched at his face: something was trying to get at his eyes—

The lights rose gradually in response to his motion; he was in his cabin, in his ship, he was all right. It was nothing but a nightmare.

He lay down again and rubbed his face with both

hands. He was soaked with sweat. That was the most re-
alistic dream he had had in a long time. The terrorism he
had seen at the very beginning of his Starfleet career had
haunted him for years, in dreams just like this one. A
shadowy figure appeared, pointed a gun at him, and fired,
then, as if he were two separate people, he watched himself die and felt himself die as a spiderweb slowly infiltrated his brain. The dream always ended as silver-gray
death clouded his hazel eyes.

He rubbed his chest, right over the breastbone, where
the bullet had entered, in this dream. "Could at least
have killed me instantly," he said aloud, reaching very far
for even bitter humor, and failing to grasp any.

The dream before the nightmare, though, that was different. It was another dream he had not had for a long
time: he had dreamed of Hunter. He tried not even to
think of her, most of the time. He had so nearly destroyed
their friendship with his immaturity; he had certainly destroyed their intimacy.

Why don't you grow up, Jim? he thought. Your dreams
don't just come along to entertain you, they're there to
give you good advice. You've been warned of your mortality, though if you're lucky you'll have a better death
than that one. But you *are* mortal—and so is she. She's in
more danger than you are, more of the time: what if
something happens to her and you've never told her how
you feel, or at least that you know you were a damned
fool?

He ordered the lights out again and lay in the darkness
trying to get back to sleep. But he knew that in the morning he would not forget the dreams he had tonight.

In her darkened cabin, Hunter looked up from the
backlighted reading screen and shivered. Had she dozed
off? She did not think so. She leaned back, stretched,
rubbed her temples, and returned her attention to the
reader. The paper it displayed was hard going, all these
years past her formal physics training, but the work was
bizarre enough to interest her. She had always thought
Georges Mordreaux was a little crazy, and this work confirmed her suspicions. The fourth paper in a series of five,
it had a publication date two years past. Hunter could
find no reference to any succeeding monograph, to paper
number five.

She wondered what had happened to Mordreaux after he quit the Makropyrios in a fit of pique and bruised ego. He always signed his papers, but never added any location.

Hunter felt too restless to concentrate on physics. She turned off the reader, folded it against the wall, and went up to the cockpit to prepare *Aerfen* for docking with Aleph Prime.

Her crew needed replacements even worse than *Aerfen* needed fixing, but Starfleet had her request and had not yet deigned to answer. Every time Hunter ran into the bureaucracy, which she did more and more frequently the more responsibility she earned, she daydreamed about resigning. She could always join the free commandoes. Or just go home and stay for a while. She was not due for a sabbatical for two more years; the best she could hope for in the meantime was a few weeks home with her family, with her daughter; and a few days by herself, in the mountains, to renew her friendship with the phoenix eagle who had watched over her while she found her dreamname.

Hunter shook her head. She could get hopelessly sentimental sometimes; if she got any more maudlin she would start thinking about Jim Kirk, and that would bring on a bad case of "if onlies."

If only he were a completely different person, Hunter thought. If only I were, too. Then it would have worked out perfectly.

Strolling toward his office, Ian Braithewaite stopped and stuck his head into the office of Aleph Prime's public defender.

"Hi, Lee, how you feeling today?"

"Better," she said. "I must have started to get a bug, but it's gone now."

"Good."

"Anything interesting coming up?" she asked. "I'm tired of pleading fines for drunken miners. Why don't you turn up a good smuggling case?"

"Don't I wish," he said.

"Want to go for coffee later?"

"Sure," Ian said. "I'll meet you after court."

He went on down the hall and to his office, to start in

on his moderately heavy load of massively boring cases, day after day, always the same.

Without a sound, without a motion, Mandala woke. She went from deep dreaming sleep to complete wakefulness in an instant. She felt cold, with the sweat of fear.

Almost as quickly as she awakened, she remembered where she was: her own cabin, on the *Enterprise*, her new assignment. Not back in the patrol, not in the midst of a fire-fight. She rubbed the ache beneath the scar on her left shoulder. She must have strained the old break during a workout. She really should find time to regrow the bone. It was silly to put up with the discomfort. And this time the twinge of pain had prodded memory and brought on her nightmare.

But it *was* just a nightmare. She had faced and overcome its dangers just as she had beaten other perils, real ones, and the struggle and victory had suffused her with a fierce joy.

Hikaru slept peacefully beside her. The faint light gleamed on his shoulders. He lay face-down with his head pillowed on his arms, turned toward her. Yesterday, they had both realized they wanted, and needed, to spend as much time together as they could, even if he were soon to leave the *Enterprise*.

He was so gentle . . . Mandala did not like to think of him hardened by the violence he would encounter in his next assignment. But she could not say so to him. Her reasons were too selfish; and she would, in effect, be telling him to give up his ambitions.

He might be strong enough to come through the experience unchanged. It was possible. But it was about as likely as his chances of advancing farther without making the transfer at all.

She pushed away the depressing thoughts, for she still felt exhilarated by her dream. Her heart beat quickly; she was excited. She leaned down and kissed the point of Hikaru's shoulder. She kissed the corner of his jaw, his ear, his temple. His eyes opened, closed, opened.

He drew in a long breath. "I'm glad you woke me up."

"I'm glad you woke up." She brushed her fingertips languorously up and down his back. He shivered.

"You got me out of some nightmare," he said.

"Bad?"

"It seems like it . . . but I can't remember anything about it, now."

She moved closer to him and put her arm around his shoulders, cuddling him. He hugged her tight, burying his face in her long loose hair, until he had shaken off the unease, and began to respond to her.

She leaned over him, letting her hair fall down in a curtain around them. When it tickled his neck and shoulders, he smiled. She caressed him, drawing warm patterns with her fingers and cool ones with her ruby ring.

"You are so beautiful," Mandala said, and bent down to kiss him again before he could think of anything to say.

Jenniver Aristeides and Snnanagfashtalli sat across from each other in the duty room, playing chess. They both preferred the classical two-dimensional board to the 3-D versions; it was somehow cleaner and less fussy, but it retained its infinite complexity.

"At least if I ask Mandala Flynn for a transfer she won't spit in my face," Jenniver said.

"No," said Fashtall. "She is not like the other one, she is not the spitting type."

"It's just that I have such a hard time getting anybody to believe I don't like to pound people into the ground every chance I get." Jenniver shrugged. "I guess I can't blame them."

Fashtall raised her sleek head and gazed across the table at her, the pupils in her maroon eyes widening. *"I* believe," she said. "They will not say they do not believe you, when I am around. And no one will spit in your face."

"He never actually did, you know," Jenniver said mildly. "He couldn't reach that far anyway."

"Mandala Flynn's predecessor is gone," Fashtall said. "And Mandala Flynn is our officer. If she does not give you a transfer to Botany, she will tell you a reason, at least. I do not think she will hold you in place longer than she must, if she knows you are unhappy."

"I'm scared to talk to her," Jenniver said.

"She will not hurt you. And you will not hurt her. Have you watched her, at judo? No ordinary human on the ship could defeat her, not even the captain."

"Could you?" Jenniver asked.

Fashtall blinked at her. "I do not play fair, by those rules."

The Changeling laughed. Reflecting that Fashtall had far more sense of humor than anyone else gave her credit for, Jenniver moved her queen's pawn.

After a moment, Fashtall growled.

Jenniver smiled. "You're not even in check."

"I will soon be. Driven by a pawn!" She made another irritated noise. "You think a move farther ahead than I, friend Jenniver, and I envy you."

She suddenly turned, the spotted fur at the back of her neck rising, bristling.

"What is it?"

"Something fell. Someone. In the observatory."

Fashtall bounded out of the duty room on all fours, and Jenniver followed, running easily in the absurdly light gravity. She passed Fashtall and reached the observatory first.

Mr. Spock stood swaying in the middle of the dimly-lit room, his eyes rolled back so far they showed nothing but white crescents, his hair disarrayed, blood running down the side of his face from a gash in his left temple, and, most strangely of all—once Jenniver noticed it—out of uniform, wearing a flowing, dark-brown tunic rather than his uniform shirt. She hurried toward him: her boot crunched on a shard that cracked like plastic. She hesitated, afraid as she often was that she had inadvertently damaged some fragile possession of the frail people around her. But the floor was littered with the amber fragments: whatever the damage was, it was not something she had caused.

Spock's knees buckled and Jenniver forgot the broken bits around her: she leaped forward and caught the science officer before he fell. She held him up. Fashtall rose on her hind legs and touched his forehead.

"Fever," she said. "High—much too high even for a Vulcan."

Spock raised his head. "My observations . . ." he said. "Entropy . . ." There was a wild, confused look in his eyes. "Captain Kirk—"

"Fashtall, you go wake up Dr. McCoy. I'll help Mr. Spock to sick bay."

Snnanagfashtalli's white whiskers bristled out: a gesture of agreement. She sprang over the broken instrument and disappeared into the corridor.

"I am all right," Spock said.

"You're bleeding, Mr. Spock."

He put his hand to his temple; his fingers came away wet with blood. Then he looked at his sleeve, brown silk, not blue velour.

"Let me take you to sick bay," she said. "Please."

"I am not in need of assistance!"

She thought she was being cruel but she could not think of anything else to do but obey him. She was supporting most of his weight: she let him go, as slowly as she dared so he would have as much chance as she could give him to keep his feet. But as she had feared, his legs would not support him. He collapsed again, and again she kept him from falling.

She looked at the wall across the room, not meeting his eyes: if she pretended she had not noticed, perhaps he could pretend she had not seen.

"I am going to sick bay," she said. "Will you come with me?"

"Ensign Aristeides," he said softly, "my pride does not require quite so much protection. I would be grateful for your help."

Leonard McCoy paced back and forth in his office, wondering what he had done to deserve such insomnia. The inexplicable period of unconsciousness in the transporter room, whatever that was all about, had done nothing to alleviate his tiredness; it only made it worse. And it made him worry about it more. He felt as if he had gone on a binge such as he had not indulged in since he was a peach-fuzzed undergraduate, despite his reputation—and his pose—as a hard drinker of the old southern school. But he had not had anything stronger than coffee—and precious little of that since he had begun having trouble sleeping—since coffee and brandy at the officers' reception for Mandala Flynn: hardly an indulgence to come back and haunt him two months later.

"Dr. McCoy!" Snnanagfashtalli rose up gracefully on her hind legs from the running position. "Mr. Spock is ill. Fever, at least three degrees Centigrade—"

"He always has a fever of at least three degrees Centigrade."

"As do I," Snarl said, flattening her ears. "In human terms."

Snarl was not a being to trade witticisms with; McCoy grew very serious very quickly.

"Where is he?"

"He remained conscious, so Ensign Aristeides is helping him to sick bay."

"Good. Thank you." McCoy felt relieved when Snarl pricked up her tufted ears again.

Jenniver Aristeides strode in, carrying Spock. The Vulcan lay unconscious in her arms, his long hands limp, his head thrown back. Every few seconds a drop of blood spattered on the floor.

"He passed out just a minute ago." Though the ensign loomed head and shoulders over McCoy, she spoke hesitantly. "I thought it was better to bring him than wait for a stretcher."

"You showed good judgment." McCoy sighed. "I was afraid of this, he's worked himself right into a fit of the vapors."

Epilogue

Jim Kirk sat by Spock's bedside, turning the strangely shaped bit of broken equipment over and over in his hands. He had never seen anything remotely like it before and he could not figure out what it was—or what it had been. This was the only piece large enough to inspect; the other shattered fragments lay jumbled together in a box nearby.

McCoy came in and sat down, rubbing his eyes tiredly.

"Bones," Jim said, "I'll call you when he starts to wake up. Why don't you go get some sleep?"

"That's just the trouble, I've been trying," McCoy said. "Whatever Spock did to himself so he wouldn't need sleep, I think he gave it to me, too."

Jim rubbed his fingertip along the smooth curved amber surface, stopping at a broken edge.

"I've felt uneasy for the last couple of days," McCoy said. "As if something awful is about to happen, and I can't do anything about it. Or it's already happened, and I don't even know about it."

Kirk grinned. "You've only felt it for a couple of days? I've been like that since we got within grabbing distance of that damned singularity." He glanced at Spock, who

216

had not moved at all since Kirk had come into the room. "Is he going to be all right, Bones?"

"I think so."

"Aren't you certain?" Kirk asked, startled, for he had only asked the question to get a reassuring answer.

"I'm reasonably certain," McCoy said, "but I don't see how he got himself into this state to begin with. I've been expecting somebody to have to cart him in here with exhaustion for days—"

"You knew he was going without sleep—"

"Yeah."

"—and you didn't tell me?"

"What would you have done? Forbade it?" McCoy grinned. "I didn't tell you because of medical ethics. Doctor-patient confidentiality. Not wanting to get my head bitten off by my captain."

"All right, all right. But what's wrong with him, if it isn't exhaustion?"

"It *is* exhaustion, but it's the sort I'd expect if he'd been through tremendous physical exertion. A couple of Vulcan marathons, say—a hundred kilometres through the desert. The scalp wound is completely inexplicable. He didn't get it when he fell—he reopened a graze that was already partly healed. And it was patched with hybrid skin synthetic. Spock knew I made some to match his genotype. He could have used it himself. Only he didn't; the packet was still in storage, unopened." He stopped, and shrugged. "Shall I go on?"

"No. I can do that myself. He was out of uniform—I've *never* seen him out of uniform on the ship. And—" He hefted the weird piece of equipment—"this is nothing I've ever seen before. Scotty doesn't know what it does. It's mostly bioelectronics, which are so new they're hard to come by. I've never signed a requisition for them, and there's no record that we ever brought any on board the ship."

Mr. Spock, his awareness rising slowly through the depths of sleep, gradually became aware of the voices around him. They were discussing him, but as yet he could make no sense of the individual words. He tried to concentrate.

"Something very strange is going on," Jim Kirk said. "Something I don't understand. And I don't like that at all."

"Jim!" Spock sat up so quickly that every muscle and joint and sinew shrieked: he was aware of the sensation but impervious to it, as he should be, but for all the wrong reasons. He grabbed Jim Kirk's arm. It was solid and real. Relief, and, yes, joy, overwhelmed the Vulcan. He slid his hand up Jim's arm; he started to reach up to him, to lay his hand along the side of his face to feel the unsettling energy of Jim's undamaged mind.

He pulled back abruptly, shocked by his own impulses; he turned away, toward the wall, struggling to control himself.

"Spock, what's wrong? Bones—"

"Well, you wanted him to wake up," McCoy said drily.

"Nothing is wrong, Captain," Spock said. He eased himself back down onto the bunk. His voice was steady enough not to reveal that he was on the brink of laughter, of tears. "I am merely . . . very glad to see you."

"I'm glad to see you, too." Kirk's expression was quizzical. "You've been out quite a while."

"How long, Captain?" Spock asked urgently.

"A couple of hours. Why?"

Spock relaxed. "Because, sir, the singularity is in the process of converting itself into a very small black hole, what you would call, in Earth tradition, a Hawking black hole. When the conversion is complete, the system will explode."

Kirk leaped to his feet and started out the door.

"Captain—" Spock said.

Kirk glanced back.

"The *Enterprise* is in no danger," the Vulcan said. "The process will continue for another six days at least."

"Oh," Kirk said. He returned to Spock's side. "All right, Mr. Spock. What happened?"

Spock reached up and touched the bullet wound in his temple. It was barely perceptible, for McCoy had put more skin synthetic on the gash, and sealed it with transparent spray. His brown and gold silk shirt lay crumpled on a table across the room . . . and Jim held the remains of the time-changer in his hands.

"You were in the observatory," Jim said. "Snarl heard you fall. Jenniver Aristeides brought you to sick bay. Do you remember?"

What Spock remembered, he recalled all too well. He glanced from Jim to Dr. McCoy. As they were now, neither had existed in the alternate time-stream. And Spock had quite clear memories of a time-stream in which his observations proceeded smoothly: the singularity indeed did appear, and though he could not deduce its cause, it was clear from the beginning that it would soon self-destruct and cease to be a danger. The *Enterprise* had never been called to Aleph Prime. Dr. Mordreaux had never come on board, and Spock had detected no acceleration in the increase of entropy.

And then he had reappeared in his observatory, dragged back to the *Enterprise* through space and time, to the place he belonged, and, simultaneously, it seemed, the miscalculation of his stamina caught up with him. Journey, or exhaustion, or both, caused him to lose consciousness.

"Spock?" Jim asked gently. "Do you remember?"

"No, Captain," Spock said quite truthfully. "I cannot understand what happened." He had not expected to remember the events in the time-loop he had turned back on itself and wiped out of existence. But he did.

He had learned how fragile the continuum was. He had not restored it to its original form. He had only managed to stitch it back together where it had torn most seriously; he had put patches over the worst of the rents, and hoped they would hold: perhaps he should not be so startled that the seams were not quite straight and the grain not quite smooth. If the inconsistencies were no worse than an inexplicable astronomical phenomenon that would have to remain a mystery, and conflicting sets of memories in his own mind, then perhaps he should accept them gracefully, and gratefully.

"I apologize, Captain. I cannot explain what happened."

"You've got a bit of a concussion," McCoy said. "Your memory may return when you've recovered from that."

Spock sincerely hoped it would not, but he did not say so.

Kirk hefted the broken section of the time-changer. "Maybe you can at least explain what this is."

"Of course, Captain. It is an instrument which helped me to complete my assignment." Though that was technically accurate, it was close enough to a lie for Spock to feel ashamed of himself for it.

"Where did you get it?"

"I made it, Captain."

"There aren't any bioelectronic components on this ship!"

"Hey, Jim," McCoy said, "lay off, will you?"

"Sure, Bones, as soon as Mr. Spock answers my question."

"That was not a question, Captain," Spock said. "It was a statement. However, it is quite true that the *Enterprise* carries no bioelectronics. If I may point it out, though, one of the most interesting properties of bioelectronic crystals is that they can be grown." He reached for the time-changer.

Kirk glared at him, then, quite suddenly, grinned. "Well, Mr. Spock," he said. "I never thought of you as having a green thumb."

Inexplicably, McCoy groaned. "That's it! Out!"

Spock glanced down at his hands. He did not understand Captain Kirk's remark, for if the captain were, for whatever peculiar reason, to think of Spock's thumbs, he must surely note that they were, in fact, slightly green.

"Spock," Kirk said, serious again, "you're not telling me everything, and I don't much like that."

"Captain . . . in the vicinity of a singularity, the only thing one can predict is that events will occur that one could not predict."

"I take it you don't care to elaborate on the nature of these unpredictable events."

"I would prefer not to, Captain."

Kirk scowled, and Spock thought he was going to refuse to give him the remains of the time-changer. Abruptly, Kirk grinned again and held the device out to the science officer.

Spock accepted it.

"All right, Mr. Spock. I trust you, and I trust in your judgment that whatever you can't explain won't affect the safety of this ship or anybody on it."

"Your trust will not be betrayed," Spock said.

McCoy folded his arms across his chest. "Now that you two have exchanged expressions of undying confidence, I want you—" he glared at Kirk—"to get out of here, and I want you—" he transferred his irritated gaze to Mr. Spock—"to go back to sleep. Right now. That's an order."

Jim laughed. "Okay, Bones. Mr. Spock, can we get out of here?"

"Yes, Captain. My observations are complete."

"Good." Kirk stood up and turned to leave.

Spock pushed himself up on one elbow.

"Captain—Jim—"

Kirk glanced back.

"Thank you," Spock said.

As he rounded a corner, Jim Kirk saw Mr. Sulu ahead of him, walking toward the turbo lift.

"Mr. Sulu!" he called. The helm officer did not turn around; Kirk called to him again.

Sulu stopped short, and faced him. "I'm sorry, Captain. I was . . . thinking about something."

They continued down the hall side by side.

"Are you going up to the bridge?"

"Yes, sir. I go on duty in ten minutes."

"I'm glad it's your watch," Jim said. "Mr. Spock's work is finished and we can get out of here. I'd rather have you at the helm than any of the other helm officers, when we're maneuvering near a singularity."

"Why—thank you, Captain," Sulu said, obviously astonished by the spontaneous compliment.

Sulu's been looking preoccupied lately, Kirk thought. And he needs a haircut very badly. He's starting a mustache, too—what's this all about? He's beginning to look like he belongs in the border patrol, not on a ship of the line. Of course, he has been under a lot of stress . . .

He almost made a joke about Sulu's hair, a joke that Sulu would of course take as a suggestion to get at least a trim.

Why do you want him to cut his hair? Jim Kirk asked himself. It doesn't make any difference to his work; it isn't as if he's going to get it caught in the rigging.

He thought, again, Grow up, Jim.

"Are you happy on the *Enterprise*, Mr. Sulu?" he asked.

Sulu hesitated. His tone, when he answered, was as serious as if he had been thinking the question over very hard for a very long time. "Yes, Captain. It's a better assignment than I ever hoped for, and the best I'm ever likely to have."

Kirk started to demur, to shrug off the implied compliment, but he saw an alternate interpretation for what Sulu had said. Kirk knew Sulu's record well; he knew how a desk-bound bureaucrat would look at it. "Insufficient variety of experience" would be the most likely analysis, despite the fact that no one could ask for more variety of experience than serving on the *Enterprise* provided. Unfortunately, the record was what counted, and Sulu knew that as well as anybody.

Kirk realized abruptly: *If he wants to advance, it's almost inevitable that he'll transfer off the Enterprise. You're going to lose the best helm officer this ship has ever had, if you don't do something, and do it fast.*

"I've been thinking," Kirk said. "And what I think is that it's about time we talked about making sure your record reflects all the responsibilities you have, not just the formal ones. It would be a damned shame if somewhere down the line you wanted a position and it went to some semi-competent instead just because they went up the ladder in the usual way and you didn't."

Sulu's expression gave Jim considerable excuse for self-congratulation.

"The solution isn't to normalize your record," he said. "It's to make it unique, so you have to be judged on your own terms. I think a good first step would be a field promotion to lieutenant commander. There's no question but what you'd get the promotion anyway in a few years, but a field promotion is unusual enough to stand out even to a red-tape shuffler."

"Captain . . ." Sulu sounded rather stunned.

"It would mean more responsibility, of course."

"That would be all right," Sulu said. "I mean—it would be wonderful!"

"Good. Let's get together and talk about it. You give fencing lessons in the afternoons, don't you?"

"On alternate days. The other times I take a judo lesson from Lieutenant Commander Flynn."

"What time are you finished?"

"About sixteen hundred hours, sir."

"Then, what do you say to seventeen hundred, tomorrow, in the officers' lounge?"

"I'll be there, Captain! Thank you, sir."

Kirk nodded. They reached the turbo lift, got on, and started upward toward the bridge.

"By the way, Mr. Sulu, I think that's going to be a very distinctive mustache once it gets a little longer."

Color rose in Sulu's cheeks.

"I mean it," Kirk said.

"I wasn't sure that you'd approve, sir."

"I grew a mustache myself, a few years ago."

"You did? Why didn't you keep it?"

"I'll tell you if you promise not to tell anyone else."

"Of course I promise, sir."

"It came in red. Brick red. Most ridiculous thing I ever saw in my life."

He laughed, and so did Sulu.

"I don't think mine will come in red, Captain," Sulu said.

The lift doors opened and they went out onto the bridge. Kirk grinned at Sulu.

"No, I don't suppose you'll have to worry about that possibility."

Kirk took his place; Sulu relieved the junior helm officer and checked over the controls.

"Mr. Sulu," Kirk said, "plot us a course out of here."

"Yes, sir!"

It took him only a few seconds: he had been prepared to get the ship away from the singularity at almost any moment; he was ready for any sort of emergency.

"Course entered, sir, warp factor one."

"Thank you, Mr. Sulu."

Like a freed bird, the *Enterprise* sailed out of the grasp of the singularity, through the flaming curtains of disintegrating matter that surrounded it, and out into deep space.

Captain's log, Stardate 5001.1:

We are now a day away from the singularity, and the unease that gripped the *Enterprise* and my crew throughout the entire mission there has faded, leaving in its place a feeling of relief and even contentment. Morale is better than it has been in some time, particularly in the security section: though I personally find the new commander rather prickly, she does her job splendidly.

I have decided to take the *Enterprise* through the border region between Federation space and Klingon territory, which is guarded by Captain Hunter's fleet.

The Klingons have been more aggressive than usual; they have inflicted some losses on the squadron, and until replacements arrive, the appearance of a ship of the line in the area cannot do any harm.

Administrative notes: I have forwarded to Starfleet my recommendation for Mr. Sulu's field promotion to lieutenant commander. As this will make him one of the youngest officers of that rank without formal front line experience, I may have to wrestle down a few bureaucratic hair-splitters in order to get it approved; on the other hand, if serving on the *Enterprise* doesn't qualify as some form of front line experience, I don't know what does.

On the recommendation of Lt. Commander Flynn, I have also approved the transfer of Ensign Jenniver Aristeides from Security to Botany, and Mr. Spock has asked her to take charge of a project he wants to begin, that of growing more bioelectronic components. Before now, Aristeides always seemed to me to be hardly any more the emotional type than Mr. Spock, but she is clearly delighted by her new job.

Mr. Spock is recovering from severe overwork. He has assured Starfleet that the singularity will soon wipe itself out of the universe. My science officer shows no more sign than before that he is willing to discuss the "unpredictable events" that occurred during his observations. Despite a certain temptation to ask him if this is information we were not meant to know—a question that would undoubtedly grate upon his scientific objectivity—I'm not inclined to press him for more answers. It's possible that he simply made some sort of mistake that would humiliate him to reveal.

Whatever *did* happen seems to have involved only Spock himself; whatever it was, it has not affected the *Enterprise* at all.

And that, of course, as always, is my main concern.